"You, Miss Catherine Shreveton, Are An Unprincipled Hoyden, A Complete Ninnyhammer, And A Menace To Society."

"I beg your pardon!"

"You may, but you shan't receive it. No horse—and I mean this without question—no horse anywhere is worth risking life and limb. And that is something your uncle would be the first to tell you."

"My lord, this is hardly necessary," Catherine protested, as she was hoisted onto the marquis' big bay.

"Be quiet," Stefton returned evenly.

"You are causing undue talk! There is nothing the matter with me, I assure you. I was merely winded a moment."

"Miss Shreveton, I do not suffer fools gladly. You could have been killed."

"This horse would never have killed me!"

"I was not speaking of the *horse*," he said.

★

A GRAND GESTURE

Also by Holly Newman

Gentleman's Trade
Honor's Players

Published by
WARNER BOOKS

A GRAND GESTURE

Holly Newman

WARNER BOOKS

A Warner Communications Company

WARNER BOOKS EDITION

Warner Books, Inc.
666 Fifth Avenue
New York, N.Y. 10103

 A Warner Communications Company

Printed in the United States of America

First Printing: May, 1989

10 9 8 7 6 5 4 3 2 1

Tender-handed stroke a nettle,
And it stings you for your pains;
Grasp it like a man of mettle,
And it soft as silk remains.

Verses Written on a Window in Scotland

Aaron Hill
1685–1750

CHAPTER
ONE

My Dearest Mary,

I have invited my twin nieces, Lady Iris and Lady Dahlia to London for the Season. As daughters of my brother Aldric, fifth Earl of Whelan, they possess the rank which demands a London Season.

Recently, however, it was brought to my attention that I have two other Shreveton nieces—both of marriageable age—who have come out provincially yet have not had the opportunity of a London Season. One is Susannah, daughter of my youngest brother, Captain Glendon Shreveton, and the other is Catherine, your daughter and only child of my dear departed brother, Ralph. I am certain that you are aware that the Shreveton family holds a very respected place in Society, indeed. We owe it to Society to introduce our children. I really can not allow either Susannah or Catherine to be overlooked in this manner.

I have decided that this Season will be much enlivened by the presence of four young Shrevetons and it is my intention to undertake this project. Under my aegis all of my Shreveton nieces can be assured the proper notice from the polite world.

1

*If you will send my dear niece, Catherine, to London,
I will introduce her to the ton. Do not worry for the lack
of suitable gowns. I intend such articles to be gifts I
grant all my nieces.*

*I am confident that Catherine, though the eldest and
possessing the least in prospects, will be able, under my
tutelage of course, to make an eligible parti—though perhaps
not as brilliant as her cousins. If you will forgive my plain
speaking, at least she will have a better chance than in
the wilds of Yorkshire.*

I remain with respect, etc.

> *Alicia Harth*
> *Countess of Seaverness*

Lady Burke's knuckles were white and her hands shook
as she lowered the letter. The brown eyes she turned toward
her daughter Mary glittered with anger.

Seeing her mother's expression, and knowing full well
her Irish temper, the Honorable Mrs. Ralph Shreveton's
hands fluttered beseechingly. "Lady Harth has no way of
knowing Catherine's true position, Mama. She knows Ralph's
portion was small. It would be natural for her to think
Catherine has never had a Season because we are too poor!"

"Fustian."

"No, it's true."

"Mary, she's implying Catherine's a—a—a nothing!"

Mary looked down at her hands which were twisting her
handkerchief into a ball. "Maybe it would be better if she
were," she said softly.

"Mary!"

The younger woman blushed and looked up quickly, stilling
her nervous fingers by pressing her hands deep in her lap.
"Well, she will be two-and-twenty this spring." The note of
defiance mixed with exasperation in her tone was unusual.

Lady Burke's eyes narrowed as she looked at her daughter,
then a ghost of a smile touched her lips, and she relaxed.
"Aye," she said slowly.

And you just forty and looking no more than thirty, she
thought; *and as giddy as a seventeen-year-old when Squire*

ftwich comes to call, but pokering up like a fifty-year-
d turbaned matron when Catherine's about. No wonder
e lass strives to be away from home when the squire comes
.

Gwen drummed her fingertips on the arm of her chair,
aring at the sunlight shining through the tall parlor win-
ws that showed dust in the air as silver glitter and made
tterns of light on the Aubusson carpet, lending jewel-like
arity to its mellow old colors. Mary had been widowed ten
ars, long enough for grief to turn to fond memories—as ..
ould. Over the years, Mary had been content with her
ughter; however, the time was past that Catherine needed
ddling. Mary was far too young to exist merely from day
day.

Gwen was confident the squire wished to marry her
ughter. The problem was Mary herself. She wouldn't
ntemplate remarrying with Catherine not settled, and
thing was in the wind from that quarter.

It was not for lack of beauty or money that Catherine was
t yet married—rather from a lack of concern. Two-and-
enty Catherine would soon be; however, a nothing she
as not. To a string of forlorn young men who had crossed
r path, she was the elusive beauty. None were able to
pture her attention, let alone her heart; yet no matter how
ag she talked or danced with them at the local assemblies,
ey were always proclaiming to be head over heels in love
th her warm brown eyes, laughing freckled countenance,
d masses of auburn hair shining like burnished copper in
ndlelight or fire in the sun. That was part of the problem.
ere was too much proclaiming and little enough sincerity.
d Catherine knew it. The only sincere aspect of Catherine's
itors was their awe at discovering that Catherine was
hooled as a horse trainer for her uncle, Sir Eugene Burke,
.—and would be his heir.

Gwen made an exasperated noise. Her grandchild playing
being a stable boy! She blamed herself for that. She could
ve put a halt to it, but she liked seeing her son and
anddaughter happy. Catherine was the child Eugene and
wife, Deirdra, couldn't have; Eugene, the father Catherine
ely missed. They would perhaps both have been better

pleased had she been a boy. Gwen often thought they forg
she wasn't. She was more involved with the business
raising, training, and selling Burke horses than a wom
should be. And, to make matters worse, on her last birthd
Eugene announced that she would inherit his entire esta
including the stables.

Gwen turned to face her daughter, a thoughtful expressi
on her face. Mary smiled timidly back, afraid to break i
her mother's thoughts.

Perhaps it would be wisest for Catherine to go to Lond
for the Season. She knew Catherine had no desire for a ta
of town life. Yet how could the chit choose to be a coun
spinster without knowing the alternatives? But how to ma
Catherine see that? And how to make her obey the wishes
the haughty Countess of Seaverness?

Grimly Gwen considered it might do to send Catherine
Lady Harth just to bring that woman down a peg. She w
vaguely aware Lady Harth's assumptions had merit sin
nothing had ever been done to present Catherine; due, s
guiltily knew, to her own distaste for making such
effort. Still, with Catherine gone a bit, the little roman
between Mary and the squire might have an opportunity
given the proper nudge—to blossom and come to fruiti
Not that Mary would see that as a strong argument; howev
it bore considerable weight with Gwen. She looked
her daughter, sitting on one of the brocade-covered chairs
the window, smoothing a wrinkle from her blue-and-whi
striped muslin gown. Squire Leftwich would be an excelle
match.

If Gwen was to see to her daughter's happiness, l
granddaughter would have to go to London. "Do you tru
wish her to go?"

Mary, who was again studying her hands, looked up
her mother. This time her gaze didn't waver. "Yes."

Gwen sighed, nodding her head as she tossed the letter
the little table by her chair.

That both ladies should agree was only the beginni
They knew that if Catherine were approached with the id
she would merely say, "How nice, but no, thank you," a
if she were actually to see the letter, she wouldn't come off I

h horse for days and would reproach her dear parent and
ndmother for even contemplating such a scheme.

'I believe Deirdra is the key,'' Gwen said after consider-
e thought. They'd discussed the problem for over an hour
l always come back to Eugene. He had a control over
herine's waywardness that neither her mother nor her
ndmother possessed, and Deirdra had control over him.
his own, he would not encourage such a trip, deeming it
ainine nonsense.

'She can turn the lock on this matter. Of that I am
tain. After all, she is Irish.''

Mary, though not convinced that being Irish had anything
do with the situation, merely nodded her head vaguely
l inquired if she should request the carriage be brought
und. Gwen asked her not to be such a ninny, saying they
uld make their call at their usual hour.

'For depend on it,'' she said, ''to do anything out of the
inary would only cause comment and make Catherine
picious, which we would not be wanting to do.''

'Should we not tell Lady Harth the true facts of Catherine's
ition? It cannot be right to allow her to make plans based
n false assumptions,'' Mary suggested later that afternoon
they drove through the village of Umberfife to Fifefield,
Burke estate.

'Nonsense,'' Gwen replied, scarcely glancing at her
ghter seated opposite her in their carriage. ''What right
s she have to make such assumptions? It would be worse
he thought her to be rich and she really wasn't. No one
sneer for long at money, my dear.''

'Do you remember, Mama, when Ralph and I were first
rried and made that visit to his family? It was easy to see
y did not care for Ralph's choice for a bride, and Lady
rth made sure I knew it. She is Ralph's eldest sister, but
ot at all like my dear Ralph in temperament. Though, in
honesty, I do feel her haughty nature is assumed in
f-defense.''

'Self-defense?''

'Yes.'' Mary blushed and looked guilty for she hated to
ak ill of others. ''She is—well, she is clumsy. There is
other way to put it. Since she is prone to breaking things

by her clumsiness, she's adopted a formidable mien to h
behind and haughtily pretends none of her accidents happe
And hardly anyone else tried to be kind to me. Aldr
Ralph's oldest brother, was under the thumb of his fi
wife, Lily. A most domineering, hateful woman, I could
imagine. She looked down her nose at me and made
most hateful comments that Lady Harth echoed for th
were bosom-bows. Penelope, Ralph's other sister, tried
be pleasant but she was breeding and spent much of ea
day in her room. I was never so miserable.''

Mary smiled suddenly, a faraway look reflected in her s
brown eyes. ''Lady Harth's loudest complaint was tha
was a nobody—that even Penelope had the sense to marr
baronet.''

''What? Mary, do not tell me you allowed that woman
continue in her misguided beliefs for over twenty years
Gwen said, shocked.

Her daughter shrugged helplessly. ''You remember h
Ralph was. He loved a good joke, and he thought the f
that I was really the daughter of a baronet was terri
funny. I was quite overwhelmed. All I wanted to do was
away. If Ralph had not remained by my side, and if
youngest brother, Glendon, had not been there to keep us
laughter, I doubt I would have survived it.'' Mary's vo
choked on her last words, her eyes glistening with unsh
tears.

Gwen sniffed. While her daughter might feel a misera
stay with Ralph's family was worthwhile if it gave h
amusement, she thought otherwise.

''Pardon, Mama, did you say something? I'm afrai
wasn't attending,'' Mary said, dabbing her eyes with
handkerchief.

''No, merely an old woman muttering to herself. N
don't question me further. See, we've arrived at Fifefi
Manor,'' Gwen said, feeling the rush of pride she alwa
experienced when she visited the Burke estate.

The house Sir Eugene Burke's grandfather had purchas
for his line was in keeping with his character. It was a larg
three-story, gray stone edifice built in the late sixtee
century. For all its unprepossessing color and hulking sha

eld a charm of its own, which was due to its asymmetry
composition as much as to the pair of octagonal bay
dows that rose through two stories. The estate had changed
ds several times before it came into Burke's keeping,
each owner made changes to suit his whims and needs.
a consequence, the house belonged to no era but
mmanded respect and mention in the guide books both
ause of its unique design and its illustrious owner.

When the footman handed her down from the carriage,
ven looked away from the house toward the stables, from
ich the real fame of the Burkes derived. The Burke name
s a byword in the sporting community, for Burke horses
re known as excellent mounts for hunting and pleasure. A
rke horse was not a horse to be ridden by anyone. It took
competent rider to handle such a high-strung, vibrant
mal. This added to the horses' value. They were trea-
ed possessions, and often family heirlooms were sold by
impecunious individual in order to maintain the animal.

Gwen's breast swelled with love when she saw her
ndsome son by the stable courtyard archway. He was in
ious discourse with a gentleman of Corinthian proportion
elegance, who was attired in a prodigiously modish,
lticaped greatcoat with a high crowned beaver set rakishly
p glossy black locks. The men were turned away from her,
viously studying the horse being put through his paces in
training paddock.

Gwen's eyes narrowed and she raised a hand to shield
m from the winter sun's glare. Could it be? Her breath
istled through her teeth, clouding the cold air before her
th white vapor. That *boy* on the horse was Catherine! And
front of a member of the *ton*!

Gwen grabbed Mary's elbow and propelled her toward
house. "Look at that hoyden! Lady Harth's letter was
ll timed."

Mary pulled against her mother to stop her forward
ogression so she might see. A timid "oh" escaped her
s; then she turned to her mother and resolutely straight-
ed. "We did grant her permission to ride astride, so we
st be complacent about the breeches. It would hardly be
mly to raise her skirts to such heights."

"Yes, yes, I am aware of that," Gwen returned test
"But not in front of strangers!"

"What?"

"Look, there—by the stable archway..."

Mary cringed. "Maybe, Mother, he won't recognize
as a girl, dressed like that, with her hair tucked un
her hat," she offered weakly, shoving her hands deep i
her muff.

Gwen harrumphed and raised her skirts to climb the st
before the house. "Just pray he's looking more at the ho
than the rider. If this London venture's to be any succe
we don't need any rumors circulating." She continued
grumble under her breath as she passed through the doorv
into the hall.

Mary followed meekly, risking one last glance in
direction of the stables and paddock. She bit her lip
helpless frustration when she saw the elegant gentlen
gesture toward the paddock. Then, compressing her lips
determination, she went into the manor house.

Sir Eugene Burke watched the horse and rider with pri
"So, Stefton, what do you think?" he asked the gen
man standing next to him.

The Marquis of Stefton folded his arms across his br
chest. "I'll own I prefer a gray or a black," he draw
consideringly, "however, that horse could cause me to m
an exception. Have you coursed him?"

The corner of Sir Eugene's mouth kicked up in
humor. "Not personally, but I have good reports—excell
action, good clean jumps without a falter."

"Who schooled him, Michaels or Stoddard?"

"Neither. You're looking at the one who claims t
credit." Sir Eugene's grin broadened as he noted the m
quis's black eyebrows rise in disbelief.

"That squib of a lad? Come, Gene, you're doing it
brown. I didn't cut my eyeteeth yesterday."

"On my honor. Done a wonderful job with that hor
He'll fetch a good price in London."

The marquis studied the rider carefully. "Got light han
a good seat..." He frowned a moment, then turned back

Eugene. "Would you take it amiss if I offered the lad a
ance as a jockey for me?"

Sir Eugene appeared to consider the matter for a moment.
With your reputation," he said lightly, "her mother would
ke exception to the idea—it is hardly an occupation for a
ntly reared female."

"Female!" Lord Stefton's head whipped around and he
ared at Sir Eugene. "Are you saying that boy is *a woman*?"

Sir Eugene nodded. "My niece," he answered complacently.

"Have you gone daft, man?" The marquis shed his
nguid posture to peer intently at the rider. Every idea of
opriety was affronted—delightfully so. He found himself
ssessed of a lively curiosity as to the personality of his
end's niece. Unexpectedly, the image of himself as a
und keen to the scent flashed in his mind, effectively
using his initial interest.

He gave Sir Eugene a sideways glance. It was taken for
anted no woman could possibly ride a Burke horse. Sir
gene, he knew, did nothing to disabuse the world of this
tion. Most likely he knew full well this increased the
ystique—and therefore the value—of the horses.

"Why are you telling me this? I cannot believe you wish
e to spread such insight among the *ton*," he drawled
yly.

Sir Eugene tore his eyes away from Catherine to look at
e marquis. "Hardly," he said levelly. "I don't know why
mention it now, other than some desire to show my pride.
e'll be my heir. She's like a daughter to me." He
ughed, looking affectionately at Catherine. "Or perhaps I
ould say, more like a son."

The sounds of Gwen's carriage being driven into the
bleyard drew his attention and he glanced away from
atherine toward the source of the sound. "That's my
other's carriage. She must be inside. Excuse me, Stefton,
must pay my respects. Are you sure you won't stay the
ght?"

"No, though I thank you for the offer. My luggage and
let are ten miles down the road. I only stopped on my
turn from visiting a friend in Northumbria to see if I might

steal a march and acquire one of your horses before th
spring sale.''

''Well, stay long enough to share a mug of ale and war
yourself. Dawes will show you the way to the library.''

The marquis nodded absently as Sir Eugene turned
leave, his attention returning to the rider on the big ba
horse.

Gwen and Mary surged past the butler into Deirdra
sitting room, a sunny yellow room with broad window
overlooking the park, stables, paddocks, and fields beyon
that constituted the main part of the farm.

It was Deirdra's favorite place, for there she could sit a
sew and look out over Eugene's world though her ow
delicacy of constitution precluded her participation. She w
a fragile woman with a heart-shaped face and an almo
translucent complexion save for the natural roses in h
cheeks. She possessed the merriest blue eyes, always read
to crinkle at the sides when she laughed. Her fine brow
hair insisted on slipping out of its confining pins so sl
always looked as though she'd been rushing about. Th
impression was intensified by the rapid, birdlike movemen
of her hands as she talked, carrying her beyond spoke
thoughts.

She was mending Sir Eugene's shirts when Gwen a
Mary entered, and she turned swiftly like a startled fawn whe
the door opened. Her brief expression of startled surprise turne
to warm welcome when she recognized her visitors ar
urged them to come in by the fire. She carefully folded h
husband's shirts and rang for refreshments.

Gwen chuckled at Deirdra's occupation and leaned bad
into a deep gold brocade armchair across from her. ''Sti
refusing to let a seamstress touch his shirts? Well, be caref
you don't ruin your eyes.''

Deirdra giggled. ''Oh, faith, if I don't have a care ar
sew only when the light is best, Eugene scolds me like
child.'' Her hands fluttered. ''He looks black at me enoug
for enjoying the mending. I can't help it, I must be bus
and mending is ingrained in me from childhood.

''But tell me,'' she continued, leaning forward, her fac

intent, "is the rector's youngest quite recovered now from the measles? I haven't gone out for nigh on a week now and I find it disconcerting not to know all that has happened. I sometimes think Eugene is too cautious of my health. Though I catch cold easily, I am otherwise strong."

"That may be, but don't you be getting any ideas, my girl," Gwen said gruffly, trying to mask her emotion for the slip of a woman seated before her.

Deirdra had been a truly energetic woman until her accident ten years ago. Deirdra had come to her mother-in-law's house to announce the joyful news that she was finally breeding. When Ralph drove her home that afternoon a sudden storm blew up, with more wind and sound than rain. A stray paper, carried by the wind, blew across the eyes of one of the horses. The startled horse reared and bolted. The trap careened madly after the horse until the entire assemblage tumbled into a ditch not far from Fifefield. Raymond Dawes, the son of Sir Eugene's estate agent, found them. Ralph was dead, his neck broken when he was thrown from the carriage. Deirdra was alive, but she lost the child she was carrying and contracted pneumonia. The incident took its toll on her health. In her activities she was a mere shadow of her former self, though outwardly as gregarious as ever.

"Yes, the child is better. Now it looks like the squire's two boys have it," Mary answered sadly. "The poor man, he is in such a state. To see his two babes, usually so full of life, still and quiet frets him to flinders." Mary's voice broke slightly, caught up in her thoughts of the squire.

Deirdra and Gwen exchanged knowing looks and smiled.

Together they talked on of happenings in the village in a pleasant, gossipy manner until Deirdra's butler brought them tea, and left, closing the big white double doors softly behind him. It was a signal to the elder Lady Burke, and she leaned forward in her chair.

"Deirdra, love, we must admit this is not a mere social call on our part. We need your assistance," she said nodding over in Mary's direction.

Deirdra's eyes opened wide. "Oh! Anything, need you ask? But whatever for?"

Gwen smiled, leaning back once more in her chair and

bringing her hands together forming a steeple with her fingertips. "You said earlier you often do not know what is going on with people because you are so secluded here." She paused for a moment and glanced briefly at Mary who was sitting straight in her chair with an intense expression on her face. "But I dare swear," she went on, "you see our Catherine more than we."

Deirdra grinned. "Yes, that is most likely true."

"Does she appear content with the horses? Has she ever mentioned to you any other wishes? Dreams?" Gwen asked.

Deirdra's brow clouded for a second. "Alas, no. And if I be understanding you right, you mean, does she think of marrying."

"Yes. Though she has never voiced such dreams to us, we wonder if they do cross her mind."

"I've often teased her that she should have a man of her own rather than share mine." Deirdra's laughter tinkled merrily. "For so it does seem at times."

Gwen sighed. "And the lass is nigh on two-and-twenty. That is what we have come to talk to you about." She straightened in her chair. "Mary has a letter from Ralph's sister, the Countess of Seaverness, offering to present Catherine this Season."

Deirdra's eyes grew round. "However did this come about?" she asked, looking from Gwen to Mary and back.

Gwen turned to her daughter. "Perhaps, Mary, you had best show Deirdra the letter."

Mary reached into her reticule, her face a study of conflicting emotions. "I do believe she means well," she said anxiously, extracting the letter and handing it to Deirdra.

Deirdra read quickly. When she was finished, instead of the outrage Gwen and Mary expected, she fell to whoops of laughter.

"Oh, I am sorry—" she sputtered at last. "But to be thinking of Catherine in this way, it is so outrageous! I can just imagine the picture Lady Harth has of her. It is rich, I vow!" She was suddenly serious. "Oh, you do take this seriously."

Gwen was the first to recover. "You're quite right. It is outrageous. Nonetheless—disregarding the snobbish tone of

Lady Harth's letter and her false assumptions—we do wish for Catherine to go to London. To be so totally immured in the countryside is disastrous for her chances of meeting any gentleman worthy of her. Even Eugene had his fling and Grand Tour before he settled here. But how can we get her to London in the face of that?'' Gwen asked, pointing to the letter Deirdra held.

Deirdra had to admit her headstrong niece wouldn't take kindly to such an invitation.

"That is why we've come to you. We think if Eugene could be brought to sponsor the idea, then the rest is assured!"

"What is it I am to sponsor?" a deep voice asked.

The three ladies looked up quickly at the gentleman standing just inside the room. Gwen frowned and Mary blushed, but Deirdra clapped her hands excitedly and would have run to him had not Sir Eugene forestalled her by taking long swift strides to her side, taking her fluttering hands in his own, and urging her to stay still.

Mary's eyes misted slightly at the sight of the tenderness between her twin brother and his wife, while Gwen regarded him dispassionately.

He was dressed for riding in dun-colored breeches and brown coat with a scarf tied negligently about his neck. His was not the studied casualness currently in vogue; his was natural. He was a man who didn't care about fashion. He didn't have to.

How alike her children were in looks, Gwen thought. And Catherine, too, had the same large deep brown eyes and square chin. In Catherine and Eugene the square jaw was strong, and supported the belief a square jaw denoted a stubborn personality.

"Ralph's sister, the Countess of Seaverness, has offered to present Catherine this Season along with her three other nieces," Deirdra told him brightly, then started to giggle again. "She assumes Catherine has never had a Season and is still unwed because she has little portion and no beauty!"

Eugene raised an eyebrow but vouched no comment.

Mary, nervous at the growing silence, took up the issue. 'We believe she should go despite Lady Harth's ideas.''

"I fail to see where I enter into the matter. If the chit wishes to go, I see no reason why she shouldn't."

"My love," Deirdra said softly, tugging her husband's hand to get his attention, "I think what Gwen and Mary are afraid of is Catherine will not go if she thinks you need her here. And she has said she does not wish to wed. She prefers the company of horses." Deirdra gave him a soft smile.

"Nonsense. Of course she will one day wed. She would be a prize for any gentleman!"

"Aye, she's a prize, but will the prize ever be claimed?" Gwen asked sarcastically, annoyed with her son's offhand manner. "You forget she is already one-and-twenty. Do you see any prospects about? No! Unless you consider the young men with the regiment stationed in York, or perhaps some of those greedy country fops she meets at the Harrogate Assemblies who fall in love with her beauty, but truthfully only wish to marry her because one day your estate will pass to her. Those are Catherine's choices now." Gwen was growing more frustrated at her son's urbane countenance. "Oh! How I wish you had not told everyone your intentions."

Sir Eugene's brows snapped together. He scowled at his mother while he considered her words. He never thought of Catherine's age and, he realized, he never thought of her ever leaving Umberfife. He had meant it for the best when he made Catherine his heir. As for leaving her Fifefield and the stable, well, it was the only way to keep it in the family. He and Deirdra would have no children. Catherine and her husband would keep the Burke tradition alive and one day his grandnephews would inherit. But he had no wish for her to wed a fortune hunter. . . . If his mother was correct. He looked quizzically at his wife. Her eyes big as saucers, she nodded. He looked back to his mother.

"It was not meant that way," he said, irritated at his mother as well as himself.

"There is reason for Catherine to go to London," Deirdra said slowly. Three pairs of eyes turned to her. She smiled broadly. "You mentioned it yourself earlier, Lady Burke. Did you not note Gene had a Grand Tour before taking over Fifefield?"

Eugene and Mary were puzzled by Deirdra's line of thought; however, Gwen caught the nub of the matter.

"Of course, he did not want to go either, eager as he was to take over. However, afterwards, Gene, you said it yourself, it was the best thing you could have done. You knew how to judge horses and the trip taught you to judge people as well!" Gwen said, warning to the idea. "If you were to tell Catherine it would help her run the stable, she might go willingly."

"Yes, and I know just how to spur on that willingness, too," Deirdra said.

The other three looked at her expectantly. She shook her head. "I shan't tell you, for it must be something between Catherine and me. But mark my words, she will go." She began to giggle again, clapping her hand over her mouth to keep from laughing aloud, her eyes dancing with mischief.

CHAPTER
TWO

Catherine's attention was focused on Zephyros, the deep-chested bay she rode. She was particularly proud of Zephyros and anxious to show off his paces to Raymond Dawes. She was confident the stallion would be the prize of the string he took to London that spring. She wanted to make sure he knew it too.

Dawes leaned his forearms negligently on the top of the fence and watched horse and rider, a slight smile softening his ruggedly chiseled features. As Sir Eugene's agent in London, he was rarely at Fifefield for long and on those occasions he returned, he was closeted for hours on end with Sir Eugene in the estate office.

Slowly the patronizing smile he had adopted faded as he watched the performance in the paddock before him. He leaned farther forward, resting his chin on his crossed arms. Catherine, glancing at him briefly, was jubilant. She knew Dawes was now no longer indulging her and was seriously concentrating.

With a self-satisfied smile on her face, she put the horse to some difficult jumps. She failed to note the elegant gentleman by the stableyard, so intent was she on impressing the agent.

"Well? Isn't he marvelous?" Catherine finally asked riding up to him and slipping from the big bay's back. "Zephyros could carry a good-sized man for hours without tiring, and still look graceful and light doing so!" She stroked the bay's nose affectionately and turned bright shining brown eyes on Raymond Dawes.

"Mayhap you have the right of it," he said slowly as he straightened and reached out also to stroke the horse.

"Is that all you can say? Don't you have any other comment?" Catherine felt disappointed. Her eyes glazed over as she turned back to stroke the horse's neck. "I think he's one of the best we've had and should fetch a high price! I must own, if I did not have my Gwyneth, I should be loath to part with him at all!" she said with a toss of her head.

Dawes scowled for a moment and looked out across the fields, then back to the big bay. The animal was beginning to prance at standing still for so long.

"Wouldn't be right."

Catherine cocked an eyebrow in inquiry. "Oh?" she asked softly, a hard edge to her voice.

"He's too big for you."

Catherine gave him a wrathful look, stamped her foot and started to protest, but Dawes forestalled her.

"I said you were right afore when you said he could carry a good-sized man. Should, too. Not enough horses of his size and quality around. Fetch a top price, like you said."

"Well, why didn't you say so before?" Catherine asked exasperated.

"No sense repeating what you just said. Don't know why you want to hear again what you already know."

Catherine frowned at him a moment longer until her own sense of the ridiculous overcame her and she had to laugh.

"Enough, I call craven! I'm taking him back to the stables now. Would you open the gate, please?" she asked.

Dawes fell into step beside her. "Miss Catherine," he began after they'd walked a way toward the stables in silence. "I still say it isn't right, but you do have a way with horses."

Catherine looked sharply at her uncle's agent. This was rare praise indeed! Some of the sparkle came back to her eyes then and she breathlessly launched into a recital of all the horses she had schooled that were in the string for the spring sale. She did not stop until they reached the stableyard and turned over the bay to one of the young stableboys.

It was then that she noticed the stranger lounging there, watching her. She blushed to the roots of her hair as she saw a small half-smile curve his lips. He touched his hat in a slight bow her way and she felt a sudden heat course through her chilled body. He was quite simply the most devastatingly handsome man she had ever seen. Belatedly she realized his gaze was lingering on her figure, and glancing down at her attire, she blushed anew. Never before had she regretted her breeches. Now she felt awkward and strangely stripped bare.

"Miss Catherine?"

"What? Oh, sorry, Raymond. I—I was just thinking I would like to see a sale in London," she babbled. "I'd like to see who gets my dears. Isn't that a client you should attend to?" She gestured jerkily in the stranger's direction and began to back away toward the house.

"Who? My lord!" Dawes exclaimed, striding over to the marquis. "I beg your pardon. Have you been standing here long?"

Catherine took that opportunity to take to her heels toward the house in a very unladylike fashion.

The Marquis of Stefton, assuring Dawes he had not been standing long, watched her flee with masculine appreciation for her slender yet nicely curved form. She would indeed be a handful, he acknowledged to himself before turning his attention to Raymond Dawes.

* * *

Entering through a side door, Catherine was met by
young footman who told her that Lady Burke was desirou
of seeing her. Receiving this intelligence, she did not g
directly to her aunt's sitting room. Her mind was too mucl
in a turmoil, her body trembling—though not from th
cold—and she was uncomfortably aware of her attire. Skip
ping nimbly up the backstairs—taking some steps two at
time—she called to Bethie, one of the housemaids, to fetcl
hot water to the little room allotted to her. Though her dea
relations grudgingly consented to her wearing breeches t
ride in, she was careful not to wear the offending garment
in the house and kept a few muslin dresses at Fifefield. Sh
shuddered at the thought of what their reactions would be i
they knew a visitor had seen her in her breeches.

She rapidly washed and, with thinly held patience, suffere
Bethie to dress her glowing auburn curls in an artful knot o
top of her head with trailing ringlets, when she learned he
mother and grandmother were below with Aunt Deirdra an
Uncle Eugene. *A regular family conclave,* Catherine though
with a hollow laugh. She fidgeted impatiently while Bethi
laced up her yellow sprigged muslin gown, much as the bi
bay had pranced when she stroked him. Bethie begged he
to stay still a moment and she'd be done in a trice.

When Catherine entered Deirdra's sitting room som
minutes later, the conversation in the room ceased abruptl
and four pairs of eyes turned to her. Catherine felt uncom
fortably like a small child discovered in a prank, but coul
not think why. There was her mother looking distressed, he
grandmother with a bland expression (that always spelle
trouble), her Uncle Eugene giving her a curiously inter
look. Of them all, only Aunt Deirdra seemed her norma
self. It was she who broke the silence Catherine's entranc
caused.

"Catherine! You'll never guess!" Deirdra giggled an
patted a space on the yellow brocade sofa next to he
"Come here, for we have the most fabulous news!"

Catherine could not resist the infectiously gay quality c
Deirdra's voice and slowly moved across the room to sit b

er aunt. Deirdra clasped both of Catherine's hands in her
wn and looked intently at her.

"You must know, we have all felt a little guilty of
epriving you of a London Season, as by rights you should
ave had one years ago. We are so complacent here, we
rget we have all seen London and the sights, whereas you
ave not. Happily now we may bury our guilt, because you
re to go to London!"

Catherine tilted her head to the side. "Are *we* going to
ondon?"

"Not we, dear," broke in her grandmother despite Deirdra's
arning glance. "Just you."

"Yes, yes," put in Mary breathlessly. "Your father's
ster has asked for you to come to London so she may
resent you."

"But, Mama," Catherine said, "we have been through
is before. I have no desire for the frivolities of London."

"Think of the many young gentlemen you will meet."

Catherine blushed and stood up stiffly. Gwen, cursing her
wn interference, wished Mary to perdition and wondered
gain how she ever came to have such a gentle ninnyham-
er for a daughter.

"I do not desire to be wed. There is too much to be done
ere." Catherine swept an accusing glance around the room.
Now, if you will excuse me—"

"Hold!" Sir Eugene said from his place by the window.
is dark face held a black anger that caused Catherine to
ink and take an instinctive step backward as he approached
r. "You are displaying a marked disrespect for your
ders, which I am afraid I cannot like," Sir Eugene said,
king her chin in his hand and forcing her to look up at
m.

He spoke in an even tone but Catherine knew she had
red badly, and no matter how much he let her wind him
ound her finger from day to day, when he was displeased
was best to make what amends one could.

"Now sit down and keep a civil tongue in your head," he
dered.

Deirdra giggled then, and Catherine sank back down to
r seat as all eyes were turned from her to Deirdra.

"Oh, really, my love, it is not as bad as that. Now loo
what you have done! We will be lucky to get a peep out o
her, now." Deirdra patted Catherine's hand soothingly, know
ing full well that no matter how repressive her dear Ger
could be, ultimately Catherine would not stay silent.

"Now, where was I? Ah, yes—the most droll thing ha
occurred, though I must admit, neither Gwen nor Mary se
it quite in the same light as I do, but no matter. Anyway, th
Countess of Seaverness says there are four Shreveton gir
who have not been presented, and she would like to make
grand gesture and present all four to Society at once in
single Season. I dare swear the woman has no idea what sh
will be letting herself in for, to have four young women
her home with all the problems of shopping for four, th
entertaining, the suitors. Why, I do think it would be vast
fatiguing. But I must confess, my dear, what positively ha
me in whoops is that it's obvious by her invitation sh
thinks you have never been to London in the past becaus
you are too poor and very plain! I believe that is what ha
put Gwen and Mary in queer stirrups, but I see how sh
came to have such a mistaken idea."

Catherine's mind was in a whirl, but she knew she cou
not make any more untoward comments. She was rath
piqued at the cavalier manner of her aunt, of all people, an
gasped slightly when she read the letter Deirdra placed
her hand.

"Is it not plain from this she thinks of me in a differe
light than my cousins? I am sure she would not care if I d
not take her invitation. It seems only a gesture. Besides, sh
would be sadly disappointed in me. I have no desire to
wed, and I think I have reached the age where a woma
must realize her situation in life and take it with goo
grace," she said, trying to assume a mien of quiet dignit
"I—" Catherine broke off abruptly when she caught sig
of her uncle's flushed countenance.

"Enough! We will have no more discussion," Sir Euge
said angrily as he paced the floor. "You will go to Londo
because I say you will go!"

All the ladies looked at him in surprise. It was out
character for him to take a stance against Catherine. He ha

owever, been suffering a twinge of guilt since his mother
ad brought Catherine's situation to his attention. He knew
e frequently disregarded Catherine's feminine nature. He
ad desperately wanted a son to share his plans for the
ture; Catherine, with her tomboyish ways, had filled that
le, and he had continued to allow her to do so, partly
ecause she shared his love of horses, and partly—if truth
e told—because he received an odd satisfaction from
ncouraging her to go against the established role for wom-
n. He would not have wanted his Deirdra to be any other
an the warm, deeply feminine woman she was. He came
the conclusion he was to right his wrong immediately, for
atherine's own good. He stopped his pacing and glared
wn at her.

"You will listen to Mother, Mary, and Deirdra, and you
ill do as they say and go to London." With that parting
ot, he strode out of the room.

Deirdra shook her head in dismay, smiling slightly as she
atched her beloved husband leave. She exchanged slight
ances with Mary and Gwen before turning once more to
atherine.

Catherine, for her own part was dumbfounded. Never
fore had she seen her uncle exhibit such a closed mind. It
arked a flame of resentment and she compressed her lips
stubbornness. Mary, bereft of a handkerchief, wrung
r hands in agitation and looked pained. Gwen sat very
right in her chair, carefully schooling her face not to show
y sympathy to Catherine for Sir Eugene's treatment of the
uation. She did not know whether she was distressed by
bluntness or relieved to have the situation set forward so
plicitly.

Deirdra, after watching for some moments the ebb and
w of emotions across Catherine's face, deemed it time to
tle the emotionally charged atmosphere.

"Tea should be ready," she said as she pulled the bell
e next to her. "I believe Cook baked some spice cakes
ay, which I dearly would like for I am famished."

Sir Eugene's mind churned as he descended the stairs and
ssed the hall to the library. His mind was still caught up

on the knotty problem of his niece when he entered, and was with a start he remembered his guest.

"Stefton, my apologies. I have been shamefully remiss. A slight domestic problem." He smiled. "When one surrounded by female relatives it is not an uncommon occurrence," he said humorously.

The marquis inclined his head in acknowledgment of the apology, then sipped his Fifefield brewed ale. "We have known each other many years, Burke. No need to stand on ceremony, I assure you. Dawes and your staff have been most accommodating."

Sir Eugene poured himself a mug, paced the room a moment, then sat down across from his guest.

"You saw my niece. Now I must ask that you forget you ever did—particularly her unusual attire."

The marquis raised an eyebrow in polite inquiry, then shrugged. "I have a lamentable memory. Consider it forgotten."

Sir Eugene frowned down at the mug he held. "Catherine is my heir."

"She is a fortunate young woman," Lord Stefton murmured.

"I don't know." He rubbed his hand along the back of his neck to ease tight muscles. "I am sending her to London this spring to be presented—probably at least three years too late. Her aunt, the Countess of Seaverness, is taking her."

"Lady Harth?"

"Yes. You look surprised."

"Surprised? Yes, though perhaps amused would be a better word. I didn't know you were related to Lady Harth."

"My sister married Ralph Shreveton."

"Ah, one of the younger brothers of Aldric Shreveton, our illustrious Earl of Whelan," Lord Stefton drawled meaningfully, for it was well known that since his second marriage—this one to his solicitor's daughter—the earl had become staid and vulgarly middle-class.

Sir Eugene barked a short, harsh laugh. "Precisely."

"I account Viscount St. Ryne, Lady Harth's son, a particular friend of mine. It is my understanding his current absence from the country is a direct result of his mother's

tchmaking propensities. He holds it she is attempting to
ke up for his uncle's disastrous liaison.''

Sir Eugene shrugged. "I care not for Lady Harth's
sons—my concern is for Catherine. She is old to be
sented. I would be distressed to learn she was considered
ape-leader.''

"May I inquire her age?''

"She will be two-and-twenty this spring.''

"Definitely an ape-leader,'' Lord Stefton said callously.

Sir Eugene opened his mouth to issue a scathing retort,
n shut it, his lips compressed against ill-considered
rds.

"A wise decision,'' Stefton said, amused.

Sir Eugene's face cleared and he leaned earnestly toward
rd Stefton. "You are an influential figure in Society.
rhaps if you—''

A warning silver light flared briefly in the marquis's gray
s. He would have thought Sir Eugene above such pandering.
ou flatter me. It is my understanding, however, that
—ah—reputation encourages debutantes to stay out of
orb.''

"Hear me out a moment. I am not suggesting you should
ke her one of your flirts; however, if you could see your
y clear to speaking with her a moment at some ball or
er, it would raise her credit in the eyes of Society. It may
p remove the stigma of her age. I tell you, Stefton, I
uld not ask if she were a blushing seventeen-year-old,
d do not be afraid she would languish for your attentions,
I don't believe you're in her style.''

A frown creased the marquis's brow and his lips thinned.
t in her style! he thought, irritated. He studied Sir Eugene
ntly, finally a wry smile lifted the corners of his finely
seled mouth. He had come close to taking himself too
iously, for he admitted a twinge of pique at the thought
t some woman might be immune to his charms. He
nembered Catherine's animated expression when she talked
Dawes and the sweet curves displayed to advantage in her
se-fitting breeches. It might be interesting. . . .

"Shall I bring her into fashion?'' he nonchalantly asked
host.

A horrified look captured Sir Eugene's features. "No! mean, I do not wish you to put yourself out in any way.

Lord Stefton waved a hand to dismiss his concern, th that wry smile spread to his eyes and he took another sip ale. "I promise, she shall not be overlooked."

"Aunt Dee, I can't see what there is to laugh about Catherine exclaimed later that day as she paced the floor Deirdra's sitting room. "Nor why everyone, particular Uncle Gene, must needs run my life. I have no desire to p on airs and simper and coo as other empty-headed femal jockeying for the supposed honor of some man's name a then being virtually auctioned off like a horse at Tattersall's

Deirdra watched Catherine in silence, allowing her expend her nervous energy before attempting to talk to h She dispassionately noted her niece's cheeks were stained deep rose from her agitated state and wondered if the ch realized how beautiful she was when she was angry. Quiet she drew an embroidery stand in front of her and beg separating the bright strands of silk.

"I have no need to be wed and I cannot like othe meddling in my affairs," Catherine finished.

"Are you so sure we make plans just for you?" Deird returned placidly.

Catherine stopped her pacing and looked over her sho der at her aunt.

"Are you so sure of yourself? Mayhap you are being trifle selfish," Deirdra continued, speaking softly to ca her as Catherine and Eugene would calm a high strung co

Catherine came slowly forward to sit beside Deird "What do you mean?"

Deirdra sighed and leaned back in her chair. She smil fondly at her niece. Somehow she was feeling the elde aunt, though only twelve years separated them.

"Squire Leftwich has wanted this year past to wed yo mama, and she is not against the idea; however, she will do so as long as you are not settled."

"But I am."

"Not in a mother's eyes, my dear. Your grandmot thinks your mother is being too missish but, well hones dear, having you around is a constant reminder to her of age. While you are not by she is as giddy as a young in the throes of her first romance. Your grandmother ieves, and I agree, if you were absent a few weeks, the le romance could come to fruition.'' She bent her head a ment to thread her needle. ''You must also consider your eritance. Frankly, you need a bit of town bronze. Your cle Gene, remember, took the Grand Tour before he took er Fifefield and came to learn about people, which has de him all the sharper in dealing with those who would chase a Burke horse. You are only spiting yourself by not ing advantage of the opportunities. Why, I am sure your at must move in the first circles, among just the people o would purchase our horses. Think of the connections!'' e was silent for a moment as she regarded Catherine, her d tilted to one side and her hands for once still in her

Making a decision, she picked up her needle and guided hrough the fabric before her. ''No one says you have to per and coo. Play a part if you wish. Take the town by rm, or be exactly what the countess expects you to be—a hing.'' Deirdra shrugged slightly. ''It is really of no tter. But do stop thinking we are trying to run your life. are merely attempting to throw opportunities your way. , however, cannot tell you what you should discover m this situation.''

Catherine frowned. ''I still cannot like it, though there is ch in what you say.''

She suddenly remembered the stranger by the stableyard the way he had stared at her. A slight blush flared over cheeks in memory of the strange sensations he'd aroused. stubborn look came over her face and her jaw jutted out lishly. ''But I will not be on display!'' She rose and led the room again before stopping before Deirdra. ''I k I will be what Lady Harth expects: a plain, meek use.''

Deirdra giggled, though not for the reasons Catherine ught. For all Catherine's vivacious nature, there was a ak of shyness in her that would allow her to be cruelly t unless she had some protection. Playing the mouse

would make it her game, and give her confidence as
came to know the people around her. Deirdra doubted
ability to maintain such a role indefinitely, for her spi
were too high.

"If that is your wish. We'll let it be our secret. Y
uncle, your grandmother, and your mother would only
hurt if they knew, for they have so much pride in you.'

Catherine nodded vaguely, her mind already busy fo
ing, testing, and discarding or shelving ideas for the
tended role. Deirdra giggled again and reached out
draw her niece to sit by her so they could begin planning
campaign.

CHAPTER
THREE

So abundant was the faith the family placed in Deir
no one questioned Catherine's sudden complacence, anc
the few weeks before Catherine was to leave for Lon
there was much coming and going between Fifefield
Linley House. While Gwen and Mary were planning morn
dresses and ball gowns, Deirdra and Catherine were bu
sewing plain gowns and discussing hair styles and mann
Deirdra was hard pressed to contain her mirth through
those fleeting weeks. Catherine never considered her lo
one way or another and was certain she looked as dowdy
her dress. Deirdra knew differently. Nothing could hide
mask Catherine's natural appeal, and those who loo
beyond the gown to her face could not fail to see her cha
Those who did not see beyond outward appearances, Deir
dismissed as of no importance.

Sir Eugene made all the arrangements. Catherine wo
draw on his account while in London and would jour

here in the company of Raymond Dawes and his wife
Maureen.

For an abigail, Deirdra offered the services of Bethie
Callahan, the daughter of her housekeeper. She was a
spirited frizzy-haired strawberry blonde who served Catherine
at Fifefield. She had been married to a young soldier who
died in battle the year before, shortly before peace was
announced. So, at twenty, she was back at Fifefield. Deirdra
saw her as young enough to enjoy Catherine's plans, but
wise enough to keep her eyes and ears open in order to
advise her mistress.

She was a good choice. She entered into their plans
eagerly, and with Bethie's aid, it was no great matter to
pack the plain gowns. Catherine wanted to leave all the
fancy beautiful dresses at home; however, Deirdra and
Bethie forestalled her, saying no one knew when they might
be wanted.

If the truth be told, by the time the carriage passed by the
massive brick columns surmounted by the wrought-iron arch
that marked the end of the drive from Linley House,
Catherine was in high gig. It was a cold, yet clear and dry
day in the beginning of March. Perfect weather for leave-
taking and starting a long journey—or so Sir Eugene said at
breakfast that morning.

Sir Eugene and his lady arrived at Linley House early to
be in on the last-minute hustle and bustle of leave-taking.
Deirdra flitted about like a butterfly, her merry laugh tinkling
everywhere. Her high spirits kept a flustered Mary from a fit
of vapors, soothed Gwen's rough snappish manner, and kept
Catherine excited about the trip. In short order Deirdra had
the entire household gathered on the front steps of the
rambling red brick mansion, all eager to see the young miss
off. So it was in a flurry of embraces, blessings, exhorta-
tions to dress warmly, a few sniffles, lectures, and many
smiles, Catherine departed.

When the last glimpse of Linley House and her waving
well-wishers were out of sight, Catherine pulled herself in
from leaning out the carriage window. Her cheeks were a
bright rosy color from the cold and her eyes sparkled.
Maureen smiled complacently at her charge, thinking she'd

be the rage of London, so lively and pretty was Miss
Catherine. Gentlemen could not fail to be enchanted with
her high color and flashing eyes. A well-set-up young lady
she was to her mind. Netta Scorby, the seamstress in
Umberfife, had spent many a long hour with Lady Burke
poring over the latest ladies' magazines to get ideas for
Catherine's wardrobe. They turned out some beautiful dresses,
Maureen heard, and well she could believe it seeing the
midnight blue traveling dress with light blue frogs that
Catherine wore. It was certainly all the crack.

No, Miss Catherine would not be coming back to Umberfife
unbetrothed. Like as not there'd be a notice in the *Morning*
Gazette before the Season was out.

Maureen Dawes, well satisfied with the start of the
journey, leaned contentedly back against the brown velvet
squabs and closed her eyes.

While familiar landmarks were still to be observed out the
windows and the skies remained clear, Catherine's sunny
mood prevailed. But it was not to be expected this fortuitous
combination would continue to exist the further south they
journeyed. So it was, as the clouds gathered and the
atmosphere became dank and chilly, Catherine's thoughts
clouded.

Catherine had never been farther away from home than
York and Harrogate. She loved her home, village, and
surrounding countryside. She was content. Or so she told
herself since that assembly in Harrogate when she overheard
three of her dedicated suitors speculating on the size of the
dowry that her Uncle Eugene was bound to grant. They
further compounded their greed by cold-bloodedly discussing
her expectations on his death.

She'd been eighteen at the time and giddy over the
attentions she received. A cold weight settled in her chest
then, and she decided to find fulfillment in life from the
horses she rode and schooled. She still flirted outrageously
and danced every dance, but her heart remained encased in
its cold vault.

Occasionally she discovered herself daydreaming *what*
if..., though this she squelched and denied, even to her

elf. That was fairy-tale time. She decided that the realities of life in the nineteenth century precluded love.

Love. Instinctively she shied away from the word, strangely afraid of the emotion and its connotations. Love meant letting go, abandoning oneself to another. It was a frightening idea. Aunt Deirdra loved her husband, and she knew her mother had loved her father. They deferred to their husbands' every wish, and both—though in different ways —were weak, helpless creatures. Catherine knew it was foolish, but she was afraid that love would rob her of life, would turn her into a meek, placid creature who did nothing in life but live for her husband.

This absurd fear of love warred with her internal confidence to meet any jump straight on, to throw her heart over first. The ambiguity of her situation was not lost on her and it gnawed at her. She would like to let go and enjoy herself, to take a risk on finding love—yet her pride and shyness prevented her. She fretted over the duality of her emotions, feeling somehow lesser for her fears, yet confident of their nature.

The blacker the sky, the colder the air, the more Catherine's thoughts spiraled down.

The next morning saw neither improvement in the weather nor in Catherine's mood. As she stood before the looking glass in her chamber at the Rose and Crown, she felt no satisfaction at seeing a reflection of herself in a plain, dun-colored gown with her hair pulled severely away from her face denying its natural tendency to wave. She felt she looked the plain mouse. However, seeing herself so attired, and knowing the masquerade began at that moment, she suffered a strange disquiet.

Catherine stood before the mirror so long without moving or saying a word that Bethie became nervous. "Are you all right, Miss Catherine?" she asked uncertainly.

"What—oh, yes, thank you, Bethie." She turned toward her abigail and smiled. "I must confess our plan for me never seemed real until now." She faced the mirror once more, turning from side to side to see herself better. "I am a figure of fun! What do you suppose will be Maureen and Raymond's reaction? I venture they will not like it."

Bethie giggled, "No, Miss, but as much as they disapprove, they know they have no say over you."

Catherine sighed. "True, and how much that knowledge will hurt them. Raymond has never altered the image he has of me as a wild twelve-year-old following him around the stables. Well, enough. Where is my bonnet, Bethie?" She looked about her.

"Here, Miss. There, now we're ready." Bethie said tying the ribbon under Catherine's chin.

Catherine turned back to the mirror briefly, her earlier reverie gone and replaced with an objective attitude. The gown and the bonnet, a washed-out dun color like the dress, served to focus attention on Catherine's tanned complexion, earned from long hours in the saddle without benefit of a hat. Her mother and grandmother had plied her with creams and salves to negate the harsh drying effects of the elements on her complexion. They'd achieved only a modicum of success. She was not an alabaster beauty. Catherine's skin was soft and smooth, in perfect condition—save for a golden glow that only served to highlight a speaking pair of dark brown eyes and burnished auburn hair. Colors looked good on her, but there would be no problem looking plain and unattractive in the white gowns considered *de rigeur* for the debutante.

"Yes, I'll do. My gloves? Thank you. You have everything in order now? Good, then run fetch the post boy to carry these boxes down while I confront Mr. and Mrs. Dawes."

Bethie giggled again and told Catherine she couldn't blame them, if she didn't mind her saying so. It was hoydenish, what she was doing.

Catherine shrugged slightly and went out the door Bethie held open. She did not again look back in the mirror. The die was cast. She lifted her chin and stood straighter as she sedately descended to the coffee room below.

Much to her relief, Maureen Dawes was its only occupant. An empty plate bore mute testimony to her husband's earlier presence. Maureen looked up and smiled.

"Good morning, did—" She got no further when her

ind registered what her eyes were seeing. She stared at atherine.

Catherine carefully schooled her expression to a serious ien and returned a faint good morning to Maureen before king a seat. She kept her eyes downcast in a modest and nassuming manner.

"Catherine?" Maureen's voice shook.

"Yes?"

"What are you doing?"

"Why, eating my breakfast."

"Don't play May-games with me, why are you dressed in at hideous fashion?"

Catherine put down her fork and for the first time looked aureen in the eyes. "Because I wish to be," she answered ftly.

Maureen blinked rapidly and Catherine watched her as a ries of conflicting emotions crossed her round plump face. he felt sorry for her. She took her responsibility so serious- and was well aware—as was all of Umberfife, Catherine ought with a grimace—that she was being sent to London contract a brilliant alliance. Catherine watched her chap- on come to a decision. She braced herself; she was not to e swayed, not now.

"Well, it will not do at all. What would your family say they saw you so rigged? You go right back upstairs and hange into one of those nice costumes Mrs. Scorby made p." Maureen moved her hands before her as if to shoo atherine up the stairs; however, Catherine stayed where ie was and placidly sipped her coffee.

"No."

Maureen gasped. "Now see here, Miss, I am in charge of ou and I want none of your hoydenish manners. You'll do s you're told and very prettily."

Catherine sighed. "I suppose it is from being married six ears that you have developed this dictatorial manner. Nev- rtheless, may I remind you that you are a scant two years lder than I, and frankly, I cannot think that makes you esponsible for me. I am legally my own mistress, and I hall do as I please, and it pleases me to dress as I do."

At that last Catherine felt a twinge of conscience, bu
pushed it aside.

Maureen's jaw dropped and she sat there gaping like a
landed fish. Catherine was hard pressed not to laugh. She
knew Maureen meant well; however, she was not going to
let anyone ride roughshod over her any longer. They had
gotten her to go to London; beyond that she dug in her
heels. She was determined to have a say in her own affairs.
She smiled demurely at Maureen and returned to her meal.

Maureen was made of resilient northern stock, and while
she did not know how to handle this different Catherine, she
was not at a standstill. She rose hurriedly, her napkin falling
to the floor unnoticed, and scurried out the door in search of
her husband.

Unfortunately for her peace of mind, she did not find the
looked-for help in that quarter. Dawes, upon hearing his
nearly hysterical wife's account of the past few minutes,
merely took her arm to walk around the courtyard, much as
he would have walked a horse, allowing it to cool.

"You're not to worry yourself," he said after some
minutes. "She was bound to take some queer start."

"Raymond Dawes, how can you say that?" asked his
much exasperated mate.

"Stands to reason, ain't been broken to harness yet."

"Not bro—she is not a horse! It is past time she was
married. She's too fine a girl to be a spinster. She'll not get
a nice gentleman looking like that!" Maureen's chest heaved
and her cheeks were flushed from righteous indignation. She
made to move away from her husband back to the coffee
room, but Raymond held her fast.

"Stay. Early days yet. All this fuss just put her back up
more. Give her a long rope, she'll tire. 'Sides, that aunt of
hers will have something to say about how she dresses.
Bound not to let her look the frump."

Maureen halted and looked up at her husband. That for
him was a long speech and he did make sense. "But it isn't
right!" she wailed.

"Not saying as how it is or it isn't."

"Do you really think her ladyship will set things right?"

"Bound to. That Shreveton family, they set great store by

ppearances. Except for Viscount St. Ryne, they always buy
e showy horses. Ain't much on wind or length of limb,
ut they look grand.''

Maureen sighed and Raymond turned her around and led
er slowly back to the coffee room.

It could not be said Maureen was totally mollified, but
he could admit defeat for the while. Catherine was glad to
e spared further recriminations, though she was curious
nd a bit piqued by Dawes's unconcern. She was suspi-
ious, yet try as she might, a logical explanation eluded her.
he endeavored to push it out of her mind—still, it was a
ng way to Grantham.

The Marquis of Stefton sat sprawled sideways in the
carred and scratched wooden arm chair in the best private
arlor offered by the Lion's Mane Inn. One leg dangling
ver the arm of the chair swung restlessly. The substantial
mains of an evening repast offered by the obsequious
nkeeper to his illustrious guest were pushed negligently
vay from the space set before him. The marquis sat, idly
virling a wineglass between strong tapering fingers. His
one-gray, heavily lidded eyes were turned away to gaze out
e window of the first floor private parlor that fronted the
n and overlooked the courtyard below.

There was little activity of note. Once, a dog ran across
e courtyard followed by a young boy, but the marquis
carcely noticed the pair. He was lost in his own brooding
oughts and stared unseeing at the vista before him.

He was dressed all in black and his Hessians gleamed in
e flickering light of the candles. The marquis's black hair,
ut shorter than fashion preferred, was disheveled and
urled around his brow like a satyr's wild locks. The strong
lanes of his face, square jaw, and prominent blade nose,
ere not handsome in the classic Adonis sense, yet his
sage was one that set the hearts of women—young and
ld—fluttering. His handsome swarthy features were now
arred by a pronounced scowl that drew his thick black
rows together, creating deep furrows in his high forehead,
d etched brackets by the corners of his firm mouth.

It had not been a promising day. First there had been

Panthea clinging to him in an absurd fashion; and then th
damned outside wheeler throwing a shoe and as luck wou
have it, not only did the landlord have no extra horses
lend him but the only farrier in miles had been called
some insignificant country squire's estate for the day. *Pro
ably to attend the shoes of some sluggard of a beast,* th
marquis thought laconically.

Finally, the crowning irritation had been the discove
that the only inn around also housed that bastard Kirkso
and his cronies. No, it had not been an auspicious day.

The marquis tossed off the last of the wine in his gla
and bent to the table to grab the bottle, his mind returning
the person he perceived as authoress of the day's misfortune

Damn the woman! Did she think no one would see he
That she wouldn't set tongues wagging? Or did she hope
compromise herself in the eyes of the *beau monde,* ar
thereby force him to offer for her? She was deluding herse
if that was her game. He hadn't cut his eyeteeth yesterda
and she was no virginal ingenue to cry over lost innocenc
She'd played the footloose widow too long, and too mar
eyebrows had been raised by her behavior in the past f
there to be fear of ruination. Done that years ag
chuckleheaded female. She had been an amusing, decor
tive mistress; now she was beginning to bore him. That th
lady wished to sink her claws in deeper and be the Marchic
ness of Stefton and the next Duchess of Vauden w
obvious. Bets were being laid at White's as to the odds
her success.

Stefton knew he must one day marry; however, the id
of Panthea Welville in his mother's position was extreme
distasteful. When she heard he was to leave town for
fortnight, what must she do but pay an unwarranted, ar
highly irregular visit to his home.

Panthea clung to him, begging him to stay in Londo
with her or take her with him wherever he was going. S
even manufactured a fine sheen of tears in her eyes and s
her lower lip trembling as she spoke with heartfelt accent
She should have taken to the boards. Not for once did s
deceive him, for she had forgotten how on one occasio
she'd affected such a pose for their joint amusement. H

manner nauseated him and caused him to leave the metropolis later than he cared to. In his black humor he had pushed his horses to their limit to make up for lost time, until one of the horses threw a shoe a half day's journey from his ancestral home, so that he was forced to put up for the night and present himself at his parents's home on the morrow.

Fortunately, despite all her protestations and ardent coaxing, Stefton had not told Lady Welville where he was going. It would have been like her to appear on their doorstep unasked, and that was one circumstance he wished to avoid.

Stefton shook himself out of his reverie, once again drained his glass and reached for the bottle.

Perhaps, he mused, it was best the nag threw a shoe. It gave him time to vent his anger and present the loving son to his parents—unmarred by other matters.

So deep was he in his own thoughts, he scarcely noticed the carriage as it drove into the courtyard, and might not have given it more than a cursory glance had it not been for the magnificent team of horses pulling the equipage. Perhaps new guests were the diversion needed to lift his spirits. He stood, sipping his wine thoughtfully as he closely studied the carriage, the long-tailed black horse led by the groom riding behind, and the coach's occupants.

Catherine was exhausted, her head throbbing, as the carriage drew up before the inn. Only a day's journey left; at that moment however, she wanted nothing so much as a little refreshment and a chance to rest on something that did not sway and jolt. She entered the inn dazed, with Maureen Dawes and Bethie Callahan close behind, leaving Dawes and Tom Coachman to look after the horses. Her impression of the hostelry was one of cozy warmth and cleanliness. As tired as she was, she failed to notice the three inebriated gentlemen lounging just inside the taproom, as the slightly rotund innkeeper huffed and puffed his way toward her.

She summoned a smile for that worthy as he stopped before her, wringing his hands on the large cotton apron that served to protect his buckskin breeches. His round face was flushed and his bald pate glistened. Had she been less tired,

Catherine would have been amused by his mannerisms an•
dubbed him a scuttling beetle of a fellow.

"Good evening. I believe you have rooms bespoken fo
us by Sir Eugene Burke," she said softly.

The innkeeper bowed, but before he could answer,
slurred voice came from the direction of the taproom.

"Too old for a daughter and don't look like a wife—n
rings. Hey—" the voice said more loudly after jabbing on
of his compatriots in the side and winking broadly. "Wha
are you, his bit of muslin?"

The two other gentlemen laughed uproariously. Stunned
Catherine glanced briefly in their direction but otherwise di
not deign to acknowledge that she had heard the comment
She noted the three gentlemen sprawled around the tabl
were fashionably dressed, though a trifle castaway in coun
tenance and appearance. Her tormentor seemed much th
eldest of the group, at least five-and-thirty. His companion
appeared in their twenties, the youngest a pretty fair-haire
youth Catherine deemed only slightly removed from th
grubby schoolboy state.

Encouraged by such ready laughter and another quaff c
ale, the heckler hailed the innkeeper. "I thought this was
respectable inn. What's this becoming, a bawdy house?'
Again he collapsed into laughter as he swilled his ale.

Catherine frowned and her eyes narrowed as she contin
ued to face the innkeeper. That gentleman was flustered
True, he did have rooms bespoken by Sir Eugene Burke, y•
he hesitated; his was a prominent establishment. It woul
not do to let it be thought it was also an abode for commo
tramps. He looked from the gentlemen to the drab femal
standing before him. It didn't seem in keeping with h•
calling to be dressed so severely. A disguise? He blinke
rapidly and rubbed his hands down his aproned front.

Catherine caught the hesitation in his manner. Her colo
rose, her eyes glinting dangerously. "I am his niece," sh
said through clenched teeth.

That brought another wave of laughter from the gentleme
sprawled across the oak table in the taproom. "Niece! H
horses look better than you do!"

Catherine whirled to face the source of the needling drunken voice and curled her lip contemptuously.

He raised his mug in mock salute.

Maureen and Berthie began to exclaim loudly; however, Catherine hushed them and turned to the innkeeper once again.

"I am Catherine Shreveton, Sir Eugene Burke's niece, and I am on my way to London to visit my aunt, the Countess of Seaverness," she said levelly.

At that the youngest of the three tormentors gave a crow of laughter and slapped his knee. "Stab me if you ain't got the right of it, Kirkson, and that just proves it," he said, hiccoughing. "Everyone knows all Shrevetons are blonde like me. I ought to know my own kin, and you don't look like any to me." He blinked at her owlishly.

The innkeeper began to wring his hands. Sir Eugene was a valued customer. Nevertheless . . . "Now see here, miss—" he began.

He got no further. Kirkson, rising from his chair by the door, came up behind Catherine and grabbed her around the waist.

Panic clutched at Catherine. She beat him wildly about the head with her reticule, twisting and turning to break free from his grasp.

Maureen screamed in outrage and pummeled his back. Bethie attacked his shins with her heavy country shoes and clawed at his face, calling him every sort of beast and screeching at him to let her mistress go. The innkeeper wrung his hands then wiped them against his apron again as he feebly protested.

Ignoring the innkeeper, Kirkson swore viciously, relinquishing his grasp of Catherine as he turned to fight off her protectors. Dodging another kick, he pushed Bethie toward the gentleman claiming Shreveton kinship.

"Orrick, take this tidbit and keep her out of my way!"

With Bethie gone, he swung around to face Maureen, his elbow connecting with her right eye. Maureen howled in pain, momentarily blinded by tears of pain. Kirkson shoved her roughly away. Maureen staggered backward and fell awkwardly into a corner of the hall. He turned back to

Catherine, who raised her arm to hit him again. He caught
her wrist, cruelly twisting it, and wrested her reticule away.

"Here, George, catch!" He tossed the purse to the third
gentleman, who still sat at the table, clutching his sides in
laughter.

Catherine's initial fear was replaced by cold anger as she
felt Kirkson's arms go around her. She tried to squirm away,
but he held her fast. He laughed at her attempts, her
twisting motions increasing the ardor in his eyes. Pulling
her close, his mouth came down on hers hard, his teeth
grinding painfully against her lips.

Catherine had never kissed a man and felt a suffocating
horror engulf her. She was dimly aware of George pulling
money out of her reticule and tossing it into the air. Some of
it fluttered into the fireplace, flaring briefly. In wild despera-
tion, Catherine viciously bit Kirkson's lower lip. He drew
back swearing and momentarily loosened his grasp.

It was enough. She broke loose. As he made to lunge for
her again, she picked up his mug of ale and threw it at him.

"*Brava!*" said a voice from the balcony.

All eyes turned upward to the figure leaning on the
balustrade. Catherine's mouth dropped open, dumb surprise
robbing her of motion. It was the gentleman she'd seen a
month before at her uncle's!

"By-the-by, Orrick," the gentleman went on in a bored
tone as he flicked open a small, gold snuffbox with one
hand and delicately took a pinch, "I don't believe anyone
would call St. Ryne fair, and I've heard tell those young
brats of Aldric's have their mother's mousey brown looks."

The innkeeper looked up at his distinguished guest and
blinked rapidly, his eyes widening. "Gentlemen, please!"
he squeaked.

"Stay out of this, Stefton," Kirkson warned after a
cursory glance in the marquis's direction. He advanced
steadily on Catherine. Young Orrick, momentarily taken
aback by Stefton's remarks, was surprised when Bethie
kicked him in the shins. He let her go, yelping in pain.
Maureen scrambled awkwardly to her feet and ran out the
door.

Eager to help her mistress, Bethie evaded Orrick's lunge

d grabbed a candlestick, throwing it at Kirkson. He
dged it with ease, but her actions afforded Catherine the
portunity to gather her wits.

Catherine ran to the fireplace and grasped a poker to
andish before her. Her bonnet had come off in the scuf-
ng, and her hair was tumbling down. She was breathing
pidly, her cheeks flushed, her eyes dark and sparkling.

"You bitch," Kirkson growled. "Think you're too good
r us, eh? I'll get you. It will be a pleasure to tame you,
y dear."

"Careful, Kirkson, don't say I didn't warn you; I'd lay
u odds she is who she claims to be," Stefton drawled as
walked to the stairway.

The innkeeper glanced rapidly from the girl to the mar-
is and back again. Nervously, he cleared his throat and
asped his pudgy hands before him. "Sir! Sir! I must insist
u leave this young woman alone. Please desist, sir!"

"I would have said that earlier if I were you," Stefton
d the innkeeper as he reached the bottom stair. The man
cked away in confusion at the condemning expression on
e marquis's face.

Kirkson backed Catherine into a corner. Stefton could see
wild martial light flaring in her eyes as she prepared to
fend herself. Orrick and George Primly were whistling
d hooting encouragement to Kirkson. Bethie, her eyes
de with fright as she stood with her back to the front wall,
oked pleadingly at the marquis.

"You are becoming a bore, Kirkson," Stefton said languidly.

Kirkson laughed, intent on capturing his prize. Catherine
ung the poker, but it was an awkward weapon. He
isted it out of her grasp, tossing it across the room.
took another step closer to her. With his advance, she
rank back into the corner as far as she could.

Suddenly, her languid supporter from the balcony was
hind Kirkson, his shoulders bunching as he pounced on
rkson like a large black panther, grasping her attacker by
collar and pulling him roughly off balance.

Raymond Dawes, followed by Tom Coachman and Maureen,
shed into the room. Stefton, seeing Sir Eugene's man,
ung Kirkson over to him.

"Dawes, perhaps you would be so kind as to dispose of this filth."

Raymond did not wait to question. He drew back his arm then delivered a shattering right hook to Kirkson's jaw. The man staggered backward, then slowly crumbled to the floor unconscious.

Tom Coachman grabbed George and young Orrick as they tumbled over each other in their efforts to escape, and banged their heads together.

Maureen and Bethie supported a trembling Catherine.

"I have stayed here many times, as you know," Raymond breathing heavily, said to the innkeeper, "and I suggested this establishment to Sir Eugene. I shall inform him of my error." He turned to Catherine, his face a study of anger, chagrin, and remorse. "Miss Catherine, I am sorry I chose so ill. Shall I have the horses put to and we go elsewhere?"

The innkeeper sat down heavily on the stairs, his head in his hands. "I am ruined," he muttered. "Absolutely ruined."

Stefton from his vantage point by the fireplace leaned against the mantelpiece and watched Catherine through hooded eyes. He had been intrigued by her spirit as she fought Kirkson with such icy determination, and he had found himself coming to her aid out of admiration for that determination and strength. Yet now, he saw her as she suffered the emotional backlash. He saw her blanched complexion, her trembling, and as she closed her eyes to fight off a last convulsive shudder, he saw her bite her full lower lip and draw a bright red bead of blood as she strove to overcome her raging emotions and drop a calm mantle over herself. When she finally opened her rich chocolate brown eyes to answer Dawes, Stefton unconsciously straightened. This was no missish debutante. Most women of his acquaintance would have continued their weeping and protestations. This woman was different.

A sudden tightening in his loins took him by surprise, for he was not some callow youth discovering the mysteries of the fruitful vine. He admitted a strangely dispassionate curiosity as to his reactions to this woman. The upcoming Season, he mused, could prove vastly entertaining.

Catherine's voice when she answered Raymond was low

nd husky. "No, we shall remain here for the night as my
ncle arranged." The necessity of making decisions brought
Catherine to her senses again. "I am certain we can look to
he landlord to assure us we shall be well tended. Is that not
orrect, my good man?" she asked in a firm yet soft voice.

The innkeeper, hardly daring to trust his good fortune,
umped up, hurriedly bowing several times and kissing
Catherine's hand, assuring her in broken stammering phrases
hat all would be as she would like. She hardly seemed to
otice, but waved him to the stairs.

"Just show us to our rooms at the moment. I believe I
vill rest before dinner."

Stefton, watching the whole, surprised everyone—including
imself—by laughing out loud.

CHAPTER
FOUR

"Oh, Miss! Miss Catherine, look!" Bethie squealed,
ousing Catherine from a drowsing state.

Reluctantly, Catherine opened her eyes. Seated opposite
er, Bethie's body was awkwardly twisted, her nose pressed
gainst the glass carriage window.

"What is it?" Catherine inquired in a distracted manner.
Three days of rocking and swaying in the carriage, passing
umerous towns, villages, pastures, fields, and windswept
eaths, had dimmed her interest in her surroundings. Her
ind was occupied with memories of the embarrassing
vents of the previous evening and the disconcerting, pene-
ating gaze of her rescuer. The decidedly vexatious realiza-
on that her thoughts dwelled more on Lord Stefton than on
e effrontery of the inebriated gentlemen gave her a throb-
ing headache and an unwarranted snappish demeanor. The
entleman cut up Catherine's peace in a manner entirely

foreign to her experiences. Every time she'd been aware of those steel gray eyes upon her, she felt a strange tightness in her chest overlaid with a tingling that rippled through her threatening to descend all the way to her toes! Humbly Catherine admitted that perhaps there was some merit in her relatives' decision to ship her off to London. The incident of the previous evening made patently obvious to her the necessity for acquiring the town bronze Deirdra mentioned.

Nonetheless, the notion that gentlemen of Kirkson's ilk should buy and ride a Burke horse was distasteful. Well after last evening's imbroglio, she doubted Dawes would accept his coin for any horse. Particularly not after the nasty black eye Maureen now sported.

Poor Maureen! That black-and-blue bruise completely mortified her. If it had been possible, she would have confined herself to her bedroom until the telltale color faded. As it were, from somewhere she'd managed to conjure a bonnet with a wide, deep brim to shade her face. Furthermore, at every carriage stop she walked with her head down and a hand raised to clasp the bonnet brim as if to save it from escaping in an errant wind. Catherine would have laughed at Maureen's machinations if she wasn't aware of how deeply affected the woman was by the injury.

Bethie, on the other hand, seemed to have been invigorated by the incident. There was about her a renewed sense of excitement. All day she'd been in high gig and looking forward to arriving in London.

"Miss Catherine," Bethie said again, this time turning around to tap her mistress's knee, "It's Lunnon! Quick—look before we descend the hill for I'm afeard you'll not see such a sight again."

Dutifully Catherine leaned forward to look out the window, an indulgent smile on her face. Then she gasped. In the distance was the blue ribbon of the Thames River winding around tall buildings and spires that caught the late afternoon sunlight. Further to the east, the sky was steel blue, heralding approaching rain. Against the darkening sky the buildings glowed with golden color. The city was beautiful, and for the first time, Catherine felt a tiny surge of excitement growing.

"See, Miss?" Bethie softly asked, a look of awe in her es.

"Yes. Thank you," Catherine returned, smiling happily r the first time in days.

"What are you two going on about?" Maureen asked, aning toward them to look out their window. She sniffed. Looks like we'll have rain before we reach town."

"Oh, Maureen," Catherine said, laughter bubbling up in- le, "but doesn't it look beautiful from here?"

Maureen Dawes looked at her queerly before settling back ainst the brown velvet squabs. "Rain clouds is rain ouds—and mark my words, you'll not be thinking it so ce when you have to get out of this carriage into the rain. hat a fine impression you'll make on that aunt of yours en, all wet and dripping."

Catherine shrugged. "I'm not interested in making a od impression."

"Shame on you, Catherine Shreveton! What a thing to y when your aunt has opened her house to you and is fering to present you and all."

"Well, it's true. And just think what sort of relatives I ust have if that young gentleman of last evening—Orrick, asn't it?—really is my cousin."

"I'm sure he's just young and mixed up with bad compa- . I certainly intend to discover who his parents are and form them of his disgraceful behavior," Maureen said verely as her hand came up to touch her sore cheek ngerly. The hand dropped back into her lap and she sat raighter. "I'm certain they will see he is punished."

"Oh, really, Maureen," Catherine said, laughing, "he is ot a schoolboy."

"Nevertheless, I shall see they are made aware of his sgraceful behavior."

Catherine shook her head doubtfully and turned back ward the window. Unfortunately, they'd already begun eir descent from the hill and the delightful aspect of ondon in the distance was lost from sight.

Maureen Dawes's prediction of rain before they reached ondon was all too accurate. The heavy downpour painted

the city in drab shades of gray and brown and created larg
muddy puddles of water on the cobbled streets that splashe
the carriage to its windows, obscuring the dreary view fron
sight. Inside the carriage, a damp chill prompted the inhab
itants to draw closer for shared warmth. Maureen succumbe
to morose reflection on her injury, but somehow, Catherine
and Bethie's spirits remained high. Later, descending fron
the carriage at Harth House on Upper Grosvenor Stree
Catherine did not hurry to cross the pavement to climb th
wide stone steps. Instead, she found herself enjoying th
rain, much to the consternation of Maureen, who urged he
to bestir herself, for she could not enter the house befor
Catherine, and she did not like standing in the rain waitin
for her reluctant charge. Standing beside his wife, Raymor
was a drenched, muddy mess; yet he acted as if it was of n
concern, thereby further irritating Maureen.

Lady Harth's butler instructed that Bethie and the luggag
be conveyed to the house's back entrance. Then, his thi
nose flaring, he escorted Catherine and Mr. and Mrs. Dawe
into the hallway.

"I shall inform her ladyship of your arrival," he sai
austerely, adding, "if you would be so kind as to wait.
The sneer on his face told Catherine he had indeed notice
their wet and muddy clothes and had no intention o
showing them to a comfortable room to wait in.

A loud yelp of pain followed by a thump and the crash o
breaking china came from behind the closed double doors o
a room farther down the hall, past the stairway. The butle
winced, closing his eyes briefly as a look of resignatio
twisted his arrogant features.

"What was that?" Catherine exclaimed, moving towar
the closed door.

"Do not concern yourself, Miss," the butler said hurrie
ly, placing himself between her and the door. "A commo
household accident."

Gone was the urbane, superior butler. In moments he'
been changed into a harried, nervous man. The transforma
tion was so complete and instantaneous that Catherine foun
herself halting in surprise and wonderment.

The doors behind the butler opened and a red-face

weating footman came out of the room. He was awkwardly
carrying a tray of broken china before him as he moved in a
bandy-legged fashion, the front of his uniform wet from the
waist down.

"Mr. Pennymore, I'm giving notice," he said, shoving
the tray into the butler's hands.

"Let's not be hasty, John, please," implored the butler,
hurriedly putting the tray on one of the empty side tables.

"Hasty! My manhood's scalded and you tells me not to
be hasty?"

"John!"

Catherine bit her lip to contain a giggle while behind her
Maureen gasped in shock and a pained look of empathy
pursed Dawes's mouth and twisted his features.

"She don't even apologize, just reprimands me for calling out in me pain. No sir, I'll not stay another day in this
madhouse. I'll just be changing and collecting my wages."

"A rise, John? How about a rise?"

"No sir, it ain't worth it," proclaimed the footman as he
turned to make his way carefully down the hall.

"Double your wages?" Pennymore offered desperately.

The footman stopped for a moment, then carefully turned
to look at the butler. "It depends on how me fragile
condition heals," he said loftily and continued down the
hall.

Watching him leave, Catherine valiantly struggled to
repress an urge to laugh—without success.

Pennymore smoothed his thinning hair back into place
and turned around to stare down at her as if she were some
insect under a magnifying glass. He had transformed once
again and was the epitome of the arrogant butler.

"If you will wait here, I will—as I told you before we
were so rudely interrupted—inform the countess of your
arrival." He sniffed dismissively, then turned to proceed into
the room.

Her curiosity increasing with each moment, Catherine
began to examine her aunt's home. She walked down the
hall. It was elegant in its architectural design—a black-and-
white marble floor, marble pillars, a graceful curving stairway, and deeply patterned plaster medallions on the ceiling

highlighted with gold leaf, were among its features—yet th
house seemed strangely barren. The hall was devoid o
decorative accoutrements. Niches in the wall, obviousl
designed for statues, were bare. Side tables, intricatel
carved and layered in gold leaf, stood well out of the way i
almost inaccessible corners, devoid of vases, trays, or othe
items.

Stark. That was the word, Catherine decided, she woul
use to describe Harth House—elegant yet stark. It made he
wonder if her aunt was really as wealthy and snobbish a
she had assumed. The lack of expensive bric-a-brac coul
connote a reversal in the family fortunes and the necessity o
selling off family heirlooms.

Catherine suddenly felt uncomfortable in her masquerad
and determined to act cheerful and friendly, for it wa
possible Lady Harth could ill afford to present four niece
and was truly doing so out of some misguided notion o
family honor.

Or perhaps she really was quite mad, as the footma
suggested.

It was with decidedly mixed emotions that Catherin
heard the door open, followed by the rustle of silk skirts
She took a deep breath, placed a smile on her lips, an
squared her shoulders.

A tall, angularly built woman garbed in a mustard
colored gown stopped ten feet away. She folded her hand
before her, tilted her head back, raised one thin eyebrow, an
stared down her aquiline nose at Catherine.

Catherine's smile faltered, a blush surging up her neck t
her cheeks, staining them deep red. Suddenly she wa
uncomfortably aware of her rain-drenched clothes and he
cold, damp feet. She shifted position restlessly before th
woman's considering stare. Anger flared within her, and sh
abruptly raised her head to meet the gaze of her Aun
Alicia. It was then she saw the other woman, who wa
wearing a gage green gown—a plump woman with an ope
and sadly smiling countenance. She reminded Catherine o
her father. Confusion swept through Catherine. She droppe
her gaze to the floor.

Pursing her lips at her sister's stiff, unwelcoming demean

, Lady Orrick swept past Alicia to enfold Catherine
a welcoming embrace. She clucked her tongue. It never
iled that after one of her sister's *accidents* she always
rned formidably arrogant. It was as if she blamed the next
:rson she saw for her own clumsiness.

"I just can't believe it! Ralph's little girl—after all these
:ars!" Lady Orrick cooed delightedly, her sharp eyes
pidly scanning Catherine and her entourage. She nodded
ice to herself in satisfaction, though she was curious as to
e child's drab raiment. The girl's mother, she remem-
:red, dressed conservatively but at least possessed a nice
nse of color and style.

Lady Orrick turned back to gauge Alicia's reaction.
bviously, her sister saw nothing amiss in their niece's
tire, so busy was she assessing her niece as a person. Lady
rrick's eyes narrowed; their sparkle dimmed. She was
it pleased by the looks exchanged by her sister and
atherine in awkward silence, though the answering chal-
nge she saw on Catherine's face intrigued her.

"Passable," the tall, angular woman finally declared,
epping closer. "Those freckles are deplorable, but you'll
). I am your aunt, Lady Harth, Countess of Seaverness.
ou may call me Aunt Alicia," she declared briskly. "This
your Aunt Penelope, Lady Orrick."

"Orrick?" sputtered Maureen Dawes, drawing all eyes
ward her for the first time.

Catherine whirled around, reaching out to grasp Maureen's
rist, silently imploring her to be quiet. "We—we encountered
young gentleman along the way by the name of Orrick. He
as blonde, blue-eyed, probably about twenty. Is he any
lation?" Catherine said rapidly, pulling down on Maureen's
ind and all the while smiling brightly.

"Yes, that would be my son Stephen, your cousin."

"Really?" Catherine said brittlely, "How—how—in-
resting!"

So far, Lady Orrick was the only person to welcome her
ith any warmth at all. She could not repay this gentle
oman, who so resembled her father, by talebearing.

Lady Orrick studied her niece's expression, and the con-
:rnation she saw written on Mrs. Dawes's round vis-

age, with interest. No doubt Catherine's meeting with he
son had been less than amicable. She hoped the ugly bruis
on Catherine's chaperone's face was not some souvenir o
their encounter. Well, that story she would get later fror
her scapegrace offspring.

"Let me introduce you to some of your other cousins,"
Penelope said, skillfully drawing Catherine past Alicia to
ward the others standing in the hall. Despite her sister'
ridiculous standoffish manner, the child needed welcoming

Lady Harth regally nodded agreement, then turned to fac
Mr. and Mrs. Dawes. "Thank you for escorting my niec
from Yorkshire. Give my butler your direction as you leave
I will see that you are adequately recompensed for you
efforts."

"What! Well, I never—" began Maureen indignantly.

"Thank you very kindly," interrupted Raymond, "but Si
Eugene Burke has already paid our expenses."

Lady Orrick looked back over her shoulder at Raymon
Dawes. She owned she had not paid much attention to th
fellow previously, but the name of Sir Eugene Burke pique
her interest. What did he have to do with her niece?

"Excellent," Lady Harth told Dawes, neither recogniz
ing nor caring about the identity of Sir Eugene Burke
"Good day."

Catherine, hearing the last, looked over her shoulder t
see the Dawes turning to leave and hastened to bid ther
good-bye. Aunt Alicia was certainly strange, and Catherin
couldn't decide if her initial summation of the woman wa
accurate or if her revised idea that she was genteell
impoverished yet proud was correct. Nevertheless, she su
mised she'd stepped into a very unusual household.

Aunt Penelope patted her arm, drawing her attention t
three beautiful blonde young women standing at the base c
the stairs. After a quick glance at the gray-streaked blond
hair showing beneath her aunts' lace caps, she began t
understand how her cousin Orrick could doubt her Shrevet
ton lineage.

The youngest two women were as matched as bookend
differing only in the color of the ribbons trimming the
identical floral printed muslin frocks. They were perfe

ecimens of china doll beauty, and radiated as much
armth as a statue. They looked at Catherine with twin
pressions of boredom.

"Catherine, these are your cousins, Lady Iris and Lady
ahlia, daughters of your uncle, the Earl of Whelan. Don't
' to tell them apart, I can assure you it is impossible!"
dy Orrick said gaily, though privately annoyed by the
ins' attitudes. "To accommodate us, they wear some
icle of clothing that enables us to differentiate between
em. Girls," she said, looking at them pointedly, "please
lp me make your cousin Catherine welcome."

Iris and Dahlia looked at each other in private, unspoken
mmunication, then turned back toward Catherine, their
rfect bow-shaped mouths lifting upwards at the corners in
actly the same manner.

"Charmed," the one with the blue ribbons murmured.

"Delighted," the one with the red ribbons added.

Lady Orrick frowned briefly and steered Catherine away
om the twins. Her brow cleared and a warm smile lit
r face as they drew near her shy third niece. "This is your
usin Susannah, daughter of your uncle, Captain Glendon
reveton."

Susannah approached Catherine hesitatingly. She was tiny
d delicately boned, her hair a richer golden blonde than
at of the twins, her eyes brown instead of blue—brown
es that were as large and soft as a young doe's. Catherine
ontaneously smiled at her. Relieved, Susannah smiled
ck.

"Aunt Alicia, shouldn't we be dressing for the Wyndersham
usicale?" Red Ribbon interrupted. Blue Ribbon nodded
reement, smiling sweetly at Lady Alicia.

"The Wyndershams! Of course, at once. We can't let
therine's late arrival discommode us further. Quick, girls,
stairs, at once."

"Alicia!" Penelope protested, "surely you're not plan-
ag on Catherine's attending an affair her first night in the
y."

"Most certainly not! She'll need to be decently attired as
fits a Shreveton before she may go anywhere."

"You would have her stay here, alone, when she has ju
arrived?"

"But, Penelope," protested her sister, "since you ha
been so disagreeable as have other plans for this evening
have no further recourse."

"Alicia!" Lady Orrick placed her hands on her amp
hips and glared at her elder sister.

"Oh, very well," Lady Harth said sourly, "Susann
may stay with Catherine."

Lady Orrick pursed her lips briefly. "That's not wha
had in mind," she said severely.

"It's all right, Aunt Penelope" Susannah interjected.
would like to stay."

Penelope frowned doubtfully.

"And I assure you, I will not mind if they all go out
Catherine said. "It was a long journey," she added coaxing

"Very properly said," Lady Harth stated, nodding
approval. "Susannah, show Catherine to her room."

"Immediately, Aunt Alicia," Susannah said, making
little curtsy.

Penelope's frown deepened. When she had seen the twi
work their manipulative ways upon Alicia to get her to gi
them a London Season, Penelope suggested to her sister th
she present all of their nieces who had not been presente
She desired that the twins succeed beyond their expectatio
and perhaps learn a lesson against manipulating othe
Unfortunately she neglected to consider the possibility
continued manipulation on the part of Aldric's daughter
Now she worried that the twins—flaunting their position
daughters of an earl—would make life miserable for the
cousins.

To make matters worse, she would not be in London
deflect the worst of their mischief. She had promised h
daughter, Marianne, to be present at her third confineme
Penelope shook her head in self-disgust. This was ve
ill-planned.

She watched Susannah and Catherine turn to ascend t
stairs. She knew they could be cruelly ignored in favor
the spoiled twins. Twin cats, that's what they were. Sti
Catherine did not seem to be as drab a little thing as th

had all supposed, and it appeared she had a quick wit as well as a kind heart. *It really is too bad that I must leave tomorrow,* she thought. *I would be willing to wager that Catherine will prove to be a more beautiful flower than either Iris or Dahlia.* Well, she would return to London for the ball Alicia would be giving later in the Season in the debutantes' honor. It was an event she was beginning to anticipate.

Susannah led Catherine to her room, then stood uncertainly in the doorway. She was lonely in Aunt Alicia's household, and she had hoped Catherine and she could form a friendship, for Iris and Dahlia were neither friendly nor kind. She felt she was suffering through each day until the Season was over and she could return to her parent's home in Portsmouth.

She shifted nervously from foot to foot, her large brown eyes wide, as she watched Catherine warmly greet a smiling, frizzy-haired maid. In awe she watched them giggle together like school friends. Then she witnessed the strangest thing of all. Catherine removed her dowdy bonnet, tossing it carelessly into a corner of the room before she reached up to the tight bun at the back of her head and rapidly pulled out a handful of hairpins. A glorious tumble of wavy auburn hair fell past her shoulders. Catherine leaned forward to shake her head then flung her head back, raking her fingers through the thick auburn waves as they settled back away from her face.

"What a relief!" Catherine massaged her scalp,, her eyes half-closed, a smile of sheer bliss curving her lips upward, her face aglow.

"But—but—you're beautiful!" Susannah blurted out.

Startled, Catherine turned toward the doorway. She had forgotten all about her cousin. Truthfully, she assumed she'd want to leave her presence as quickly as the others did. Behind her, Bethie giggled again. She cast a glance of reproof at her maid before crossing the room to take her cousin's hands in hers. She looked into her eyes, mentally framing a careful reply, when she noted the shy vulnerability in Susannah's wide-eyed gaze. Impulsively, she squeezed

her cousin's small hands reassuringly, a bright smile sending
sparkle to her eyes and dimples to her cheeks.

"Can I trust you to keep a secret?" Catherine asked.

"Of course," Susannah said, puzzled.

Catherine hooked an arm around Susannah's waist and
drew her into the room, seating her on a brocade-covered
bench at the foot of the bed. Catherine studied her shy
cousin a moment then nodded, and began to pace the room.

"I came to Aunt Alicia's under duress. I never desired a
London Season. I was coerced into coming by my well-
meaning family."

"*Family?* But Aunt Alicia said you were all alone—
except for your mother."

"Hardly," Catherine said drily, coming to sit next to
Susannah on the bench. "My mother and I live with my
grandmother, and a few miles away live my uncle and his
wife. Shortly, if my aunt Deirdra's predictions are true, I
will also be acquiring a stepfather and two stepbrothers.
Actually, I wouldn't mind that, for Mother is lonely and too
cowed by my grandmother. And Squire Leftwich does care
for her. He and his sons need her, whereas Grandmother and
I really don't," she finished ruefully.

Catherine stared into the dancing flames in the fireplace.
"Unfortunately," she said slowly, "Mother has this notion
that she cannot look to her own happiness until she knows
am comfortably situated. Such nonsense. Anyway, Aun
Deirdra and Grandmother felt the squire might be more
inclined to press his suit, and Mother more inclined to
accept, if I were not around."

"I see."

Catherine glanced at Susannah's serious expression be
fore turning back to her contemplation of the flickering
flames in the hearth. "Then there is the matter of my
inheritance," she added, frowning at her thoughts.

"*Inheritance?*" Susannah asked, then blushed, "I'm
sorry—I don't know what—really, it is no business o
mine."

Catherine returned her full attention to her cousin, laugh
ing at Susannah's evident confusion. "Do not be embarrassed.
know Aunt Alicia has painted a gloomy picture of my life

ut her renderings are without basis—they are cut from the cloth of her imagination. That is what bothered me the most about coming to London, the knowledge that Aunt Alicia considered me a nothing.''

"Well, you are not alone there, for she does not think much more of me—if she thinks of me at all!''

"Ah, but by your looks alone, you are a true Shreveton. But I digress. Let me tell you about my inheritance, for it lies at the base of my presence in London. Have you ever heard of Burke horses?''

"Yes, of course. Father would love to own one but says it wouldn't be fair to the animal, because he is at sea so much, you know, and there would be no one about to exercise it. Mother said she would, for she loves to ride, but Father told her that no woman can control a Burke horse.''

"Fustian,'' Catherine said and rose from the bench. "I school Burke horses.''

"I beg your pardon?''

"It's true, I assure you. My uncle is Sir Eugene Burke, and I shall be his heir,'' Catherine added with pride and satisfaction.

At Susannah's shocked expression, Catherine laughed and went on to tell her enthralled cousin about the events leading up to the start of her sojourn to London, and her reason for the dowdy disguise.

"It really is how Aunt Alicia expected me to appear. Why should I disappoint her?''

Susannah laughed, feeling more at ease with her cousin though vestiges of awe remained.

"I must admit, however, that last evening I had cause to regret my attire,'' Catherine said ruefully.

Susannah encouraged Catherine to tell her the story. Catherine tried to give her a brief summary; however, Ethie, methodically unpacking Catherine's trunks, continually threw in elaborations that forced Catherine to elaborate a kind.

"And you say Sir Philip Kirkson gave your Mrs. Dawes that black eye? And that Cousin Stephen was involved? Aunt Penelope will be mortified to learn that.''

"Which is precisely why we won't tell her.''

''But what about this gentleman who tried to warn Si
Philip to leave you alone? Who was he?''

Catherine quickly turned away from Susannah to hide the
telltale blush that flared brightly on her cheeks. ''Um,
think he was called Stefton,'' she managed, fighting down
the strange surge of tingling that rippled through her body a
the thought of his dark satyric visage and black locks tha
curled across his brow.

''Stefton? The Marquis of Stefton? He actually inter
vened?'' Susannah asked, rising and crossing to Catherine'
side to place a hand on her shoulder.

''Ultimately, yes,'' Catherine said slowly, puzzled by he
cousin's reaction.

Susannah shook her head, her hand falling from he
cousin's shoulder. ''How odd,'' she said softly, a pensiv
expression in her eyes. ''From what I've heard of him, he'
more inclined to pull up a chair to watch than to lift a finge
to defend anyone.''

''Well, he very nearly did just stand back, and truthfully
at the end, he found the whole quite comical, for he laughe
heartily.'' The memory of amusement glinting in her silve
eyes coupled with his rakish, thoroughly masculine smil
set her limbs quivering. Angrily she banished the imag
from her mind.

''I believe he took the entire incident as a sideshow fo
his enjoyment,'' she said firmly. ''I am convinced the onl
reason he did anything at all was because he and Kirkso
have some great dislike for each other and he knew it woul
be the perfect way to nettle Kirkson. Of course, he waite
until mere moments before Mr. Dawes burst into the room,
Catherine finished waspishly. Then she paused for breat
and grinned. ''But enough of what has gone before. Yo
and I need to plan for what we must do in the future.''

''Do?'' Susannah asked doubtfully.

''Yes,'' Catherine said, coming to sit by Susannah on th
end of the bench, ''for unless I miss my guess, the two c
us will have to band together so our more *illustrious* cousin
don't ride roughshod over either of us.''

''That is true,'' Susannah declared fervently.

''How is it that Aunt Alicia invited us to come to Londo

r the Season? She doesn't seem the type to open her doors readily.''

Susannah laughed. "Now that is a tale, and it owes its nesis, I believe, in her son's self-exile.''

"Exile!''

"*Self*-exile. Aunt Alicia has been after her son, Justin, to arry for two or three years now. Claims it is his duty. She es to promote a match by throwing countless suitable ung women at him during dinner parties, house parties, lls—everywhere. To escape his mother's matchmaking propensities, and hopefully teach her a lesson against meding, he left England for a protracted visit to some family properties in the West Indies.''

"Wise man.''

"I'm not so sure," countered Susannah. "Justin—Viscount Ryne—is a prime catch in the marriage mart, and for ars Aunt Alicia has been asked to every social event cause she is the mother of a prime catch. Only she didn't ow that was the reason until Justin was out of the country d the invitations to her began to fall off drastically. It's rfectly understandable. That incident at tea was not unique. nt Alicia is clumsy. Frightfully clumsy. Who would invite walking disaster to a party if they did not need to?''

"I'll bet I'll hear some blisterin' stories belowstairs then,'' ethie said eagerly while placing Catherine's stockings in a esser drawer.

Susannah laughed. "I'm sure you will.''

"How did Aunt Alicia go from dwindling invitations to esiding over the coming-out of four nieces?''

"It started with Iris and Dahlia. Evidently they wrote a ry heartrending letter to our aunt lamenting how they ould not be able to use some Norwich silk shawls she sent em for Christmas because their stepmother would not stir herself to present them or take them to places where ey could wear the shawls and show them to advantage. nt Alicia hates the new countess for she is middle-class d makes no excuses for it. And because she bore Uncle dric three male babies whereas Lily Abshire, who was the rl's first wife and mother of the twins, died in childbirth.

And the first countess was a great friend of Aunt Alicia too.''

''So in a fit of pique at her sister-in-law, Aunt Alic[ia] decided to present the twins. But why are *we* here?''

''I believe that was Aunt Penelope's doing. Evidently s[he] realized that the twins were trying to play off of Au[nt] Alicia's dislike for their stepmother, so she thought she['d] help them succeed well beyond their expectations.''

Catherine nodded in understanding. She rose from t[he] bench to slowly pace the room as she listened.

''She somehow planted the idea in Aunt Alicia's he[ad] that she would be readily admired for presenting four niec[es] in a single Season. Making a grand gesture. She w[as] correct.''

''So, enter Susannah and Catherine.''

''Yes,'' Susannah replied quietly. She folded her hands [in] her lap and leaned back against a bedpost.

Catherine stopped her pacing by the window. Outside t[he] rain continued, a steady patter against the glass obscuri[ng] the street below. ''Well, I believe it is obvious that o[ur] cousins are still simmering about our encroachment on *the[ir]* Season. They wished to be the only flowers in the Shreve[ton] bouquet; instead, the Shreveton arrangement contains flo[w]ers *and* thorns.''

''But sometimes, Miss, it's the plants wot have thor[ns] that have the prettier flowers,'' Bethie said sagely, tucki[ng] the last of Catherine's things away in a drawer.

CHAPTER
FIVE

''Please watch the linens, Miss Catherine!'' Bethie i[m]plored three mornings later as she watched her you[ng] mistress gesticulate with her cup of hot chocolate as s[he]

lked with Susannah, who was seated with her on the end
the bed. The little maid tossed a muslin dress over her
m to take belowstairs for pressing. "Mrs. Harmond takes
very dim view of stains on the linens and will hold me
countable if there's so much as a drop of chocolate on
m," she said, crossing to the bedroom door.

"Fustian," Catherine said as Bethie closed the door
hind her. She took a sip of chocolate. "It's me the
usekeeper must find fault with in order to curry favor with
dy Iris and Lady Dahlia. After all, they are the daughters
an earl. What do you think, Susannah? Shall we just spill
drop to give Mrs. Harmond something to decry? It might
better than having her search out something."

Susannah laughed. "Cynicism does not become you,
usin. Besides, you'll spoil the game. Most of the fun lies
looking for faults, not in finding them.

"True." Catherine slowly uncurled her legs from under
r and swung them around to the floor. "Or, in the case of
nt Alicia, making up faults and assigning them to another."

"I think she does that to force attention away from her
msiness."

"What do you mean?" Catherine asked, looking back
er her shoulder at her cousin.

"She acts as if it doesn't exist and ignores all accidents
e creates, but I'm sure at one time she was unmercifully
sed. Most likely she now strikes first before someone
n strike at her. Recall how she was at the dressmaker's?"

"When she knocked over all those bolts of fabrics?"
therine nodded. "I thought the modiste would burst her
ys! Especially when Aunt Alicia stepped on that white
e and left a dirty footprint." She stood up and walked
ward the fireplace.

"But notice, she did not comment on Aunt Alicia's
msiness," Susannah said, tightening the fastening of her
ssing gown.

"Of course not. Aunt Alicia is a valued patroness! And
nember when she wouldn't go into the apothecary's? She
emed it beneath her. She probably was afraid she'd break
nething in there, what with all those bottles, vials, and
sks. Sometimes I can almost feel sorry for her—it must be

lonely to be so formidable yet so clumsy. I remember th
evening I arrived I thought the sparsely decorated house wa
due to lack of funds. Never would I have dreamed that o'
proper and aristocratic aunt was prone to accidents and ha
long ago broken all the decorative accoutrements of th
house.''

''Accidents! Sometimes she's a walking disaster! It's i
wonder she has trouble retaining servants. Frankly, I'
surprised John stayed after that hot tea incident.''

Catherine laughed and nodded. ''It does make me cur
ous, though, to meet the earl. What sort of man could p
up with her?''

''He'll be here for our ball. Aunt Alicia couldn't get hi
to stay in London for the Season. Though she may I
formidable to others, he does not dance merrily to h
piping,'' Susannah pointed out.

''Neither does her son, for that matter.'' Catherine refill
her cup from the silver chocolate pot Bethie had placed
the table near the fireplace, then offered it to Susanna
Susannah nodded and Catherine carried the silver pot to he

''Remember that Miss Brownlow who was also at th
dressmaker's?'' she asked as she poured chocolate into h
cousin's cup. ''Her attentions to Aunt Alicia were nausea
ing. It was patently obvious she would like to be th
Viscountess St. Ryne and the next Countess of Seaverness.
She set the empty pot down, then wrapped her hands arou
her cup, savoring its warmth. ''I don't blame Justin f
leaving the country. In Yorkshire I experienced the san
kind of pursuit—the pursuit for what I can bring financial
to a marriage. My appearance, who I am, that was just i
added bonus. It is very lowering and the reason I hav
decided to forgo that institution.''

''Thus the real reason for this masquerade,'' Susanna
said softly.

''Yes,'' Catherine admitted, smiling sadly.

Bethie's soft knock at the door interrupted them. Catherin
bade her maid enter, then turned to see Susannah doubtful
shaking her head.

''Cousin, that is not a route to happiness.''

Catherine grinned ruefully. ''I know. I just don't lil

people—no matter how well-meaning—trying to run my life. I do miss riding Gwyneth, my horse, though. I much prefer riding to walking. I swear I have never walked so much as I have the last few days in London!''

''If only there were some way you could ride—without destroying your character.''

''You know, Miss, maybe there is,'' Bethie put in slowly as she picked up the hot-chocolate tray.

''How?''

''A disguise for a disguise.''

''I'm afraid I don't understand.''

''Wot if you rode heavily veiled? You know, in an outfit no one's seen?''

''It would certainly set tongues wagging,'' Susannah said, handing the maid her chocolate cup.

''True, but the gossip will be speculating as to my identity, not gossiping about Catherine Shreveton,'' Catherine said, thinking of the possibilities. ''I could have an elegant riding habit made and ride through the park heavily veiled—a mystery woman.''

Bethie nodded excitedly.

''I don't know, Catherine. If Society were to discover the hoax, you would surely be ostracized,'' Susannah warned.

''Would that be so bad? Then I could return that much sooner to Yorkshire.''

''Then again, if it were discovered that you are not the little charity case Aunt Alicia has been presenting you to be, Society may turn on her, thinking she is trying to save you or her son,'' her cousin pointed out.

''I hadn't thought of that. Though Aunt Alicia is stuffy, I don't believe she deserves that interpretation. Well, we will just have to be sure no one discovers my secret. First of all, I must have a new riding habit. Something positively dashing!''

''That's the ticket, Miss Catherine!'' Bethie said, gathering up the last of the chocolate dishes and carrying them to the door.

''And how do you propose to get out from under Aunt Alicia's eye in order to find such a costume?'' Susannah asked.

Catherine smiled. "I think I can count on Iris and Dahlia to help."

"Those two cats? They'd never do anything for us willingly."

"Precisely. But they will go out of their way to see that we don't get what we want, so we'll just have to convince them that we love shopping with them."

"I don't know that my acting abilities are that great," Susannah said drily.

Catherine laughed. "Leave that to me. Lately I've had plenty of practice."

Four hours later, Susannah and Catherine were walking down Bond Street. A few paces in front of them walked the Ladies Iris and Dahlia, both sporting sour expressions. Behind them all came an excited Bethie and the grim-faced Emma, Iris and Dahlia's maid. The twins were dressed in pastel pink and blue gowns while Susannah and Catherine marched behind them in serviceable white muslin gowns with dark blue spencers.

Since breakfast Catherine and Susannah had stayed close to the twins, agreeing with their decisions, and eager to share a shopping excursion.

"We know you two, with your beauty and rank, will attract the most eligible gentlemen to your sides. It is a great boon to us," Catherine stated earlier that morning, "to share a London Season with you, for we are bound to meet far more eligible young men than it would normally be possible for us to mingle with."

Susannah did not know where to look while Catherine complimented their cousins. Suddenly a family portrait hung over the fireplace became of consuming interest. She kept her face averted, pretending to study the painting avidly, not daring to look in Catherine's direction lest she burst out laughing.

Iris and Dahlia, however, did not laugh. Though they took the compliments as their due, the realization that they would have to share the acquaintance of gentlemen with their country cousins was distasteful in the extreme. They began to plot ways to avoid Susannah's and Catherine's company.

Not long after they entered Bond Street, Iris, who was dressed in pink, began to complain of a headache. Susannah and Catherine murmured words of condolence while Dahlia became exceedingly solicitous of her sister's welfare, querying her every twenty paces or so on the state of her health. Iris's lamentations became stronger until Emma decreed they all must return to Harth House for Lady Iris's sake.

Lady Iris argued that she only needed to rest awhile. Perhaps at Gunther's, she suggested, where she could partake of a cooling ice. "But please, do go on without me," she said prettily, effecting a wan smile. "It is too fine a spring day to waste."

"Oh, we couldn't, not at all!" Catherine protested. "What would Aunt Alicia say?"

"No need to worry her. I'm sure I am just fatigued and in need of a little rest and refreshment."

"I'll escort my sister to Gunther's. We wouldn't think of depriving you two of this outing," Dahlia said, clasping her sister's elbow and turning her back the way they came.

"It is a beautiful day, isn't it," Catherine said doubtfully. Susannah leaned toward a shop window, ostensibly reading a shop placard.

"I'm sure I would feel worse if I knew you all returned to Harth House on my account," Iris said faintly. "Please, continue."

Catherine looked doubtful. "Well, if you are sure," she said slowly.

"We insist," Dahlia said, beginning to hasten her pace.

"All right," Catherine said with a show of reluctance.

"I hope you feel better soon," Susannah said, finally turning around, her lips pursed in a struggle to hide a smile and contain her mirth.

Susannah and Catherine watched the twins and their abigail hurry down the street. When they were out of sight, the cousins and Bethie began to giggle.

"You are so naughty, Catherine!" Susannah said, as she attempted to recover her composure.

"I'd be willing to lay odds that I know the real reason they are headed for Berkeley Square."

"I would not give you an argument there. They have more than a passion for Gunther's ices."

"Yes, a passion for all the young bucks who stroll the area," Catherine said drily. "But enough of them. At least we have achieved our goal—*Freedom*!"

The cousins linked arms. "Well, where to now?" Susannah asked.

"Now we discover a dressmaker—someone fashionable who is not patronized by the Countess of Seaverness," Catherine said, scanning the shop windows and noting the type of people who went in and out of the various shops along the street.

"No one fashionable is patronized by Lady Harth," offered Bethie.

Catherine laughed. "Then that should make our task all the easier. Do you know anything about that shop across the way?" she asked Susannah, pointing to a neat establishment fronted by a green and gold sign proclaiming the services of one Madame Vaussard.

"Only that it is not patronized by Aunt Alicia."

"Then that is where we shall begin," Catherine said decisively.

"Oh, please, Oliver, buy me a gown from this silver net. It will go a long way toward appeasing my sadness at the cruel way you deserted me last week," Lady Welville wheedled, a pretty pout emphasizing her full, ruby-red lips. She draped the material across her chest in the suggestion of a low-cut bodice. Her long dark lashes drooped seductively over her blue eyes and a catlike smile emerged from the pout as she looked sideways up at him through the veil of lashes. "It could make a most—ah—enticing gown."

The Marquis of Stefton leaned back on one elbow against the small counter used to display selections of feathers and flowers and crossed one leg negligently before the other as he studied the posturing woman before him.

He intended to sever the relationship. During their outing, he thought to discover some bauble or other that she was enamored of that could serve as a parting gift—not a ridiculous gown in which she could advertise to the world her abundant charms. He didn't know why he let himself be talked into accompanying Panthea to the dressmaker's.

He watched her cup the fabric to her full breasts while suggestively running her tongue across her lips.

Perhaps, he considered, his actions stemmed from a twinge of pity for the woman who tried so hard to wield feminine charms to her advantage. Such girlish posturings were a caricature on a woman her age. Her actions lacked grace and elegance, he thought distastefully. She was no better than the coarse-mouthed ladybirds of the theater.

"Yes, enticing." He watched her preen and smile archly at him. "Very suitable for the Cyprians' Ball," he drawled.

"Oliver!"

The marquis straightened and languidly removed a stray piece of feather from his black jacket. "Really, Panthea, your taste is degenerating. While it may land you in a man's bed, it will not land you with a man's name." His words were spoken softly, though an undercurrent of cold steel ran through them.

Panthea blanched, feeling the steel slicing through her. For the past two weeks or more she had felt the marquis slipping away from her. She desperately wanted to revive his flagging interest, but now it seemed she'd erred badly. The silver net slipped through her fingers.

"You're right, of course. This fabric is just too gauche." She laughed shrilly. "You have such exquisite taste. I was right to bring you with me." She reached out one long, milky white hand toward the marquis.

He ignored her. Picking up his hat from the counter, he placed it rakishly on his head, running his hand along the brim as he checked its position through one of the long gilt-framed mirrors on the wall. When he turned back toward Panthea, she was still staring at him, dumbfounded by his actions.

"Why don't you allow Madame Vaussard to guide you in fabric and style," he suggested, a slight smile playing upon his lips. "Now, if you'll excuse me, I think I shall stroll down to Jackson's to see if I can get in a few healthy rounds of sparring."

He touched the brim of his hat in salute and opened the door.

Catherine was amazed when the solid green door of Madame Vaussard's establishment opened before her hand touched the latch and a large man, dressed in black, almost careened into her. Instinctively she stumbled backward, bumping into Susannah who, in surprise, dropped her reticule. They both stooped to retrieve it, the brims of their bonnets smashing together. Susannah started to giggle.

"Miss Shreveton, so we meet again. What a pleasant surprise."

The dark, rich-timbred voice took the cousins by surprise. Slowly they turned and rose as one, a bright shade of pink staining Catherine's neck and cheeks.

"My lord," she murmured, curtsying.

"I trust you are quite recovered from that unfortunate episode at the inn?" he inquired solicitously, his eyes never leaving Catherine's flushed countenance.

Catherine was incensed that he should mention the incident. Surely a *gentleman* would possess more consideration for a lady's sensibilities. She tossed her head up, her chin thrusting out in challenge as she met his steady regard. "I deem it best forgotten."

His lips twitched in humor. *Egad, but she is a feisty one!* He bowed his head. "As you wish. I am known to have a deplorable memory, anyway. I hope others are as inclined to forget," he finished meaningfully.

"Memory serves no purpose."

"I bow to your greater knowledge. But aren't you going to introduce me to your companion?"

Catherine had the grace to blush again. "Of course," she said stiffly, turning to Susannah. "May I present his lordship, the Marquis of Stefton. My lord, my cousin, Miss Shreveton."

Stefton smiled at her awkward introduction, but made no comment. He bowed to Susannah. "Charmed, my dear. Your father is, I believe, our illustrious Captain the Honorable Glendon Shreveton of His Majesty's navy?"

"That is correct, my—my lord," Susannah stuttered,
shing and bowing her head in pretty confusion.

He returned his attention to Catherine. "I shall look
ward to seeing you both again. Perhaps at Lady Oakley's
l?"

"Yes, I believe we go there," Catherine returned stiffly.

Stefton raised an amused eyebrow at her show of reluc-
ice, then grasped her hand, raising it to his lips. "Since I
t to forget the incident at the inn, I shall look forward to
king your acquaintance at Lady Oakley's."

He bowed again to Susannah, then turned on his heel to
inter down Bond Street.

"Arrogant, insufferable, and rude," Catherine murmured
athfully.

"And out of character," mused her cousin, complacently
iling as she watched the marquis until he was out of
ht. Bethie giggled and exchanged knowing looks with
sannah.

Fiercely denying the tingling that trailed down her spine,
therine looked at them in disgust. Clasping Susannah's
ow, she pulled her toward the shop.

Through the open shop door, Lady Welville saw the
rquis engage two plainly dressed young women in con-
sation. She was frustrated that she could not hear what
s said; however, that he was acquainted with one of them
s obvious. Jealousy clawed at her and she swore viciously
ler her breath. She grabbed her cloak and reticule and
rched toward the door, angrily shouldering aside the
k-auburn-haired woman who'd held Stefton's attention.

"What—!" Catherine exclaimed, staring after the elegantly
red woman.

"Do not mind that one," Madame Vaussard said, hurry-
to Catherine's side and leading her and Susannah,
lowed by Bethie, into the shop.

"Hannah, *ma petite chou*, do not stand there. Put that
ric away. *Vite! Vite!*" the little Frenchwoman said, wav-
her assistant toward the back room. She led Catherine
I Susannah to two Queen Anne chairs covered in a pale
en damask cloth and begged them to be seated.

"Now, how may I be of service to you?" she ask
studying them intently.

Madame Vaussard catered to women of the *bon ton* v
possessed both money and a certain panache or flair
enabled them to wear gowns a step ahead of fashion.
did not consider Lady Welville to be a suitable candio
for her creations, for the woman was, as the marquis impli
only barely respectable.

Two so badly dressed young ladies she would norma
dismiss and consign to a shop assistant, but Madame Vauss
had not become successful by judging a person on appe
ances only. A shrewd knowledge of Society, and the abi
to look beyond the obvious, were also hallmarks of
success.

These two plainly gowned women intrigued her. Tl
were both beauties, despite the scraped-back hair of
dark-haired one. She had not missed the way that one I
challenged the marquis, or how he had smiled in return

The Marquis of Stefton was not known for speak
kindly to, let alone teasing, young women. And that k
upon the dark one's hand—*oo-la-la!* There was an unf
story here that she, Madame Vaussard, would know. It v
just possible she might be looking at the next Marchion
of Stefton and future Duchess of Vauden! That was no
plum any clever dressmaker would ignore, and Mada
Vaussard was nothing if not clever.

Madame watched closely as the dark-haired one fol
her hands in her lap and tilted up her head to meet
steady regard squarely. She did not blush or look swi
away as so many simpering young misses did. She too
deep breath, as if contemplating how to begin. Mada
Vaussard took her cue and smiled reassuringly.

"I would have a riding habit made," the young won
said coolly, "the most fashionable and eye-catching ha
you can create. I would also like you to work witl
milliner of your choice to design a hat with a face-obscur
veil. In keeping with my reasons for the veil, I also requ
your promise of secrecy. Can you do it?"

Madame Vaussard blinked at the forthright request. "*Parc
mademoiselle, I fear you go too fast for me." Her estir

n of the young woman was rapidly rising. "You will,
rhaps, forgive my confusion. You are, please—?"

"I am Miss Catherine Shreveton, and this is my cousin,
ss Susannah Shreveton."

"Ah! *Bon*, you are two of the nieces that the Countess of
averness is presenting, *non*? The countess does not honor
 with her custom," Madame Vaussard said carefully.

"And you wonder at our presence here," Catherine said.
The little Frenchwoman shrugged apologetically.

"It is because our illustrious relative does not frequent your
ablishment that I am here." Catherine looked carefully at
 dressmaker. "May I have your promise of secrecy?"

Madame Vaussard smiled. "My child, a woman's dress-
ker is often privileged to knowledge not shared by others.
 ould not be successful if I could not maintain my silence."

Catherine and Susannah exchanged glances. Susannah
ded slightly, then turned to Madame Vaussard.

"My cousin's situation is most unusual."

"Ah, but isn't that what makes life interesting?"

"I am certain you have known women without money
 o strive to appear as if they are rich."

"This is lamentably true, for my bills, they go unpaid
l I suffer for it," Madame Vaussard said pointedly,
ning both young women with a considering eye.

Catherine laughed. "Do not worry, madame, I am not of
ir number; rather, I represent their opposite."

"*Qu'est-ce que?*"

"My aunt thinks of me as a charity case and so tells all of
ndon. It is not so. Have you heard of Burke Horses or Sir
gene Burke, madame?"

"*Mais, oui!*"

"He is my uncle. It is not a fact I wish bruited about. My
ire is to appear just as my aunt perceives me. I find this
iness of a London Season to be tantamount to a horse fair.
ave no desire to be examined for length of limb, soundness
wind, or breeding potential." Catherine sighed and clasped
 hands in her lap.

"Nonetheless, I would like to ride. As you might imag-
, I ride Burke horses," she said, almost apologetically.
is not an accomplishment of most women; therefore, if I

am to be seen on a Burke animal, I must be somewhat
of the ordinary.''

"Ah, *je comprends,* mademoiselle. You wish to be mys
rious, *n'est-ce pas?*"

"That's it, precisely."

Madame Vaussard tapped her forefinger against her ch
Then a slow mischievous smile swept over her face, light
her blue eyes. She'd wager her business that the marq
knew her identity, and had plans for the young woman t
did not include anonymity.

"Tell me, *s'il vous plait,* do you intend to carry
charade throughout the Season?''

Catherine nodded.

"Ah, well . . . We shall see. But come, now, let us go i
the back and get your measurements and discuss fabri
Come, come,'' she said, shooing them through a gre
curtained doorway into the back room.

Madame Vaussard remembered the marquis's smile
doubted Miss Shreveton would be overlooked in society
long. The *bon ton* might not understand why they w
paying attention to her, but they would follow Lord Stefto
lead. And soon Miss Shreveton would find herself out
her depth.

Madame Vaussard smiled secretly as she followed th
into her fitting room, already designing the perfect ballgo
for her young client. She intended to start sewing it as s
as she finished the riding habit.

CHAPTER
SIX

"After that delicious dinner, I'm inclined to be indolen
Captain Richard Chilberlain said, studying the play of c
dlelight on his cut crystal wine goblet.

The Earl of Soothcoor smirked, then nodded in agreement. He raised his wineglass in salute at his host. "Never d much use for frogs, but if I had ha'f yur money, efton, I'd hire Gascoullet away from you."

The marquis smiled cynically at his two friends. "And I ought it was my company that drew you two so often to y table. My conceit, it seems, knows no bounds. I should e Gascoullet and seek repentance."

"Ha! You'd have to have a bit o' conscience first," the rl advised. He reached for the port bottle in the middle of e table. "I've a mind to forgo Lady Oakley's ball this enin'. Bound to be a squeeze. I don't mind tellin' I'm not ady to stomach this Season's crop of marriage-minded rse-hunters." He shook his head dolefully. "What do you y to us stayin' here, drinkin' more of yur excellent port, d tryin' to take yur money in a few rounds of cards?"

"Ordinarily I'd willingly fall in with such an admirable n. But not tonight, my friends. Not tonight," the mar- is repeated softly, a ghost of a smile pulling up one corner his finely chiseled mouth and burnishing his gray eyes to silver glitter.

"Eh—what's this, Stefton?" the earl exclaimed, straighten- g in his chair. A shock of lank black-and-gray hair fell er his pale blue eyes. He pushed the offending locks back th an impatient movement while his gaze rested on his st and close friend.

"A woman, no doubt," the captain hazarded.

"I trust yu'r not still sniffin' after that Panthea bitch's l."

Stefton raised a quelling eyebrow at his friends. "Gentlemen, u talk as if I were some quivering stud anxious to unt."

"Hardly," countered Captain Chilberlain. "More like the vil out to collect more souls."

"Ah, Chilberlain, your understanding almost pleases me. this instance, however, I believe I shall be more in light a fairy godfather," he urbanely proposed.

"You, Stefton, a fairy godfather? Get on with you. I'd as f believe you'd entered the clergy," declared Soothcoor.

The marquis smiled. ''Take comfort in the knowledge ▮
Cinderella does not wish to go to the ball, whereas Perraul▮
did.''

''Damn it, Stefton, yur too bloody obscure,'' protest▮
the earl.

''No, wait, Soothcoor, I think I have it. Your Cindere▮
has no use for princes—or devils, perhaps?'' hazard▮
Captain Chilberlain, leaning back in his chair and proppi▮
a well-shod foot on the cream-colored silk seat of an emp▮
chair.

''It seems implausible, does it not?''

''And so your interest is piqued. And perhaps pri▮
offended?''

''My dear Chilberlain, now you are like the gossipmo▮
gers who speculate, then spread speculations as truth▮
Stefton drawled darkly. ''Careful lest I feel obliged to ▮
your acquaintance.''

Chilberlain feigned dismay and the earl laughed. ''▮
friendship!'' he toasted. ''And women.''

''Amen!'' said the captain.

Soothcoor and Stefton laughed, clinking glasses with ▮
captain like the three musketeers. The earl never took ▮
eyes off Stefton as he downed his wine. He wondered wh▮
exactly was the nature of the madcap mischief Steft▮
proposed. He shook his head. Society thought they kn▮
the Marquis of Stefton, with his formal, urbane manner, ▮
dry cutting wit, his unremitting boredom. They were ▮
ceived. Soothcoor had followed in his trail for too ma▮
years to be lulled into accepting his social persona. Follow▮
him through high *and* low adventures.

Stefton was an able dissembler, that was true. But m▮
of all, he was consistent. He did not play with innocents. ▮
ignored them. That's why the earl was worried.

''Well, then, how are we to know Cinderella?'' Chilberl▮
asked after downing his glass.

Stefton shook his head, mockingly disappointed in ▮
captain. ''By her rags, of course. How else?''

The captain nodded, a wry smile twisting his handso▮
blond features into deep amusement that lit his deep bro▮

eyes, crinkling their corners on his tanned face into fans. ''And what magic spell is yours to cast?''

"My spell is to make her the belle of the ball despite appearances. To have Society dance at her feet without knowing why. It should make for a most amusing evening."

"Sounds like a mass of bacon-brained nonsense to me," complained the captain good-naturedly.

"And definitely the work of the devil in you. But what about yur fair victim?" asked Soothcoor, a frisson of unease crossing his thin countenance. It was not like Stefton to seek voluntarily to harm an innocent.

"What about her?"

"Are you being fair to her? To thrust her so in the light?"

A feral grin spread across the marquis's features. "I believe she will enjoy it. She is one woman who will not succumb to fits of vapors or tears. She will be more inclined to want me to ignore her as she will strive to ignore me. And that is what will make it all the more amusing."

Captain Chilberlain swung his feet to the floor and looked across the table at the earl. "Soothcoor, I fear our evening fate is sealed. And it might prove to be interesting," he finished, casting a glance Stefton's way.

Soothcoor turned to consider the marquis thoughtfully. His friend was behaving strangely. Did he realize it? It might be that Stefton has finally met his defeat. In all events, he was correct. It would prove vastly amusing.

Catherine followed her aunt and cousins up the steps before the Oakley town house. Lady Oakley's ball would be her first appearance in Society. Now the game began again in earnest and she felt disquieted at the notion. Her gown and appearance were everything she could have wished for her masquerade, yet she did not feel satisfaction. She was restless, ill at ease, and faintly disappointed.

In the entrance hall, she was slow to release the fastenings of her cloak, hesitant to unveil the girlish creation her aunt deemed appropriate: a plain white muslin gown under a white gauze overdress trimmed sparsely with white rosettes joined by silk ribbons in a garland effect. It was a pretty

enough dress for a young girl with china doll looks. On
Catherine, though, the stark whiteness of the gown made
her countenance sallow in appearance, and the dress's youthful design was a painful comedy on her nearly two-and-
twenty years. She was a figure of fun. Unfortunately, it did
not augur well for sinking into the background and not
calling attention to herself for good or bad.

Susannah looked at her anxiously. Catherine returned a
wry smile as she finally consigned the cloak to the footman's keeping. She straightened her shoulders and indicated
with a sweep of her hand that her cousin should go before
her in the procession they made up the grand stairway to the
ballroom above. Catherine knew that her dear sweet cousin
was also having doubts as to this masquerade of hers.
Susannah worried about her in what Catherine considered an
endearing fashion. She was touched, but her resolve was
firm.

Catherine pulled her lips back into a studied smile,
without warmth touching her eyes, and concentrated on her
surroundings.

The stairs they slowly climbed behind others waiting to
be announced hinted at opulent grandeur in the rooms
above. The railings were gilt, the walls painted with pea-
cock feather designs in bold blues and greens with touches
of gold and purple. Wall sconces were intricate brass designs of snarling animals.

The little effigies amused Catherine and soon she found
herself relaxing and smiling easily at their whimsical con-
struction. She had no knowledge of how her natural smile lit
her face, compelling those around to look at her closely.
There was intelligence and animation in her visage that
outshone the poorly chosen gown she wore.

When she entered the Oakleys' ornate ballroom its rose
and gold decor and Chinese dragon chandeliers enchanted
her. She stared at them in fascination.

"Catherine!" Aunt Alicia said sharply.

"Yes, ma'am," Catherine responded with alacrity.

Lady Harth scowled, then raised an eyebrow at her niece.
"This, Sarah, is my niece Catherine Shreveton, poor Ralph's
daughter. Catherine, Lady Oakley.

Catherine curtsied, then looked up into the face of her hostess. A tall, slender woman beamed back at her. "Ralph's daughter? I do remember him. Handsome, lighthearted fellow. Always one for a good joke. Went up north and married, didn't he? So you're his daughter, are you? Don't look like him, but I'd wager you have his sense of the ridiculous," she concluded, casting her eye over Catherine's attire.

Catherine reddened and cast her eyes down for a moment.

Lady Oakley clucked her tongue. "Pretty blush. Alicia, you've deplorable taste in clothes. Run along now and enjoy the ball. We'll talk at supper or some such time. Gracious, the line's all the way to the door. A squeeze!" she crowed delightedly. "My ball is a squeeze," she said, grabbing Catherine's arm impulsively just as Catherine turned to go, "and so early in the Season. Couldn't be better."

Lady Oakley dropped Catherine's arm and blinked owlishly at her through her wire-rimmed glasses. "What are you standing there for? Get on with you now. Shoo, shoo."

Lady Harth sniffed disdainfully at Lady Oakley's eccentric manner, then gathered her nieces to lead them into the ballroom.

Bemused, Catherine followed. Never had she met a person quite like Lady Oakley in dress or manner. It occurred to her that it was the heretofore unknown existence of people like Lady Oakley that had prompted her family to claim she'd led a sheltered existence.

She looked back at the tall, gaunt woman. She was dressed in an outlandish mulberry silk gown trimmed with black embroidery at the hem and across her narrow breast. Her cap was of mulberry velvet accented with large curling black-and-white ostrich feathers that bobbed and swayed frantically as she greeted her guests. The entire assemblage was set at a rakish angle on faded red curls. About her neck she wore a gem-studded dragon necklace that echoed the outlandish oriental decor of her home and confirmed that her favorite motif was dragons.

If people like Lady Oakley were to be her experience in London, then perhaps she'd been too hasty in condemning the metropolis. No matter, her current guise allowed her opportunity to observe, she decided firmly. She sat down on the settee Aunt Alicia indicated, calmly folding her hands in her lap.

An hour later when Susannah came to her side, fanning herself after the exertions of a fast-paced contredanse, Catherine still sat there. Her back was beginning to ache from the stiff upright posture she maintained while her feet treacherously ached to join the sets that formed and move to the rhythm of the music.

"I wish you would not sit here, hidden behind all this profusion of flowers," Susannah complained.

An amused smile tugged at Catherine's lips. "This is where Aunt Alicia placed me. Do you get the feeling that if neither she nor anyone else sees me, then perhaps she can forget my existence? Even for a while? Good heavens, I can't see her threading her way through this maze of flowers to my side, can you?"

Susannah shuddered. "There would be water and flowers everywhere."

"Precisely."

"Oh, but, Catherine, it isn't fair," Susannah softly wailed.

"Oh, pooh. It is what I've always claimed I desired. And it really is amusing to watch the antics of Society. Do you know, people do the strangest things when they think no one is watching. What is really amusing is how anyone could believe they are not noticed in a crowd this size. They act as if they are secluded. One gentleman and lady put me quite to the blush with their fondling. And they were standing just over there, in that corner of the room!" Catherine pointed to a shadowed corner framed by large columns carved to resemble palm trees.

Susannah laughed. "I know what you mean. It makes me wonder why we're so often told to be carefully circumspect in all our actions lest we disgrace ourselves and be barred from Society. But come, I know you must be tired of sitting here so long. Accompany me to the punch table, for I am dreadfully parched and in need of refreshment."

Smiling, Catherine stood up, and for a moment, her face was framed by an array of spring hothouse flowers placed in vases set on tall pedestals in front of the settee. She hooked her arm through Susannah's and slowly they made their way toward punch tables, which were placed in an alcove along the opposite wall.

Stefton, Captain Chilberlain, and the Earl of Soothcoor had arrived but minutes before and many a maiden turned her eyes in their direction. Stefton ignored them all, his eyes searching the assembled company, his face set in a mask of cold hauteur to discourage casual conversation with any he passed.

He was eager to find his quarry. Eager as a dog to the chase. He was not pleased by his inexplicable anticipation; nonetheless, the feelings remained. They were also feelings he remembered from his first sight of the wench while she rode the big bay as if she and the horse were one. Almost he would choose to end the game before it began. Almost.

It was then that he saw her. He inhaled sharply. Her face was framed by riotous yellow and pink flowers that accented the red-gold highlights in her hair and the roses in her cream-colored cheeks. When she stepped from behind the flowers, he grimaced at the stark white gown she wore. It showed her creamy skin to hideous disadvantage. The dress was so ill suited to her, she might as well have been dressed in rags.

"It's worse than I thought," grumbled Soothcoor, scanning the full ballroom. "I'm for the card room. How about you Chilberlain? Stefton?"

"Not yet," said the marquis. He turned to look at Soothcoor. "And neither will you. I need you."

Startled, the earl looked from Stefton to Chilberlain.

The captain shrugged. "I don't know precisely what maggot he has in his brain, but I'm game to humor him."

"Ay, I s'pose for a wee bit, but I'll not stay around to see him dance around some bitch."

"Have you ever known me to be so obvious?" Stefton drawled lazily, though inwardly he again repressed the eager quivering. "And remember, I cast myself in the role of fairy godfather, not the handsome prince."

He watched Catherine as she approached the punch table, the animation in her features as she conversed with her cousin giving a lie—as it always did—to her appearance.

"Now, gentlemen, I suggest you mingle about the company while I engage Cinderella in a dance. When we have finished, I shall introduce each of you to her and you will dance with her in turn."

"What devilment are you up to, Stefton?" demanded Soothcoor.

"Patience," floated back his reply as he threaded his way through the assembled company toward their hostess.

"Lady Oakley, forgive my intrusion."

"Stefton!" She grabbed his wrist with long bony fingers. "I know you've just arrived. Do not tell me you are leaving already! I refuse to allow you to merely put in an appearance, cause untold maidens' hearts to flutter, then disappear. I will not allow it!" she said sternly, the swaying feathers in her cap punctuating her words.

"Such was not my intention."

"Good. Furthermore, you will oblige me by dancing."

"Certainly."

She looked at him suspiciously. "And not just with your flirts, or—or *chères amies*."

"I beg your pardon!"

"Oh, don't come all stuffy and cutting with me. I may be old, but I'm not dead. Or blind. Though sometimes I think that may not be so bad. When I look at today's fashions shudder. Positively shudder."

"You could remove your glasses."

She grinned, pushing her frames up her nose. "Yes, but I've worn them so long I'd feel positively—well, you know what I mean," she finished primly.

A grin cracked Stefton's habitual reserve. Lady Oakley was an old friend of his parents, and it was for their sake he made an appearance at her ball, which was held early every Season; in truth, he would have done so regardless, for he enjoyed Lady Oakley and her eccentricities. She was a refreshing respite from the staid dowagers and the insipid debutantes that littered Society.

"So, do you dance, my lord?"

"Of a certainty. I have even come to you for an introduction to a candidate."

Lady Oakley's pale brows vanished up behind the ruff

d curls that covered her brow. She blinked at him, her lips
arsed in surprise. "Well, then, let me think which lovely
dy I can bestow your favors upon." She quickly scanned
e room. "There is Miss Halcombie, or the blonde Monweithe
ait. All the gentlemen seem to favor that one this season.
r—"

"No," he said, interrupting her recital of the Season's
igibles. "I wish you to introduce me as a dance partner to
liss Shreveton, standing over there by the punch table.
liss *Catherine* Shreveton."

She looked in the direction he indicated, her brows again
imbing behind the fringe of hair at her brow. "The young
oman in that hideous white gown?"

He inclined his head slightly in agreement while hawklike
e observed Lady Oakley's thoughts scurry across her
ansparent features.

"I'll not pretend to understand you, sir, but neither will I
low you to change your mind, for I've not seen that young
oman on the floor yet this evening."

"I thought not," he drawled.

She glanced at him sharply, but his face was unreadable.
e shrugged. "Come, then," she said, hooking her arm in
s and leading him toward the punch table.

Susannah saw Lady Oakley approaching arm in arm with
e marquis. She lightly touched her cousin's hand. "Catherine
: forewarned. I believe the Marquis of Stefton has actually
ranged the formal introduction he promised he would,"
e said, a tiny giggle escaping her lips.

Catherine's head snapped around, her brown eyes catch-
g the intent silver ones of the marquis. Tingling excite-
ent coiled down her spine. She frowned, damning the
elings as swiftly as they came. Why must this man affect
r so? She would not have it, she determined grimly. She
ould not have it at all!

Stefton saw her tiny frown and smiled rakishly in re-
onse. His anticipation for the evening grew. His poor
arry would not have a hole left to duck into when he was
rough with her this evening, he vowed.

"Ladies, please allow me to make the Marquis of Stefton

known to you. Stefton, may I present to you Miss Shreveton—
and Miss Shreveton.''

Stefton bowed over one lady's hand and then the other"
a giggle escaping from Susannah as he bent over hers. H
looked up at her and winked conspiratorially. Next to he
Catherine fumed, her temper rising.

Lady Oakley smiled complacently, her beringed finge
clasped in front of her. ''I notice you do not dance, Mi
Shreveton,'' she said addressing Catherine. ''I cannot ha
that at one of my balls, you know. It would absolutely ru
my reputation as a hostess if my guests fix themselv
against a wall. Allow me to offer the Marquis of Stefton as
partner.''

Catherine's chest rose and fell in suppressed outrag
There was no way she could refuse to dance with t
marquis in the face of Lady Oakley's solicitation. Sl
glared at the marquis, incensed to see his smile broaden
her discomfiture. *Arrogant, odious man!* she thought.

''I am obliged,'' she said tightly, certain Stefton unde
stood her double meaning.

''Not so much as I, Miss Shreveton. Shall we join the s
just forming?'' He gave her his arm.

Stiffly she laid her hand on his, allowing him to lead h
into the center of the room.

Stefton looked down at her, his piercing gray eyes near
hooded beneath coal black lashes. ''You should try for a l
of civility, Miss Shreveton. I am rescuing you from t
ignominious distinction of being one of the only women n
to dance at a ball.''

''I do not consider it ignominious, my lord,'' she replie
keeping her eyes studiously averted from his.

''I know that, Cinderella.''

His sally was rewarded with a quick glance up at his fac
''What did you call me?'' she asked frostily.

''You heard me.''

''I fail to understand, my lord, why you bother. Y
know I do not wish for your attentions.''

''Perhaps that is what has me so intrigued,'' he murmure
bowing formally to her in the opening movement of t
dance.

She curtsied to him and they circled around each other.
"Then again," he said conversationally, "perhaps it is
r my friendship to your uncle. You do remember him,
n't you? He's very proud of you, you know. What would
 say if he saw you now?"

Catherine had the grace to blush, glad that the movement
 the dance took them momentarily apart, giving her time
recover.

"You do him little honor," he continued when they met
ain.

Catherine squirmed inwardly.

"What do you know of honor, my lord?" she ground out
 he led her down through the set.

"More than you, little one," he returned, smiling wolfishly
wn at her.

Thus silenced, Catherine averted her face, determined not
 look at him or speak directly to him again.

Her perseverance was sorely tried for he kept up a
easant monologue, seemingly unaffected by her silence.
e was further annoyed to note the fawning behavior of
her women in the set as they briefly entered into figures
ith other dancers. Stefton treated them all with cool
banity, and Catherine didn't know whether to be glad or
different, for whenever she looked at his handsome face
r heart and mind warred.

At the close of the dance he led her to the side of the
om where a gentleman in red regimentals and another in
own and dull gold evening attire stood.

"Miss Shreveton, this is Captain Richard Chilberlain and
y lord, the Earl of Soothcoor," the marquis said. There
as a curious note in his voice that did not go unnoticed by
s friends. "Gentlemen, allow me to present Miss Shreveton."

Captain Chilberlain bowed low over Catherine's hand.
At your service, Miss Shreveton. I beg of you, may I have
 honor of this next dance?"

Flustered, Catherine only managed to nod jerkily and, to
r chagrin, found herself looking back over her shoulder at
 marquis as the captain led her onto the floor. Stefton
lined his head slightly in recognition of her regard, a
ght smile playing upon his lips.

"That is yur Cinderella?" Soothcoor inquired incredulousl

"Careful, my friend, that your bumptious tongue do
not lead you astray," Stefton murmured, his eyes mere sli
as he glanced over at his friend.

Soothcoor looked at him in wonder and shook his hea
"I say again, what devil is in you tonight?"

Stefton gave him a wintery smile. "Call it a whim, or
quixotic gesture."

The next two hours passed in a whirl for Catherine. Aft
her dance with Captain Chilberlain she found herself bei
led out by the dour Northumbrian, Lord Soothcoor, the
strangely, by one gentleman after another. She scarcely ha
time to draw breath between dances. It was with relief th
she heard the orchestra strike up a waltz, for she knew sl
could not venture on to the floor without prior approval l
one of the doyennes of Society.

She gently refused the youthful gallant who solicited h
hand for the waltz and sent him off instead to procure her
glass of punch. Despite her avowed wish to remain
wallflower, she was forced to admit she had enjoyed herse
The gentlemen she was introduced to were, for the great
part, more interesting than those she met at the count
dances at home. Furthermore, there was the added fillip
knowing they did not dance with her for her wealth. But t
question remained, why did they ask her to dance? The b
did not lack for available women; in fact, there were mo
young women present than men.

Unconsciously she caught her lower lip between her tee
as she considered the matter, a faraway look in her choc
late brown eyes.

A small smile tugged at the corners of the Marquis
Stefton's mouth as he saw Catherine bite her lip. He h
retired to the card room after assuring himself that s
would not lack for dance partners, and had only ju
returned to the ballroom, searching out his Cinderella to s
how she had fared.

He was pleased to note that wisps of wavy auburn ha
were escaping the tight confines of her braided corone
They curled riotously about her piquant features, softeni

e planes of her face at cheek and jaw. She was a wide-
ed innocent beauty, and he almost regretted the game to
opel her into the forefront of Society. But not quite. She
is vastly different from the young women launched every
ar into Society. She possessed wit, courage, and determi-
tion. It was a pity she was so determined to play the role
poor country mouse.

Looking at her as she gracefully accepted a glass of
nch from Mr. Stanley, he decided he must pay a call upon
ymond Dawes. Perhaps Sir Eugene Burke's agent could
ed some light on her odd behavior.

Whatever her reasons, he was equally determined she
uld not go unappreciated by the *beau monde*. He heard
chimes ring announcing supper was being served. A
ntemplative eyebrow rose, a feral smile transforming his
e to satyric wildness. Quietly he approached Catherine
d Mr. Stanley.

"Thank you, Stanley, for dancing attendance upon Miss
reveton in my absence."

Stefton's dark, low voice floated over Catherine's shoul-
r, startlingly near. Catherine whirled around, nearly drop-
ig the punch glass she held. He removed the glass from
r grasp and placed it by a vase on a nearby pedestal. He
ked markedly at Mr. Stanley until the youth began to
get.

"No trouble at all. Delighted. Perhaps we may have our
nce later. . . . He ran his forefinger underneath the white
ck of the cravat that swathed his neck in intricate folds.
bowed stiffly, his lips still working though no words
me, then turned and scurried to the far reaches of the
lroom, placing as much distance as possible between
nself and the Marquis of Stefton.

Stefton watched him go with satisfaction.

"My lord," Catherine began crossly, "I fail to under-
nd how you so intimidate everyone."

"Because I don't intimidate you?" he asked softly.

She looked up into his handsome face, her fingers curling
o fists at her sides as she fought back the heady wildness
presence always brought forth in her. "No, you do not."

"Good. Then you will not be afraid to accept my compa-

ny down to supper. Ah, here comes your cousin. Mi
Shreveton, with your permission I shall ask a friend to jo
us so that I may dine with two lovely ladies.''

''My lord,'' Susannah said, ''you honor us.'' Blushin
Susannah turned her head slightly away to look out acro
the ballroom. She gasped.

Catherine and Stefton broke the challenging eye conta
they'd maintained to see what had so caught Susannah
attention. Approaching them was Captain Chilberlain.
rather bemused Captain Chilberlain, Catherine thought. Sl
looked over in her cousin's direction to see a twin expre
sion on Susannah's features.

''There you are, Stefton,'' the captain said, but he nev
looked in the marquis's direction, his attention, his wor
centered on Susannah.

The marquis's lips twitched but he managed to respor
gravely. ''Yes, here I am. Perhaps you would like me
present you to Miss Shreveton's cousin. Miss Shreveto
this great looby totally lacking in manners is Captain Richa
Chilberlain.''

''Miss Shreveton,'' breathed the captain. He bent forma
ly over her hand.

Catherine had never believed in love at first sight. S
was rapidly revising her beliefs. She exchanged amus
glances with the marquis, relaxing in his company as th
observed love come full bloom before their eyes.

''We were all just going down to supper, Chilberlai
Care to join us?'' Stefton asked laconically.

''What?'' The captain's eyes slowly focused on the ma
quis. ''Oh, supper, right. A grand idea.'' He turned back
Susannah, offering her his arm. ''Miss Shreveton?''

Shyly, Susannah laid her hand on his arm. He quick
covered it with his other hand, anchoring her to his sid
They smiled at each other, big, silly smiles.

''After you, Chilberlain,'' interrupted Stefton.

His eyes never leaving Susannah's, Captain Chilberla
led the way across the ballroom and down the stairs. Behi
them, a fragile camaraderie had sprung up between Catheri
and Stefton and they smiled at each other.

It was an exchange of glances witnessed by many of t

ests still in the ballroom. Tongues, which had wagged
riously early in the evening at the strange behavior of the
arquis, were now set to furiously flapping behind fans and
oved hands. A hissing sound rose throughout the room.

"It's the devil, to be sure," sighed the Earl of Soothcoor,
aking his head. "And what will be the end, I ask?"

"I beg pardon, my lord?" said a young gentlemen
nding near by.

"Nothing, laddie. We'd best do our duty and choose a
dy to escort downstairs afore Lady Oakley does it for us.
e not a mind to sit through a meal with any hatchet-faced
ench of her choosing. That would spoil my digestion."

CHAPTER
SEVEN

"Excuse me, Miss Catherine, but her ladyship wishes
u to join her and the other young ladies in the drawing
om. This being her at-home day," the footman added, by
ay of explanation, for he liked Catherine, as did many of
e more discerning members of the staff, and after last
ght's ball, there would be plenty of callers.

Catherine sighed and laid the book she was reading on the
ole at her side. "Thank you, John. I will be there
ectly," she said softly.

The footman looked at her uncertainly for a moment, then
wed. "Very well, Miss. I'll inform her ladyship."

Catherine watched the man back out of the library and
ose the door softly behind him.

She looked around the comfortable old room with its
ok-lined shelves and beautiful paintings of the Quorn. She
ed this room. Since she had discovered the library on her
st full day at Harth House, it had become a peaceful

refuge from Aunt Alicia's maddening condescension and t
twins' cunning animosity.

For the most part her relatives allowed her to spend hou
between its peaceful walls. Her aunt demanded her presen
only for shopping excursions, or when one or another of h
old cronies came to call. Such visits were always uncom
fortable, for the women came only to judge the caliber
the Shreveton young ladies and comment or complime
Lady Harth on the Grand Gesture she was making in t
name of *family* by opening her house to four nieces at one
Catherine sat awkwardly silent during those visits, her tee
clenched against any vocal reaction to her aunt's response
her guests' carefully worded queries as to her nieces' sit
tion in life. The picture she painted of Catherine's lot w
bleak indeed.

When she first arrived, Catherine found her aunt's m
conceptions to be amusing. But the humor soon lost
power to draw even a tiny smile, for Catherine's though
flew guiltily to Yorkshire and her family. The Marquis
Stefton's words smote her. It was wrong for Aunt Alicia
denigrate her mother's family as she did. It was also wro
for Catherine to allow her to continue to do so; but Catheri
was loath to try to explain to her aunt the error in h
conceptions.

She sighed again. She was turning into a coward and s
knew it. Everything was so confusing. It didn't help that s
was having difficulty maintaining the meek mien she
vowed to adopt in London. And the Marquis of Stefton
that infuriating man—had not helped with his inexplicab
ability to throw her into confusion and anger. It was diffic
to be meek and angry at one and the same time. It wou
perhaps have been better for her to allow her natu
inclinations to show rather than the sorry play she acted.
truth, it may have so irritated Aunt Alicia and the twins th
it would have hastened her return home. Her current pub
disposition did not seem likely to accomplish that cou
though, in all honesty, she was no longer as eager to retu
home.

Catherine rose slowly from the comforting security of t
worn leather chair, wondering what had prompted La

arth's summons, for she had not as yet heard the large
ass knocker on the front door heralding a visitor. She
ietly left the library and crossed the hall to the drawing
om door.

"She is selfish, Aunt Alicia. Not once did she make a
ish to introduce us to the Marquis of Stefton, as she
ghtfully should have. After all, we are the daughters of an
rl," Lavender Ribbon was saying. By the voice pitch and
e color ribbons she sported, Catherine concluded that it
as Iris.

"That's not fair," protested Susannah. Her hands clutched
e edges of her embroidery frame until the knuckles whitened.
You were both very well engaged all evening."

"*You* would defend her, after all. She introduced you to
e marquis."

"She did not introduce me to the marquis at the ball.
dy Oakley introduced us," Susannah said. Her cheeks
w two bright spots of color as she skirted the lie.

"That may be," put in Yellow Ribbon, whose voice was
gher than her twin's, "but you can't deny that she virtual-
threw herself at him. Conniving him into taking her down
supper when there were so many other women of rank
serving that privilege."

"Meaning yourselves, I presume," Catherine said blandly
om the open doorway. "Personally, I did not consider it
e privilege you obviously do. And I seriously doubt the
arquis can be manipulated by any female." She crossed
e room to sit at Susannah's side on an ornate, uncomfort-
le settee.

Susannah threw her a look of ardent relief. Catherine
iled reassuringly at her, feeling a measure of remorse for
acing her gentle cousin in the position of defending her.

"That is enough, girls. Susannah, you have always been
biddable, well-mannered young woman. Your defense of
ur cousin Catherine is laudable, if misguided. Iris and
ahlia, I understand your distress. Please remember that
ur cousin is still learning how to go on in Society. We
nnot fault her for what she has not been taught in the

godforsaken wilds of Yorkshire,'' Lady Harth counsele
gracing Catherine with another of her condescending smile

Catherine gripped her hands together, shoving them dee
into her lap. ''You are most magnanimous,'' she sa
tightly.

Her aunt nodded in acceptance of Catherine's statemen
then reached up to pat a stray hair back into place under h
lace cap. ''Now, Catherine, be taught by me. You alwa
should be mindful of rank and position in Society. Just
you would vary the depth of your curtsy depending on th
rank of the person receiving the salute, so it is with protoc
at any public event. Your cousins are daughters of an ea
while you are a daughter of a younger son. In the hierarc
of Society, your cousins Iris and Dahlia hold precedence.

The twins smiled superiorly at each other, then cast th
smile at their cousins.

''I know that precept may be hard to remember,
friendly and cozy as we are together,'' Lady Harth went o
''but strive to bear that in mind. It will save you and
from needless censure in Society.''

''Did I incur censure last evening?''

Lady Harth compressed her lips tightly. ''Luckily ye
escaped that horror,'' she reluctantly admitted. ''This tim
Most likely because Society was so caught by the novelty
my grand gesture. I received untold compliments on n
patience and constitution,'' she said with pride.

Lady Harth paused, a triumphant, contemplative expre
sion on her face. ''Mrs. Drummond Burrel even unbent
far as to promise vouchers to Almack's for all of you a
approve you all for the waltz.''

Her eyes clouded over a moment. She pierced Catheri
with a fierce stare. ''I noted you are adapt at contredanse
Dare I hope you have had instruction in the waltz? (
should we hire a dancing master?''

''I believe we may forgo the dancing master. I a
conversant with the rudiments of the dance.''

Lady Harth sniffed in disbelief, her thin nostrils flaring
wide proportions reminding Catherine of a horse. ''We sh
see,'' she said disbelievingly. ''Now, regarding the subje
of the marquis, what were you two possibly discussing th

ept him so long by your side? I trust you were not being
vlgar. That will only lead to presenting yourself as a figure
fun in the clubs.''

Catherine wildly cast about in her mind for a suitable
aswer. She could not tell her of the incident at the inn, and
ve certainly could not at this point disclose her untold
ealth. Suddenly she knew the marquis had supplied the
aswer she needed.

"The marquis is a friend of my uncle. My uncle on my
other's side of the family. I believe they share an interest
horses,'' she said as blandly as possible. Beside her,
usannah's lace edged handkerchief was drawn up before
er face. Nonetheless, Catherine saw the twinkle in her eyes
ver the edge of the scrap of cloth.

"I was not aware you had a maternal uncle,'' Lady Alicia
eclared repressively.

Catherine shrugged. "Well, he does live in the wilds of
orkshire,'' she offered apologetically.

"Since you have a *family* connection,'' Dahlia said with
lse sweetness, "do you think he'll pay a call?''

"Oh, I hardly think so,'' Catherine returned in kind. She
aned back in the settee, one arm extended along its carved
ooden back. "I believe he has fulfilled some obligation to
y uncle by allowing himself to be seen in my company.''

Lady Harth nodded. "That explains it. His intention was
raise your credit in Society, of course. To bring you to the
otice of other gentlemen. I would not have thought Stefton
ould allow himself to be so accommodating; nevertheless,
trust you are cognizant and thankful of the boon he has
anted. Truthfully, I had not expected to see you on the
nce floor last evening.''

Catherine merely nodded, not trusting herself to speak for
e sudden depression that roiled within her. It was one
ing to offer the suggestion that the marquis was only
lfilling an obligation. It was quite another to have it
gerly accepted.

Pennymore opened the door. "The Most Honorable Mar-
is of Stefton, The Right Honorable Earl of Soothcoor, and
aptain Chilberlain,'' he announced.

Lady Harth's sharp eyebrows rose, her smile as toothy as

if she were suddenly anticipating a grand feast. As sh
stepped forward she managed to both smile and hiss. "Iri
Dahlia, now you may meet the marquis and turn the meetin
to good advantage, but do not overlook the earl—his estate
are not encumbered."

Catherine was dumbfounded. Color fled her face and h
throat constricted until she wanted to gasp for breath. Sh
truly had not expected him to call. She had convince
herself he was only playing a game to relieve his habitu
boredom. She did nothing to encourage him—quite sham
fully the reverse. She'd tossed and turned in the wee hou
of the morning agonizing over her behavior to her uncle
friend. The marquis was correct when he predicted Unc
Eugene would not be pleased by her masquerade and ma
ners. She was doing her family a disservice. She didr
know why he continually set her back up until she fair
spat like some stable cat. All she knew was that h
presence—nay, just the thought of him—brought on sens
tions and emotions quite foreign to her nature. Thos
feelings were like high winds. All she desired was to prote
herself from their buffeting, to shutter herself off safe
inside herself. Unfortunately, his very name rattled th
shutters, and his presence threatened to tear them from the
hinges. And yet, he himself did nothing to cause the stor
he created. Unceasingly he displayed a gentlemanly court
sy to her despite her unruly tongue and sour demeano
Never once did he step beyond the boundaries of propriet
yet she wanted to treat him as if he had. What wa
particularly vexatious was that he knew that and derive
amusement from her predicament.

Catherine watched the door for his entrance, though sh
knew she shouldn't, that she should act unconcerned. Tightne
coiled around her throat while the insidious tingling rippl
through her stomach, descending her legs. She could n
have risen from her seat even if Harth House burned dow
around her. Not until she saw his expression this day. Wh
was his purpose in calling? Her heart began hammerin
loudly in her chest until she was certain all could hear i
furious pounding.

Pennymore moved aside to allow the gentlemen to ente

"Ah, Stefton," Lady Harth said enthusiastically, extending er hand in a peremptory manner that required the gentle- an to extend a chaste salute to her knuckles. "I haven't en you since Justin left the country. How good of you to ll."

Stefton murmured a polite response and gravely bowed w, his lips scarcely touching the back of her hand. He raightened. "Allow me to present my companions, Alan awk, Earl of Soothcoor, and Captain Richard Chilberlain, te of the Duke of Wellington's staff."

Lady Harth inclined her head briefly in recognition of the troductions before returning her attention to the marquis. Stefton, I believe you were denied the opportunity of eeting two of my nieces last evening." She smiled smugly d waved her arm in the twins' direction, knocking a llow off the sofa. "Lady Iris and Lady Dahlia Shreveton. hey are the daughters, you know, of my brother Aldric, the arl of Whelan."

Stefton bowed over their hands, his lips held firmly in a raight line as he observed them vie with one another to pture his attention. They were both sitting so near the lge of the settee that any moment one or the other would ide off its edge, and he was certain that each young lady's ck and shoulders must ache from straining to lift her head gher than the other's and to stretch out her arm farther. heir broad, stiff smiles were as identical as the rest of their atures. Bookends of bland blonde prettiness. If his mind dn't been centered on the woman seated behind him, he ould have yawned.

He turned to Soothcoor and Chilberlain to draw their tention to the twins. His mouth quirked, his eyelids ooping over his slate gray eyes as he noted Chilberlain aking his way to Susannah Shreveton's side, oblivious to e other ladies in the room. That would upset Lady Harth, d he supposed he would have to deflect her ire.

Suddenly his eye caught Catherine's, for she too had been ting Captain Chilberlain's objective, and her thoughts w on a parallel course to the marquis's. For a brief oment, their eyes held, sharing an unspoken commitment their friends. The marquis's eyes silvered and Catherine

felt another wave of tingling ripple through her body. But a
swiftly as their eyes caught, they looked away, and th
marquis was drawing Soothcoor forward to attend to Lad
Iris and Lady Dahlia.

When he looked away, Catherine felt cut adrift, flounderin
She looked down at her hands clasped in her lap, one thum
running restlessly back and forth along the length of th
other. She pressed the evidence of her disquiet deep into he
lap, irritated that there was any physical manifestation
nervousness that he might see. She pulled a bright smi
onto her lips and turned in her place on the settee so that sh
might also converse with Captain Chilberlain, distractin
Aunt Alicia from noting the abject disinterest Susannah an
the captain displayed toward their surroundings.

Stefton mercilessly drew Soothcoor forward into th
Shreveton twins lair—or so the earl was to later tell h
friend. He spent a few minutes engaged in soporific conve
sation with the twins, watching them preen, flutter the
lashes, giggle, and posture, all in an endeavor to claim h
regard. Soothcoor manfully fulfilled his duties, though h
Northumbrian accent became a thicker and thicker bur
difficult to understand. Stefton frowned meaningfully at h
friend only to have his unspoken reprimand met with
bland smile and a sly wink. During one of the many lulls i
the conversation, Stefton took the opportunity of shifting h
attention to Lady Harth.

"You have become the talk of London, madame; you a
to be congratulated. It is my understanding that sever
matrons are chagrined that they lacked your foresigh
Introducing four nieces in a Season. It is on the lips
everyone and has quite eclipsed talk of Princess Charlotte
upcoming nuptials."

Lady Harth smiled complacently. "I am only doing wh
is right and proper for the family, you know. Shreveto
have always held a respected place in Society. It is on
right that all members of the family should be known
Society."

Pennymore brought in a large silver tray laden with coffe
and tea. Lady Harth graciously waved her permission

erve as she continued to talk about the Shreveton family
nd its lineage.

The butler made the rounds of the room slowly, offering
efreshments first to the twins, then to Catherine and Susannah.
t Lady Harth's side he deftly sidestepped a recklessly
esturing arm that threatened to sweep the dishes off the
ay. At his success, a faint smile threatened to crack his
npassive visage.

Stefton chose coffee and prudently set it down on a side
ble far away from Lady Harth. "You must be pleased that
ll four of your nieces are so eminently presentable."

"Well, they are Shrevetons."

"True, though I believe Miss Catherine Shreveton has
ore of the Burke family coloring and manner."

Lady Harth laughed. "Well, she certainly lacks the
hreveton fairness."

"As does your own son, Justin," observed Stefton drily.

"That is true," she said slowly, grudgingly, "but the
arth family is distinguished in its own way."

"And I believe Aldric's sons take after their mother."

Lady Harth pursed her lips. "But they are his sons, too,
nd I believe they will one day credit the Shreveton name."

Stefton studied her through hooded eyes, a sneering smile
visting his mouth into satyric handsomeness. "Appearance,"
e mused, "can be unusually deceptive, sometimes giving
o clue as to a person's lineage, and at other times,
amping distinctive features on each descendent like a
mily crest. Your niece, Catherine, for example, bears the
istinctive Burke chin that connotes stubbornness, confi-
ence, and pride."

Lady Harth sniffed. "Her mother was a pretty enough
ountry maid; however, I don't recall her possessing any of
ose traits. Catherine is well enough, I suppose, but totally
cking in charm or social artifice."

"You consider social artifice an admirable attribute?"

"It is a necessary attribute for any young woman."

"Odd. It is the one attribute I find the most deplorable in
e marriageable young ladies who litter London every
eason. I presume it is your intent to train Catherine in this
t."

"I shall do my best, of course," she assured hi
majestically.

"Then I shall enjoy her company before she learns he
lessons."

"Surely you jest, my lord."

A sneering smile curled the marquis's lips. "Only to th
extent you do, my lady."

"You, sir, are becoming impertinent."

"Aunt Alicia!" protested Lavender and Yellow Ribbon

"Then allow me to remove myself and your troubleson
niece from your company," Stefton returned blandly, pul
ing a gold engraved pocket watch from his waistcoat pock
and checking the time. He nodded. "Yes, Friarly should b
arriving momentarily. I shall take her driving in the park.

"It will do her credit, but I fail to understand why yc
bother," Lady Harth said petulantly.

"Yes, I know you do," he returned enigmatically. H
rose to cross to Catherine's side. "Miss Shreveton, allo
me to invite you driving in Hyde Park."

Catherine compressed her lips. She'd overheard most
the conversation between her aunt and the marquis, as, sl
realized in dismay, had most in the room. She wanted
reject his invitation because it was issued by him; howeve
she chafed at her aunt's callous attitude toward her. Sl
found herself rising and agreeing to the drive with a willing
ness she didn't expect.

"I will just be a moment my lord, while I get my bonn
and cloak." She looked over at her aunt to see her agitated
plucking at the folds of her skirt. Catherine looked dov
and hurriedly left the room.

Lady Harth stood up, knocking another small pillow c
the sofa. "I have a splendid idea," she said to the room
large. "I propose a theater outing this evening. Would yc
gentlemen care to join us?"

"Delighted, my lady," Chilberlain said with alacrit
beaming down at Susannah while he spoke.

Lady Harth frowned at him, noticing for the first time h
attentions to Susannah.

Stefton raised a thick black brow and looked pointedly
Soothcoor.

The Scotsman's lips twitched sourly, but he bobbed his head in Lady Harth's direction. "Aye, I'll come," he said grudgingly.

Catherine appeared at the drawing room door wearing her blue spencer and a plain chip bonnet. "I'm ready, my lord."

"A woman with a sense of promptness. How unique," he drawled.

Catherine flushed, the embers of the anger she often felt at his presence flaring into flame.

"And what about you, my lord?" Lady Dahlia said coquettishly, interrupting Catherine before she could frame a sharp retort. "You'll also join us at the theater tonight, won't you?"

"I'm afraid not," he told her blandly. He ignored Bothcoor's scowl. "I have unfinished business to attend to this evening." He bowed to all and, clasping Catherine's elbow, escorted her to the door.

Exasperated at the marquis's smooth escape, Lady Harth sat back down abruptly, her teacup sliding off the saucer she held, splashing its contents on the hem of Lady Dahlia's gown as it crashed to the floor.

Catherine maintained a steadfast silence as they descended the steps before the house and the marquis handed her into his phaeton, covered her with a warm lap robe, and jumped up beside her. He waved his groom away from his horses' heads and they set off at a trot down Upper Grosvenor Street toward Park Lane and Hyde Park Corner. His horses were fresh and apt to be fractious, so for a few moments his attention was concentrated on getting them to work together. They settled down quickly under his firm hand and moved out smoothly, their paces evenly matched.

Catherine found herself admiring his driving skills. She knew herself to be a competent whip, but not in his league. The grays he drove were beautifully matched, and she soon found herself querying the marquis as to their breeding despite her intention to remain silent unless specifically addressed.

"I bred them myself," he said, his eyes intent on guiding his team through the traffic near Hyde Park Corner.

"You?"

"Yes. On one of my estates I have established a sm breeding program. Nothing in comparison to your uncle but I fancy I have met with a modicum of success."

"Judging by this pair, I'd say you've had some splend success!"

A small smile pulled at the corners of his mouth and t silver metal glint in his eye softened to pewter. He glanc at Catherine and inclined his head in salute. "Coming fr you, I take that as high praise indeed."

"Oh, come now, I can't think why you should. You a pitching gammon, my lord."

"On the contrary, Miss Shreveton. You forget I have se you put a horse through his paces—a Burke horse, I am understand, that you schooled."

Catherine blushed. "That is perhaps a circumstance be forgotten," she said softly.

"That is what your uncle said. Tell me, Miss Shrevetc am I doomed to be requested to forget every meeting w you?"

Catherine laughed. "No, my lord. You may rememb Lady Oakley's ball, if you wish," she told him prim though her eyes still smiled warmly.

"Almost you relieve me, Miss Shreveton."

"Almost?"

"My only problem now is my lamentable memory. believe we have discussed its existence before?"

"Yes, my lord."

"With my memory, how am I to contrive to rememb what I am supposed to forget and what I am allowed remember?"

"I can see where that is a problem."

"I shall rely upon you, Miss Shreveton, to serve as arbi of my memories."

Catherine laughed again. "Have done, my lord, I beg you. I cry craven. I shall no more ask that you for; anything."

"Thank you, Miss Shreveton. You have removed a gr weight from my mind."

"Fustian."

He glanced at her again and smiled. "Friends?"

She pursed her lips and looked at him consideringly.
nally she relented and nodded. "Friends. For the sake of
y uncle."

He accepted her statement without comment, intent again
a his driving.

Catherine studied the other carriages bowling along the
ay and spotted a few people on foot braving the cold and
reading their way through bushes to secluded benches
aced under the spreading branches of majestic old trees
st tinged with the pale green of budding leaves. By
mmer those benches would be almost lost from sight,
oviding private rendezvous for lovers and hiding places
r rapscallion children running from their governesses.
ow the benches, nestled among bushes and trees, provided
haven from the cold wind that blew through the park,
minding everyone that though it was a clear sunny day,
inter was not yet finished.

As they drove down its wide concourses more and more
rriages entered the spacious park, and several people
cognized the Marquis of Stefton and waved or inclined
eir heads in a token bow.

"Miss Shreveton," the marquis said suddenly, pulling his
rses up, "would you care to take the ribbons?"

Catherine's eyes began to glow. "Do you mean it?"

He laughed, a handsome smile replacing the satyric
pression he normally wore and giving him a more boyish
pearance. "Yes, of course I mean it." He handed her the
ins and whip, then leaned back in his seat, his arms folded
ross his chest like a groom.

Catherine expertly flicked the whip, letting the thong slide
wn the handle and catching it with her little finger. The
am responded beautifully to her commands and soon she
as unconsciously cooing to them words of endearment.

Stefton watched her handle the pair and revel in the
perience. Her exuberance pleased him, and her murmured
ords of endearment to the team touched his soul. This
oman truly loved horses. She was probably more comfort-
le in their company than in the company of her own
o-legged species. Possibly he was wrong to bring her into

fashion. This was a woman who could turn the epithet '
rustic'' into a compliment.

The sight of the Marquis of Stefton allowing himself to b
driven about the park was cause for comment. The fact th
he was being driven by a woman, and that the woman wa
driving his precious grays, drew gasps and fervent specula
tion as to the meaning behind the sight. The park fair
sizzled with the hisses of whispered conjecture. Most peop
failed to recognize the young woman as the niece of th
Countess of Seaverness, and guesses abounded as to h
identity.

. Catherine, enchanted with driving the graceful pair, faile
to see the fervor she was creating. She was suddenl
happier than she'd been in months, and it showed in h
vivid countenance.

When she pulled up the team some fifteen minutes lat
to return the reins to the marquis, her cheeks were flushe
and her eyes sparkled with excitement. "They're wonde
ful! Such light mouths, so perfectly matched in pace—
don't know what to say! Has my uncle seen them?''

The marquis smiled. "Yes, many times. He too, wa
impressed, though his words lacked your enthusiasm,'' h
finished drily, guiding his grays back onto the roadway an
into a brisk trot.

"Ah, yes ever the horse trader,'' she said with affection
ate indulgence. "Did he make you an offer for the pair?'

"No, just for their breeder,'' he returned blandly, his eye
intent on the carriageway.

A gurgle of laughter came from beside him. "Th
sounds just like Uncle Gene!''

Stefton was gratified to hear her laughter for it indicated
comfortableness in his company that he'd been at pains
create. She was a prickly one, very much like the nettle
growing on the hillside—a stroke the wrong way easi
sending her into high dudgeon. He guessed she was uncom
fortable in the role she chose to play, but did not know ho
to extricate herself from the folly of her own actions, l
alone admit to folly. He was enjoying his role as fai
godfather to a reluctant Cinderella. The novelty of the gam
held at bay the habitual ennui he felt every Season when th

:w crop of debutantes (and the returning ones bearing
:ightened anxiety lest they be left on the shelf) descended
)on London. He didn't know why he stayed in town every
:ar. Mostly habit, he surmised, *and* the entertainment
·ovided in observing the intricate movements of the
·atchmaking contredanse.

Catherine Shreveton was a reluctant dancer. The irony
·as that with her beauty, wit, and wealth, she should have
·een leading the set. But she chose not to. That fascinated
·m. Women of his acquaintance were typically too ready to
·aunt their advantages. Catherine denied their existence. He
·1ose to look for and cultivate her advantages, dredge them
·1t of hiding and place them in the light, then stand back
·1d observe Society's reaction. He'd been gratified by the
·tentions she received at Lady Oakley's after she was seen
·1ncing with himself, Chilberlain, and Soothcoor. Now it
·as his desire to see those attentions continued. He would,
·e decided, see her married off before the Season ended.

He frowned suddenly. The trick would be to see that the
·:ntleman claiming her attention was suitable for her and
·1e Burke stables she would one day inherit. It wouldn't do
·1r her to become leg-shackled to a man who was a ham-
·sted rider!

The harsh lines etched into his face relaxed. He doubted
·atherine would even consider a man who didn't ride well.
·hen again, unless she rode beside him, how was she to
·1ow? His next goal must be to get her back in the saddle.

·lady's saddle, he mentally amended when the memory of
·:r in boys' clothes astride a big bay horse came to mind.

Dark clouds began to clutter the wide expanse of blue sky
·1d the wind kicked up, sending oak leaves scurrying across
·1e carriage road. Catherine pulled the lap robe closer and
·rapped her arms about herself. Unconsciously she shifted
·oser to the marquis.

Stefton's eyebrow rose at her action, then he frowned as
·e noted her huddled form. "I had best take you back
·efore the weather turns damp and you take a chill," he
·1id, his voice unusually harsh. He turned the equipage
·)wn a path that led back to Hyde Park Corner.

"Oh, please—no need to hurry on my account. There is a

bit more of a nip in the air now, but I'm used to suc
weather. Truthfully, it reminds me of home. It is too ba
that I did not bring my cloak with me from Yorkshire, onl
Grandmother thought it a great deal too shabby and countr
for London. I daresay I could use its voluminous folds fo
warmth!''

"It might be a bit cumbersome to wear while ridin
though. Do you have a warm habit or is male attire you
only riding dress?''

"I beg your pardon!'' Two bright spots of color appeare
high on her cheeks. ''My lord,'' she said repressivel
''male attire is among the subjects I requested that yo
lamentable memory forget.''

"Did you indeed? And here I thought to place your ma
attire among my most treasured memories, for you said yo
would no more request I forget anything,'' he said in faintl
mournful accents.

"Odious creature,'' she said without heat, though she di
turn to glower at him. Catherine swore she saw his lip
twitch, but he suppressed his inclination to smile, h
attention ostensibly on the road.

"Perhaps we should stick to the subject of horses,'' h
offered. ''In my stables I'm not so concerned with breedin
hunters or carriagehorses. I'm primarily interested in rac
horses. I haven't done too badly at Newmarket. Quite wel
in fact. Well enough that I've begun to consider expandir
my stable. Unfortunately, my main problem, it turns out,
finding good jockeys.''

"That I can believe. It has always been my contentio
that a good jockey must be one with his horse. It is n
enough to be small and light.''

"I agree. But such a man is hard to find, and if you
spot one, odds are the fellow is content at his curre
employ or there are other problems precluding availabilit
It's dashed frustrating. Just last month I wanted to hire
certain boy I saw riding.''

"Oh?'' Catherine warily questioned, suddenly afraid th
direction of his conversation had changed.

"Yes. The lad was the best rider I'd seen in many a da
Seemed at one with the horse, light as a feather, too,'' h

marked, casting her a sideways glance from under drooping
eyelids.

"How interesting," she managed to comment in a stran-
led voice.

"Sad thing about that rider. Doesn't ride at all now.
shocking waste, and unfair to his own horse. I saw it once.
. magnificent animal. A high-stepping coal black mare
with the most luxuriously long mane and tail I've ever seen.
Do you know the horse I'm speaking about?

"I'm familiar with her, yes," Catherine said tightly,
anger seething through her. How dare he refer to her with
veiled innuendos? To say nothing of again alluding to her
male attire, a subject she told him was closed. *Who is he to
judge my actions?* her brain screamed, though in her heart a
twinge of conscience pulled at her. Angrily she dusted the
twinge away. She was determined not to allow one more
person to attempt to manage her life.

"Too beautiful an animal to keep cooped up in a stall.
Anyone who rode a horse like that in Hyde Park would
cause comment and envy, I daresay," he said conversationally
as he pulled into the traffic on Park Lane.

"You may say or think whatever you like!" she said
sharply.

"Have I said something amiss?"

"That horse you so subtly refer to is mine, as you well
know. Her name is Gwyneth. Whether I ride her or not is
none of your concern," she ground out. She turned away
from him to sit stiffly erect, her eyes on the road ahead.

"What would Sir Eugene say to the way you are abusing—
yes, I said abusing—and well you know it so don't look
daggers at me, my girl—what would he say to the way you
are abusing that horse?"

"I am not abusing Gwyneth," she denied hotly.

"If you are going to continue in this ridiculous role you
have chosen, send the animal back to Yorkshire, or let me
take her to one of my estates that are closer. At least there
she can run in the fields, and be exercised."

"What do you mean, 'role'?" she asked, her tone dangerously soft and even.

"The role of beggar maid," he snapped, drawing up

before Harth House. "Friarly! Friarly! Where is that co
founded fellow?"

"Probably at a local ale house for a bit of respite fro
dealing with such a boorish employer."

"Don't sound so pleased. Without him to help you dow
or to hold these nags' heads so that I may help you dow
you'll have to do for yourself."

"That suits me fine, my lord," she retorted, her ey
flashing. She turned to back down out of the phaeto
quietly thankful it was not one with a high perch. S
moved swiftly, to demonstrate to the marquis she was
bread-and-water miss, and perfectly able to care for herse
If she was a bit disconcerted by the penetrating stea
regard of his gray eyes, silvered in anger, she gave
outward sign. When her left foot touched the cobbl
pavement she flashed him a superior smile.

Then she felt a tug on her gown. It was caught on
decorative curlicue of wood and was pulled up, amp
displaying her shapely ankles and calves. She pulled angri
on the material, but it stuck fast, almost overbalancing h

Stefton raised an eyebrow at her difficulties, a slight sm
playing upon his lips as he observed the generous portion
leg she displayed to advantage. Catherine saw the directi
of his gaze and a dark red blush surged up her neck into h
face. She yanked on the fabric again until it gave a rendi
sound and fell away from the carriage. Angrily, she twitch
her skirts into place, pretending unconcern for the tear in t
side. Nodding her head perfunctorily in the Marquis
Stefton's direction, she regally turned to cross the paveme
and climb the stairs before Harth House.

The Marquis of Stefton silently watched her progre
keeping his team still without a glance in their directi
Inexplicably, he still found himself angry with her, and t
anger was a churning heaviness coupled with frustrati
inside him. What bothered him the most was that he did
know if he was more angry with her for the horse, for
role-playing, or just because she defied him. It was
novelty to discover a woman who did not attempt either
placate him and defer to his every wish or to make endl

mands. It was a novelty that, despite the anger, he rather
joyed.

CHAPTER
EIGHT

Catherine fairly marched up the steps before Harth House
d let herself in before the footman could move from his
sition by the door. She did not look back. She dared not,
r she knew Stefton was watching her.

How dare he? How dare he try to lecture her on the care
her horse! It was no business of his whether she rode,
lked, or stayed indoors! And talk about role-playing—
h! The pot calling the kettle black. The insufferable
rogance of the man. How could Uncle Gene suffer him to
his friend? No, she knew the answer to that. In her
cle's eyes Stefton's superb horsemanship would compen-
te for any deficiencies of character the man possessed.
ell, it wouldn't with her. Her intuition worked very well,
nding those warning tingles through her. Her physical
action to the man was entirely understandable. He was
rely a—a *Jack Sharp!* A man to be avoided at all costs.
e would not allow herself to become one of his flirts,
en if it did increase her credit with Society. Society was
nd not to see him for what he really was. Well, she did
d . . .

Abruptly she halted her internal ravings and the set frown
her face relaxed into a chagrined smile.

She was not being entirely fair. That niggling knowledge
d been there since she first opened her mouth to refute his
rds. In all her plans and schemes, she *had* signally failed
remember Gwyneth. Her beloved horse was the innocent
tim of her machinations.

Catherine had raised Gwyneth, touching her, feeding her,

getting her used to her presence, since the day she fir
stood upon wobbly legs splayed awkwardly, her kne
seemingly too big for her slender black legs, and her dark ey
large and wide as she blinked and looked about her ne
world. Gwyneth was the first horse she schooled on h
own, and she was the only rider ever to mount Gwyneth

Now it was over two weeks since Gwyneth had be
ridden and Catherine felt guilty for ignoring her. Still, sl
railed at the marquis for his presumption in the matter.
was none of his business. She was glad she had not to
him of her plans to ride her horse as soon as she receiv
her new habit from Madame Vaussard. He might thi
what he wished, but he was not going to ride roughsh
over her!

Truthfully, she was looking forward to the day she wou
once more be up on Gwyneth's back. The difficulty wou
be in preventing Gwyneth and herself from indulging in
dead run across the park. Such actions were not seemly a
would most certainly call censure down upon her head. Funr
a day or so past she would have welcomed the censure if
sped her back to Yorkshire. Now she was not so inclined
hasten her departure from the city, but she could not fatho
what was the reason for her change of attitude. It w
perhaps many things, really. Things she could admit
herself and things that were better off ignored. La
Oakley's ball was the fulcrum for her change in thougl
The gentlemen were not all gazetted fortune hunters—
least none that she met gave that impression—and the ladi
were not so caught up in home and hearth that their conv
sation turned only on one's looks, family, or estate. S
actually enjoyed herself at the ball, and that was not
circumstance she'd considered possible.

Catherine sighed and began to trudge up the stairs to h
room.

"Miss Catherine," Pennymore called softly to her as
carefully closed the doors to the drawing room. "T
countess requested that on your return I ask you rejoin h
and the other young ladies."

Catherine nodded. "Very well, I'll just be a moment
She sighed again and gathered her energies to continue

e stairs. She was fatigued—more mentally than physically;
ll the effects were the same. The beginning of a headache
led at the corners of her brow. This was *his* doing, she
d herself fretfully. She couldn't allow him to dominate
r life in this way. She *wouldn't* allow it!

With that thought she continued up the stairs, her head
ld high, a determined expression on her face.

"There you are, Catherine," Lady Harth said with exas-
ration when she entered the drawing room some twenty
nutes later. "You missed saying your farewells to Lord
othcoor and Captain Chilberlain, but I trust we sufficiently
tended them in your favor. Now, come and greet our new
itor."

Mechanically, Catherine looked in the direction Lady
rth indicated with the broad sweep of her hand. She
ze, a gasp cut short in her throat. Blood drained from her
e, leaving her feeling chilled.

"There's no need to introduce me to Miss Shreveton. We
t during her journey to London." A sneering smile
sted the lips of Sir Philip Kirkson as he walked toward
r and bowed. "I trust you are quite recovered from the
gencies of that trip? When last we met, you did seem a
le out of sorts. I felt it behooved me to pay a call to see
w you're getting on."

"That is very good of you, Sir Philip," Lady Harth said,
iling benignly.

Catherine winced. "Very," she echoed. She threw her
d up, her chin leading, and stared coldly at him, belying
cordiality of her words. "I'm amazed to have a place in
r memory. It was such a brief encounter and fraught with
fusion."

"The only confusion I felt was in the brevity of the
ounter. I have every hope of continuing as we began."
raised her hand to his lips, keeping that tiny member
tured an unconscionable amount of time.

Catherine snatched her hand away, turning bright red as
implications of his words percolated into her mind
ring with them the memory of his arms holding her

tightly against him as his lips ground unmercifully agai
hers.

"Sir Philip," said Lady Harth, "you are all gentleman
consideration. We are planning a small theater party for t
evening and would enjoy your company—wouldn't v
Catherine?"

"What? I—I wouldn't presume upon our short acqua
tance," Catherine demurred.

"Nonsense," retorted Lady Harth, glaring at her th
turning to smile regally at Sir Philip.

A slow, wolfish smile spread across Sir Philip's face.
shall be honored to attend."

"Mrs. Reginald Howlitch, Mr. Peter Howlitch, Sir Rich
Chartrist," Pennymore said from the doorway.

Lady Harth's eyes lit up. "Oh, isn't this all that
famous!"

"If you'll excuse me, Lady Harth, I must take my lea
now. I have some appointments in the city that can not
put off," Kirkson put in smoothly, not giving the countes
moment to respond. He kissed her hand, bowed to the oth
ladies in the room, and took himself off without greeting
other visitors as they entered.

It was not to be supposed that Catherine anticipated
theater party with any degree of equanimity. That La
Harth had decided to match her with Sir Philip Kirkson v
painfully obvious in the extreme. Her aunt raved about w
a nice, well-set-up man he was, and how he was
possessor of a modest yet eminently respectable fortu
She called Catherine a sly puss, and quizzed her on
meeting with the gentleman, to which Catherine blus
furiously, though not for the reasons Lady Harth surmis
She searched her mind frantically for some tale to tell,
luckily was spared the telling for her aunt decided t
young girls would have their secrets and this could
Catherine's.

Even Lady Iris and Lady Dahlia looked more favora
upon her. With a definite suitor for Catherine, their feeli
of jealousy abated and they could unbend so far as to ag
they had Catherine to thank for introducing them to

rquis and his friends. Lady Iris decided she bore a
tiality for the Earl of Soothcoor. Whether her partiality
s for the gentleman or for his title was a moot point. She
de it her avowed aim to turn the head of this dour peer
l have him at her feet.

The self-assured prattle of Iris's plans and goals disgusted
therine and she would have felt sorry for the earl if she
ln't had the faith that the gentleman was well able to stay
e of her coils.

Lady Dahlia decided she would pursue the marquis when
opportunity arose and charged Catherine most faithfully
t should he approach her again, she would bring her dear
sin Dahlia into the conversation. Feeling as angry with
marquis as she did, Catherine thought there would be no
ther occasion for conversation; nonetheless she vowed
would do as her cousin asked, caustically deciding it
s a just revenge on two obnoxious people.

Only Susannah looked at her sadly and with a touch of
r in her eyes. "Oh, how will you bear it, cousin!" she
laimed later that night when Catherine came to her room
a comfortable evening coze.

Catherine shrugged. "What else is there to do? I believe
kson is merely looking for some form of revenge. If I
w his reprehensible behavior in the past to affect me
v, then he has won, for that is what he desires. If,
vever, I choose to forget the incident, as I charged the
ous marquis to do, then he is stalemated and the game is
e. He will wander off to other pursuits."

"I'm afraid Sir Philip is not a man to accept a stalemate."
Catherine furrowed her brow. "Possibly, but to what
pose would continued attentions be?"

"I'm sure I don't know. But for some reason that man
htens me. His eyes, they are so empty—"

"Now you are being fanciful," Catherine said, laughing.

"If he should decide he truly wanted you, I don't believe
l stick to fair means to win you," Susannah said slowly.

"What do you mean?"

"Never go driving with him. I'm not certain you'd come
k."

* * *

Though Catherine laughed freely at what she conside­
her cousin's fancies, privately they did begin to haunt h­
Just thinking of Sir Philip caused her to shudder, a reacti­
that was the antithesis of what happened when she thoug­
of the marquis. Nevertheless, she was determined to ally ­
infamy of Kirkson with the marquis until both gentlem­
were equally vile in her mind.

That evening, knowing she was pledged to partner Kirks­
at the theater, Catherine dressed as severely as possib­
pulling her hair back into a painfully tight coronet of bra­
and donning a high-necked gown of an icy blue co­
unsuitable for her complexion. Susannah dolefully sho­
her head at her cousin's attire; however their Aunt Ali­
found nothing to object to and even told Catherine s­
looked "as neat as wax." That was not, perhaps, the type ­
encomium Catherine would look for; it reminded her o­
description of someone's housekeeper or governess. But s­
bore it with good grace and even managed to have a sli­
smile on her face when she descended the stairs to greet ­
gentlemen who were escorting them to the theater.

The carriage ride to the theater was uneventful a­
Kirkson was the model of propriety, making no comme­
or allusions to their first meeting. Soon Catherine v­
feeling that perhaps the evening would not be the unmitig­
ed disaster she feared, and she sat back in her chair to en­
the play.

"How dare she. She's positively nude!" Lady Ha­
vehemently declared. She sniffed. "And she has the auda­
ty to call herself a *lady*."

Everyone looked up across the boxes to ascertain w­
had caught Lady Harth's attention. It took but a mome­
for in a box directly across from them sat the Marquis ­
Stefton and the beautiful woman who shouldered Cather­
out of the way just as she would enter Madame Vaussar­
establishment.

To say that the lady with the marquis was not dres­
decently was, to Catherine's mind, an exaggeration. Nor­
theless, the sheer lilac silk gown revealed more of her fig­
than it hid. The décolletage plunged down to a large knot­
ribbons where the bodice joined the skirt. The fabric cov­

ng her globular breasts was minimal, and even at a distance
t was plain that no chemise came between her and the
dress. Actually, Catherine thought the dress cleverly de-
igned, for—though shocking at first glance—the gown
ainted more than it revealed. She wondered if it were one of
Madame Vaussard's creations. Dispassionately, she looked
again at the dress, studying its design, until her eyes
happened to catch those of the marquis. She was startled to
discover he was intently watching her, a frown pulling his
black brows together. She found herself blushing, and hoped
no one noticed.

A deep chuckle shook the spare frame of the Earl of
Soothcoor. "So that be his unfinished business." He looked
across Lady Iris's head at Captain Chilberlain. "I'll roast
him over hot coals, for this. Aye, see if I don't."

"With my best wishes," agreed Chilberlain.

Lady Harth sniffed again and tossed her head up, in very
ill-humor that the marquis should turn down an invitation to
attend the theater with them in favor of the likes of her. "I
am extremely disappointed in his lordship and of a mind to
cut his acquaintance."

"Who is she?" Catherine found herself asking, only to
be glared at by her aunt.

"That, Miss Shreveton," supplied Kirkson, "Is Panthea,
Lady Welville, who claims she'll be the next Marchioness
of Stefton and Duchess of Vauden."

The Earl of Soothcoor snorted rudely, his thin lips twisting
in sour distaste. "She may claim all she wants."

Kirkson raised an eyebrow. "You don't believe she'll
ucceed."

Soothcoor folded his arms across his chest and looked at
him from under tangled back and gray brows. "He'll not get
eg-shackled to the likes of her," he said firmly, then
ompressed his lips. The subject was closed.

Kirkson shrugged and laughed nastily.

Catherine shuddered at the sound, for it reminded her all
too well of the night at the inn. She edged away from him as
far as she could, which was only a matter of inches in the
close confines of the theater box.

A disagreeable expression crossed Kirkson's face at her

movement. He would teach the minx a lesson and have his
revenge for the handling he received at the hands of the
marquis and Sir Eugene's man. No man or woman got the
best of Philip Kirkson. It would serve her right to be
compromised and then left to her own devices. Or, if she
stood to gain an inheritance from her uncle, she could be
his wife—one who funded his pleasures in all ways. It
might do well for him to begin some discreet inquiries into
Miss Shreveton's fortune. She did not strike him as the poor
relation for she did not have the proper demeanor for
poverty. He supposed her attire could stem from a lack of
town education. But still that did not serve. Something was
amiss, and he intended to discover what it was. It could be
that the little Shreveton could prove very valuable to him,
very valuable indeed.

He glanced up to see the marquis still regarding them,
ignoring Lady Welville's play for his attention. It seemed
the marquis would still wish to play guardian to Miss
Shreveton, for his expression was black. So much the
better. From his position across the way, there was nothing
he could do to come to her aid.

Kirkson grinned spitefully and turned sideways in his
seat, his left arm extended to drape negligently across the
back of her chair. He leaned forward to whisper in her ear.
"I still say it will be a pleasure to tame you, my dear," he
said silkily, his voice hushed for her hearing alone.

A dark red blush suffused Catherine's face, her eyes
widening. Slowly she turned her head to look over her
shoulder. "Sir Philip, I had hoped that on learning my
identity you would have the decency to apologize for your
atrocious summation of my character, and your equally
atrocious behavior," she said sternly, fighting the waves of
color that proclaimed her acute embarrassment.

Kirkson grinned, very much aware of the marquis's eye
on them, and leaned closer still. "Knowing your name
doesn't preclude the other consideration," he murmured
bending to kiss her shoulder.

In revulsion, Catherine jerked away, overbalancing on the
corner of her chair and falling across Captain Chilberlain's
lap.

Mortally chagrined, she struggled up, knocking her chair completely over.

"Are you all right, Miss Shreveton?" the captain asked solicitously as he bent down to right her chair.

"Yes! No! Oh—I don't know," she squeaked, breathing fast. She dared not look in Kirkson's direction, and frantically wondered how she could refuse to sit down next to the man again. "I—I think I'll stand up for a while. It's terribly tiring, sitting for so long, you know," she babbled as she edged her way past the other guests toward the rear of the box.

"Catherine, return to your seat immediately," commanded Lady Harth.

"But, Aunt—"

"We shall overlook your ridiculous clumsiness. Now sit; you're disturbing everyone's enjoyment of the play."

"Yes, ma'am," Catherine murmured, moving miserably toward her seat.

Susannah pulled on the captain's coat sleeve and whispered in his ear. He looked over at Kirkson. The man was gloating. The captain frowned suddenly and swiftly rose from his seat.

"Please, Miss Shreveton, allow us to change places. I am convinced you are in a draft."

The relief that flooded Catherine was palatable. "Thank you, Captain Chilberlain, that is very kind of you," she said, hurriedly sliding into his chair.

The malicious smile on Kirkson's face slowly faded to be replaced by a cold glare. He slouched down in his seat, his arms folded across his chest, as he broodingly watched the play, oblivious to its humor.

Susannah reached over to pat Catherine's hand reassuringly, then turned shining eyes upon her captain, silently thanking him.

The Earl of Soothcoor, watching the whole, grunted and looked across at Stefton. The marquis was no longer watching their box, but he lounged in his chair as he watched the play, satisfaction plainly seen on his normally expressionless visage.

*　　*　　*

The interval came too swiftly for Catherine. She knew she would be expected to stroll the galleries on Kirkson's arm. She only hoped that in a crowd he would not make any unwarranted comments or actions. She did not know what would be her recourse if he did.

Sensing her discomfort, Captain Chilberlain whispered that he and Susannah would stay near. Catherine smiled then and thanked them, sternly commanding her stampeding pulse to slow down.

"I give you the game, Miss Shreveton," said Kirkson before he extended his arm to her. He was very much aware of the towering presence of the captain and ascertained the man's intentions. He smiled at Catherine.

Gingerly, Catherine placed her hand lightly on his arm, allowing him to draw her forward. "But I have not lost all, for there is plenty of time," he assured her, still smiling.

Kirkson's smiles never reached his eyes. Catherine felt a shudder begin to wrack her body. Ruthlessly she controlled it, though her heart continued to hammer loudly. She lifted her head up, her chin thrust forward. "I would not, if I were you, Sir Philip, waste time on idle chatter."

He smirked, but vouched no further comment.

Catherine pointedly ignored him. Instead she elicited opinions from others in their party as to the quality of the play production, and maintained a lively dialogue with Mr. Dabernathy on the thespian skills of the leading actor.

"Well met, Lady Harth. I trust your party is enjoying the play."

Catherine turned at the sound of the languid, deep voice. The marquis and Lady Welville were standing nearby, the lady draped bonelessly over Stefton's arm.

The countess pursed her lips, her eyes narrowing before she spoke. Finally she rocked backward on her heels, her breath expelling in a rush. "Very much, thank you," she said stiffly.

A raffish, thoroughly masculine smile turned up the corners of Stefton's mouth. "Very wisely done," he murmured.

Lady Dahlia pushed past Catherine, dragging Mr. Dabernathy behind. "My lord, what an unlooked-for pleasure to see you here," she simpered, smiling coyly at him.

Catherine exchanged glances with Susannah and rolled her eyes expressively. Her cousin giggled.

"Thank you, Lady Dahlia," Stefton said gravely.

"Oh, do come away, Oliver. I am quite parched and you did promise me refreshments before the next interval," Lady Panthea pouted prettily, fanning her deep cleavage.

Lady Harth snorted in disgust. Lady Welville turned to raise one thin, well-defined eyebrow, her gaze finally traveling to take in the group. The superior smile on her face froze when she finally noticed Catherine. Her nostrils flared briefly, her features turning hard.

She tugged on the marquis's hand. "Introduce me, Oliver," she said imperiously.

The marquis looked at her quizzically, but made the introductions before Dahlia reclaimed his attention. Catherine dipped a slight curtsy while Lady Welville stood stiffly, looking down her nose at her.

"Well, did you find what you wanted at Madame Vaussard's?" she asked archly, certain the seamstress was above Catherine's touch.

Catherine paused, taking the woman's measure. "Perhaps," she returned easily.

"Perhaps, she says," Lady Welville mimicked to Kirkson as if inviting him to share the joke. "What a little equivocator you are, Miss Shreveton. Personally, I found the woman's fabrics and styles much too gauche for my taste. Isn't that right, Oliver?"

The marquis yawned. "I wouldn't know. When I left you were enamored of a certain silver net."

She laughed shrilly. "Oh, la, I daresay that was before I could see it in decent light. It turned out to be really quite tawdry—as you suggested it would. You have such excellent eyesight, Oliver, I find I quite envy you," she said with a die-away air, turning to Catherine. "Miss Shreveton, I'm sure your country ways have left you totally unprepared for city fashion. Be guided by me. Have nothing to do with Madame Vaussard lest she truss you up like a tart. Of course," she purred with a cat's sleepy eyed grin at cornering its prey, "it might be an improvement."

"Panthea," snapped the marquis, a slight flush discernable under his tan, "let's get some oranges before the play resumes." He dragged her off with only curt apologies.

Lady Dahlia pouted at having her prey so quickly vanish and swung around, stamping her foot in vexation. The fringe of her shawl caught her sister in the face as she twirled about, nearly initiating an argument. All the gentlemen save Kirkson rushed forward to soothe ruffled feathers. Soon the twins were preening at the attention they garnered.

Lady Harth observed the incident with something akin to self-satisfaction. The twins were getting the attention that was their due as daughters of an earl, and Sir Philip was showing himself dedicated to Catherine. It would be a relief if he should offer for her, else Lady Harth gravely feared Catherine would be her singular failure. Lady Harth did not like failure, particularly as it precluded bragging to other matchmaking mothers and relations. She did not understand what had gone on in the box earlier between Catherine and Sir Philip. Most likely the girl took some distempered freak to a compliment he extended. Silly chit. She would not stand for any missishness from Catherine. The girl was not going to throw away an eligible suitor on a whim!

Her eyes traveled from Catherine to where Susannah stood, leaning on the captain's arm. The captain had been a mistake. He would not do for Susannah at all. She would have to find a way to nip that friendship in the bud.

It was a great deal too bad that the Marquis of Stefton had declined to be a part of the theater party. It would be quite a coup to secure his hand for Dahlia. Well, she would bite her tongue at his current choice of companionship, but she would endeavor to trick Dahlia out in just the attire to capture his attention.

Iris seemed to be progressing nicely with the Earl of Soothcoor. His lineage was good, but such a dour fellow— though his manners were unfailingly polite.

She hurried after her protégées, only knocking against one lady in her endeavor to catch up. Luckily that lady's escort saw her coming and, fully conversant with Lady Harth's propensity for accidents, swiftly removed the drink from his lady's hand, saving it by a mere fraction of a second from jostling and spilling down the front of her gown.

Unfortunately, his lady was not duly appreciative of his efforts and gave him a tongue lashing for his peremptory behavior.

Lady Welville's bedchamber was done entirely in rose colored satin, and the air was redolent with that flower's scent. Though familiar with the room and its odor, the Marquis of Stefton grimaced at the overpowering smell.

Panthea poured champagne into two tall fluted goblets, then picked one up to hand to the marquis. "To you, my lord," she said huskily, her eyelids drooping seductively.

He took the glass, silently acknowledging the toast with a sneering smile curling his thin lips.

"I sent Babbette to bed early this evening. She has a cold or something. She is constantly sniffling. I can't abide sniffling." A look of distaste crossed her beautiful features, then she smiled up at the marquis. "Would you be a pet and play abigail for me this evening? I really cannot get these hooks by myself," she said plaintively.

Stefton set his champagne glass on her dressing table and slowly turned her around, his fingers lingering on the creamy white expanse of her bare shoulders. His hand slid down to the row of fasteners, his long fingers quickly releasing them, her dress parting to reveal the white expanse of her back. She really did forgo underclothes with the dress.

Panthea smiled at him over her shoulder. "You are so quiet this evening, my lord. What ever can you be thinking of that holds you so intent?"

He looked at her, a thick black brow quirking upward.

She laughed delightedly. "For shame, sir," she said, swirling away from him, her dress barely hanging on her body. She bent down to refill her champagne glass, a side of her dress dipping, revealing one full, ripe breast. She did not pull her dress into place. She sipped her champagne, running her tongue over her lips to catch all errant beads of moisture as she looked at him through the veil of her lashes.

A slight smile playing upon his lips, the Marquis of Stefton began to remove his coat.

Lady Panthea smiled at him in return. "I swear London is getting crowded with insipids," she said conversationally as she watched him divest himself of his jacket and reach for his cravat. "Can you believe those four Alicia is trying to foist on society? La! Flowers and thorns. It is too comical."

The marquis froze, a dark scowl pulling his brows together and so hooding his eyes that only a glint of hard metal color could be seen. He walked over to her dressing table mirror and began to retie his cravat.

"Oliver?"

Slowly he turned to look at her. "Almost. Almost you made me forget my purpose this evening. You are very talented. You will easily find another willing to pick up my leavings."

"What? Oliver, what are you saying?" demanded Panthea, suddenly very frightened. She allowed the other side of her dress to fall down her arms. She pulled her arms free of the brief sleeves and reached toward him coaxingly, the dress riding on her hips.

"Very Grecian," he observed drily, stepping out of her reach and bending down to retrieve his coat. He eased his arms into the tightly fitted sleeves. Panthea stepped forward, wrapping her arms around him, preventing him from getting the jacket on completely.

"No, Oliver, don't go. Stay with me. I can make you forget everything," she breathed, faint traces of tears dampening her lashes.

"Cut line, Panthea," Stefton said harshly. "You knew it would end sometime." He twisted free of her and settled his coat on his broad shoulders.

"It doesn't have to end. I promise, I'll no longer importune you for marriage. It's not important to me now. Just having you is important, Oliver!"

"Very prettily said, but it doesn't wash, my dear. Neither do those tears you are so artfully manufacturing. But don't worry," he said, reaching into his coat pocket and extracting a velvet cloth bag. "It is not my intention to leave you unpaid for all the delights you shared." He opened the bag and drew out a diamond and sapphire necklace.

The necklace coruscated in the candlelight and Panthea's mouth went round in a silent *Oh* of wonder. Stefton smiled rakishly. He turned Panthea around so she faced the mirror, then he placed the necklace around her neck and placed a parting featherlight kiss on the sensitive place under her ear.

Panthea stared entranced at the necklace, one hand tentatively reaching up to touch it as if to see if it were real.

Stealthily, Stefton backed away from her to the door, slipping through it while she admired herself in the mirror.

At the click of the latch Panthea spun around. "Oliver! No! Oliver, wait!" She tried to run toward the door, but her trailing skirts impeded her. Impatiently she kicked them free and ran to wrench open the door. "Oliver!" she shouted, real tears now streaming down her face, tears that twisted and blotched her features into ugliness.

Below, she heard the front door open and close. She screamed and slammed her bedroom door, then threw herself across the rose satin sheets, and wept into the pillows, calling Stefton every abusive name she could think of. How could he casually cast her off like an old coat! She was not a simpering little nobody. She would reclaim his attentions and be the next Duchess of Vauden or he would rue the day he trifled with her affections!

Copious tears dampened her pillows and streaks of black from her artfully darkened lashes smudged the fabric by the time she fell into fitful slumber and dreamed of revenge.

CHAPTER
NINE

"Ah—Soothcoor, what brings you to my door? I've passed two entire days without seeing you ugly phiz. I feared you'd quite cut my acquaintance."

"No more'n you'd deserve."

The marquis gave a short laugh, clapping Soothcoor on the back. "Well, come. I was just about to sit down to nuncheon. Join me. I know how you appreciate Gascoullet's culinary skills. After all, I do not tease myself that you come for my company."

"Better yurs than Chilberlain's. Faugh!"

"A falling-out with our captain?"

Soothcoor snorted. "Canna talk to him to have a fallin' out."

"I'll admit you have captured my interest, old friend. Perceive me all attention. I hang on your words."

The earl shot him a nasty look. "I'll have non a yur cozening ways. It were deferring to you which created this mess."

"It must be serious. Your accent is pronounced. What you need is a mug of ale and a substantial meal. Kennilton!"

"Immediately, my lord," said his soft-spoken butler. He took a pitcher from the sideboard and from it filled a tankard, setting it before his scowling master. He placed platters and tureens of food on the table, serving the two gentlemen quickly and efficiently. There was little conversation between the two men, though the earl's scowl was seen to relax as he ate. When both gentlemen were replete Kennilton directed that the dishes be removed, placed a large pot of coffee on the table along with a bowl of fruit and bowed his way out of the room.

"Quiet blighter," Soothcoor observed after the butler left. "No nonsense, too. I like that."

"Now I suppose you'll be telling me that you'd care to hire him away from me. I should give you my household and be done with it," Stefton said drily, humor underlining his words.

Soothcoor sniffed and his mouth twitched. A knuckle rubbed the side of his face. "Couldna afford it and wouldna stand the press o' people you deem necessary to run a household."

"But vicariously you enjoy it."

"There's worse places."

"Ah— I Perceive we are about to return to the subject of Chilberlain. What is our captain up to?"

"Smellin' o' April and May."

"Miss Susannah Shreveton?"

"Aye. There's no bein' with him. He's forever spoutin' about her."

"Our captain a lovesick swain?"

"It is serious! And it's all yur fault, askin' us to dance with her cousin at Lady Oakley's, then draggin' us to visit the next day, and trickin' us to agree to a confounded theater party that you declined. Unfinished business. Faugh!"

"It was unfinished. Now it is not."

"Gave her the go-bye, did you?"

"Along with a very handsome diamond-and-sapphire necklace."

The earl grunted. "Well, you should o' come. Save me from having to do the pretty and from Lady Iris makin' sheep's eyes at me."

"You could have given her a setdown."

"I couldna do that!"

"Chivalry in our dour earl? What is the world coming to."

"Laugh if you want, but I seen yur reaction to Kirkson and the other Miss Shreveton."

"My dear sir, what is that to mean?"

"You know damned well. Not another word I'll say."

Stefton straightened in his chair and leaned forward, resting his elbows on the table. "Kirkson has a score to settle—with me and with Miss Shreveton. Miss Shreveton is not up to his weight, but I'd venture to say that won't make odds with her."

"Lady Harth has fixed on Kirkson as a suitor for her."

The marquis raised an eyebrow and pulled on his chin, thinking. "It might be best to turn Lady Harth's attention elsewhere. I've not heard any talk of Catherine Shreveton riding."

"Does she?"

"Beautifully. Yes. I think I need to pay a call on Raymond Dawes."

"Burke's man? What's he to do with this?"

"Maybe nothing. Then again, maybe a lot," Stefton murmured, a slight smile playing upon his lips.

An hour later the Earl of Soothcoor bade his host good-bye and set off for his club, for he'd contrived the happy notion of napping in an arm chair in the library. The marquis good-humoredly waved him off, then set off in the direction of St. George's Hospital, for in the mews in that vicinity was Tattersall's, the celebrated mart for selling horses, and the offices and London stables of Burke's, the celebrated breeder of horses.

He stopped first at the Burke stables, slowly ambling down its wide, well-swept corridor. He halted in front of the stall of an elegant black mare.

The inquisitive horse nudged him. He laughed softly and reached up to scratch her head.

"That one ain't for sale, guv'nor," said a wizened old man who rocked forward on bowed legs.

"I know. I believe her name is Gwyneth."

"Aye, sir. Did you be wantin' somethin', guv'nor?" asked the old groom, suddenly suspicious of the well-dressed, soft-spoken swell.

The marquis caught the man's hesitant, suspicious manner and laughed, clapping the fellow on the back. "You're a loyal man. Tell me, where might I find Raymond Dawes at this hour?"

"In the office. Take those stairs over there," the man said, jerking his head to the right. "It's shorter."

"Thank you." The marquis flipped a coin in the old man's direction. The man caught it easily. When he saw a yellow boy lying in his palm, his eyes grew wide as saucers. His stammered thank-yous followed Stefton up the stairs.

Stefton quietly entered the main office of Burke's and stood before Dawes's high desk.

Dawes reluctantly pulled his attention up from the ledger spread open before him. Recognizing his visitor, he surged to his feet, bobbing his head twice in deference. "My lord! Begging your lordship's pardon. I didn't hear you come in."

"It's quite all right, Dawes." Stefton glanced about the

well-appointed office, spotting two worn armchairs by the fireplace. "Let's sit down over there."

"Please, your lordship," Raymond Dawes said, coming around the desk and escorting the marquis to one of the chairs.

"You too, Dawes, I'll not crane my neck looking up at you."

Dawes hesitated a moment, then sat down opposite the marquis.

"I'm not here to buy a horse. I've come to discuss Miss Shreveton. Don't shake your head so quickly. You're a loyal man, I know, but hear me out. I believe Miss Shreveton to be acting out of character and in a manner bound to distress Sir Eugene if he but knew of it."

"How so, my lord?" Dawes asked warily.

"She insists on letting everyone believe she is a poor relation. To strengthen this belief, she dresses dowdily and scrapes her hair back hideously."

Dawes shook his head. "So she did on the road to London."

"Why?"

The agent shrugged. "Can't say truly, my lord. Family pushed her to London, I know, and that don't hold with her 'cause she ain't been broken to harness yet."

"Yes, I received the impression she was independent," Stefton said drily.

"Just so, my lord."

"I gather she hasn't been riding her horse."

"No, sir, and that has me stumped plain. Not like her. Sent 'round a note saying as much. Got back a request for patience," Dawes finished, shaking his head in puzzlement.

"Patience, hmm?" Stefton steepled his fingertips as he thought. He suddenly looked back at Dawes, dropping his hands to his thighs. "Would you trust me with Gwyneth?"

"Aye," said Sir Eugene's man slowly.

Stefton laughed. "You're right to be cautious." He stood up to leave. "Expect my groom, Friarly, for the animal at four o'clock today. Have her saddled for Miss Shreveton. With a sidesaddle," he said as an afterthought, his hand reaching for the door handle.

"Very good, my lord," Dawes said. He scratched his head. Sir Eugene would not be pleased with these goin's-on, he thought as he watched the marquis leave. He would not be pleased at all.

"Catherine, are you still working on that same handkerchief you started three days ago?"

"Yes, Aunt Alicia," Catherine returned patiently. "I told you when you instructed me to embroider my initial on these that I was not proficient with a needle."

"Nonsense," Lady Harth contradicted, "every woman learns needlework from the cradle. It is a talent we are born with"

"I'm afraid I was passed over when that blessing was bestowed," Catherine remarked drily.

"Watch your tongue, young woman, I'll not have blasphemy in my house!"

Startled, Catherine stuck her needle in wide of the mark she intended. She swallowed an oath and worked the needle back out. "I beg your pardon, Aunt Alicia," she said, her jaw jutting forward as she concentrated on her task.

"If you don't like needlework, you and Susannah should have accepted Mrs. Howlitch's kind invitation and gone with her and Iris and Dahlia to Harding and Howell's this afternoon."

"Oh, but Aunt Alicia, I believe including us in her invitation was merely a nicety. Mrs. Howlitch was just as glad we did not come."

"Nonsense."

"Well, it did seem to me that she is more interested in securing one or the other of the twins as a bride for her son Peter."

"Both girls may look much higher than Mr. Peter Howlitch for a husband. His fortune may be respectable, but I quite had him in mind more for you, Susannah."

"Me! Oh no, Aunt Alicia."

"I'm afraid Captain Chilberlain will not do at all. It would be kinder to sever that connection," Lady Harth continued reflectively, ignoring Susannah's outburst. "I am rsuaded that as a naval officer, your dear father could not untenance your union with an army man.''

''Oh, no,'' Susannah said in a rush, ''Papa is not like that all!''

Lady Harth smiled condescendingly. ''Be guided by me, y dear. It will not do,'' she tried to say kindly.

''But—''

Her aunt waved an admonitory finger at her. ''No more. e shall find you a nice husband, never fear.''

Susannah lapsed into miserable silence.

''Now, Catherine, while we are on the subject of suitors, hy have we not seen Sir Philip in two days? I quite pended upon you to affix his interest. He would be quite a ather in your cap.''

''I just do not like Sir Philip, and I would refuse any offer his making—though I very much doubt he would offer atrimony.''

''I am loath to remind you that you are not in a position having the luxury of turning down offers. If you are eaming of securing the Marquis of Stefton's hand because e showed you a few kindnesses, I beg you to awaken. I do t mean to be cruel, but you are hardly his style. Iris or ahlia would be much more suited to being the next archioness of Stefton and Duchess of Vauden. After all, ey were raised to it.''

Catherine laughed. ''No, Aunt, I do not look to the arquis to make me an offer. Far from it. I think you should ow—for it is what I told my family before they sent me re—I long ago settled on the intention of remaining a inster—''

''Rubbish!'' interpolated Lady Harth.

Catherine continued without pausing: ''—just as I long o settled on the knowledge that I will never be an complished needlewoman.'' She stuck the needle in the bric crosswise and folded the entire project up, placing it the workbasket she shared with Susannah.

Pennymore entered the parlor, his manner more agitated an was his wont. ''The Marquis of Stefton is below. When informed him you were not at home he begged me to take s card up.''

Susannah and Catherine exchanged startled glaces.

"Did you tell him that Iris and Dahlia were not really a home?"

"Yes, milady. But he advised me he is not here to se them. He's come to see Miss Catherine," the butler sai apologetically.

"Send him up, then," Lady Harth said waspishly whil casting her niece a sharp glance. "What could he want?"

Catherine could only shrug, but she sat straighter on th sofa, her feet primly positioned flat on the floor, her hand clasped in her lap.

"Excuse me, Lady Harth," the marquis said, breezin into the room without ceremony. "I've come to take Mis Catherine Shreveton riding."

Lady Harth smiled haughtily. "I'm afraid you're unde some misapprehension, my lord. My niece Catherine doe not ride. If you'd care to wait, my nieces Iris and Dahli will return shortly, and they would be most gratified for th opportunity for a nice—"

"Lady Harth," interrupted the marquis, "your niec Catherine not only rides, she is the possessor of a beautifu black mare that is in dreadful want of exercise."

The countess slowly turned to look at Catherine, her fac white. "Is this true?" she asked in awful accents.

Catherine looked daggers at the marquis, then compresse her lips tightly for a moment and nodded. Aunt Alici gasped, her mouth working furiously as if she would spea but no words would come.

The Marquis of Stefton turned to Catherine, his face an voice stern. "I have just collected Gwyneth from Raymon Dawes and she is restless. Don your riding habit and com exercise your horse."

"Ah!" Lady Harth cried triumphantly, "I can assure m lord that my niece does not possess a habit."

Catherine sighed and exchanged glances with Susanna "I'm sorry, Aunt Alicia, but I recently ordered one. It wa delivered yesterday," she admitted.

The marquis smiled and crossed his arms over his ches rocking back on his heels.

"And how did you expect to pay for this extravagance? I trust you were not thinking of coming to me for payment!"

"It has already been paid for by money my uncle gave me," Catherine said apologetically.

"Now that that's settled, run upstairs and put in on. And be quick about it," Stefton ordered, holding the parlor door open for her. "I will await you in the hall." Catherine glared at him as she passed, hurrying up the stairs. This was not what she had in mind when she planned to ride Gwyneth. But perhaps it was just as well. Ever since the habit had arrived, she'd been looking for an opportunity to put it on. She had hoped that when she turned down Mrs. Howlitch, she would have time to sneak away for a short ride. Unfortunately, Lady Harth kept her close by her side, insisting that she ply her needle.

She burst into her room, calling out for Bethie, and crossed to the wardrobe to drag out the large box hidden there, a stylish box bearing a label proclaiming it to be from Madame Vaussard's. From a drawer she pulled out boots, hat, and crop. Feverishly she worried the lacings of her skirt, inadvertently knotting them. She cried out in frustration and searched for her scissors.

"Miss Catherine! What are you about?" exclaimed Bethie, entering the room.

"Thank heavens you're here. Help me get this off. I fear I've knotted it dreadfully."

"Just a minute. Stand still. There, now slip it off," Bethie directed. "So, you're going ridin'. Finally! You've been as restless as a stalled colt. How did you manage it?"

"I didn't," came the muffled response as Bethie tossed the habit over her head. "The Marquis of Stefton got Raymond to give him Gwyneth, then he came here demanding I ride."

"In front of Lady Harth?"

"Unfortunately. Though, in a way, I'm relieved to have it put forward so. I was beginning to think our grand plans for me to sneak out and ride were never going to be a possibility."

"Stand still while I finish with these hooks."

When she finished, Catherine flopped down on the edge of the bed and pulled on her black boots. Bethie then shoved

her into a chair and pulled down her hair, brushing
furiously then redressing it in a style suitable for her hat
Catherine jammed the hat on her head, secured the layers o
veiling, then twitched the ends over her shoulder. She di
not spare a glance at the mirror, but picked up her crop an
headed for the door. Less than fifteen minutes had passed
but Catherine doubted that even that short of time woul
meet with the insufferable marquis's approval. She picke
up the long train of her skirts and clattered down the stairs

Halfway down she saw the marquis watching her. Self
consciously she slowed her pace and continued down at
more decorous gait, though her heart hammered loudly i
her chest.

The marquis's face was impassive as he regarded her wit
hooded eyes. Internally, however, he was pleased with wha
he saw. This was Catherine Shreveton as she should appea
The russet wool habit fitted her form to perfection. Th
bodice, amply trimmed with black silk braiding, rose up t
her neck and conformed to every curve. The skirt was cu
on the bias and allowed to drape her figure with soft folds
The hem and train featured a rouleau of black satin held i
place by crisscrossing black silk braid. The hat sittin
jauntily on her head was of black-dyed beaver. It wa
small-brimmed and trimmed with russet-and-black-dyed os
trich feathers. Across her face, obscuring her features, wer
layers of russet veiling, caught up in the back of the hat an
allowed to drape like a train.

The marquis's eyes narrowed as he studied the veil, fo
he'd rather see her face. He decided not to press the issue
He should be glad she did not refuse to ride. It might hav
placed him in a most uncomfortable position of forcing he
to if she had. He would not have liked to resort to suc
measures.

He curtly nodded his approval of her attire and gesture
her to proceed him to the door.

Catherine didn't know whether to be angry or glad at th
marquis's lack of response. She was certain he was bound t
rail at her for the veil and was strangely discomposed whe
he did not. She slid a sideways glance at him as she passed
searching for something—though she didn't know what. He

pulse was racing and the tingling touched all her nerve endings. Warning signs, but warning her of what? He was a most enigmatic gentleman, fluctuating in his attentions, alternating between teasing, lecturing, and ignoring. He was quite unlike any other gentleman of Catherine's acquaintance. To even begin to ponder his motivations was sufficient to leave one dizzy or with a headache. The one thing she was sure of, however, was that it would be ill-advised to develop an affection, let alone a *tendre* for the man and disastrous to let him know one's feelings. Not that she entertained any warm feelings for him, she told herself briskly. Her feelings were anything but warm, unless one considered anger and disgust warm, which she did not. All in all, he was an arrogant, insufferable, odious creature.

Except that he brought her Gwyneth.

A small cry escaped Catherine's lips on seeing her beloved horse. She ran down the front steps of Harth House, grabbed the reins from the surprised marquis's man, and threw her arms around Gwyneth's neck, happily stroking and cooing to her.

Gwyneth nudged her, nuzzling Catherine's neck.

"Stop that! Stop that, Gwyn! You'll tear the veil! Did you miss me, love? Have I been very bad?" she asked her horse, scratching her head.

"If I were you, Gwyneth," came the deep, amused tones of the marquis, "I wouldn't be so quick to forgive."

Gwyneth tossed her head, then lowered it to nudge Catherine again.

The marquis sighed. "What do horses know, anyway?"

A rippling laugh came from Catherine. "She knows I love her, don't you, old girl?"

The marquis feigned disgust and offered to give Catherine a leg up. "Today, Friarly," the marquis said as he took his reins from the groom and mounted his horse, "be here when we return or you'll swap positions with young Stephen."

Friarly blanched. "You wouldn't, milord! Stephen! B—but he's nothing but a stableboy!"

"Precisely," the marquis said sternly, wheeling his horse about.

Gwyneth danced on the cobbled pavement as Catherine

held her in, waiting for the marquis. "She is a bit restive,"
Catherine observed with affection. She cooed to her to
calm down.

Stefton eyed Gwyneth consideringly. "Can you hold her
through the city traffic?" He drew nearer to her, ready to
grab the mare's bridle.

"That won't be necessary!" Catherine snapped, angry at
his presumption.

"I beg your pardon."

"And so you should," Catherine returned bitingly, urging
Gwyneth through the press of carts and carriages.

Stefton followed, cursing himself for his damned interference. It was not his desire to set her back up. Nevertheless,
by unthinkingly casting impunity upon her riding ability he
had inadvertently chosen the fastest way to do so!

They continued in silence toward Hyde Park.

It was Bugden Hill that did it. It spread out before her so
invitingly—nay, daringly. Catherine couldn't help herself,
particularly since she knew no one would recognize her.
Then again, she thought with a giggle, since that was the
case, censure was bound to fall on the marquis's head
instead, since he was her escort. That thought greatly
tickled her fancy. The flicker of daring grew until it filled
her whole being and there was no gainsaying it. Without
warning, she turned Gwyneth off the road and urged her into
a full gallop across the greensward. A wild uninhibited
laugh burst from her lips. People on the footpath followed
her progress with shocked expressions. Gathering her reins
in one hand, she raised the other in salute. Gwyneth moved
easily underneath her, flying lightly over the lush terrain.

Catherine finally turned Gwyneth's head back the way
they came, slowing her to a decorous hand canter. She was
exhilarated and at peace with herself for the first time in
weeks. Carriages and other riders were stopped in their
perambulations and joined in little knots to comment and
speculate on her headlong gallop across the park. The
knowledge that her identity was unknown gave her a heady
sense of power. She slowed Gwyneth to a walk, inclining
her head to the curious throngs she passed.

Only the marquis was alone. He sat his horse, waiting for er return. He was seemingly at his ease, one hand resting n his thigh. It was not until Catherine drew neared that she ealized his expression told another story. It was a stony lask, his eyes granite gray and as cold as winter's fiercest inds. Catherine drew in a deep breath and sat straighter in er saddle, determined to buffet the storm of his righteous e as well as she did any storm of nature's creation.

"You were correct," Catherine said lightly when she ulled up before him, "Gwyneth was in shocking need of xercise. I have been terribly remiss."

Slowly his rock-gray gaze traveled over her, chilling atherine more effectively than any words of remonstration ould. He touched his heels gently to his mount, urging him orward into a trot. Chagrined, Catherine fell in beside him.

"Well, aren't you going to say anything?" she asked at st, now more than a little nervous.

He turned his head, emptiness in the cold stare, then rned back to the road. "What would you have me say?"

She fidgeted in her saddle, her nervousness transferring to wyneth, who sidled as a sudden windblown broken branch ittered across their path. Swiftly, like the falcon diving for s prey, the marquis's hand clamped around her bridle, ulling Gwyneth up short and nearly pitching Catherine orward onto her neck.

"Stop that!" she yelled, furious at his interference. She ised her crop to swat his hand away until something in his xpression made her stop in midmotion. She slowly lowered e crop, her breathing coming faster. Never was she more ankful for the face-obscuring veil hiding her confusion d embarrassment. Her cheeks felt warm and there was a spicious blurriness to her vision. She flung her head back, aring at him though she knew he couldn't see her face. he blinked back the moisture that filled her eyes save for e few drops that coursed down her cheek.

Slowly he released his iron grip and Gwyneth tossed her ad, jangling her bridle. He sat back in his saddle, some of e harshness fading from his visage. Silently, of one ac- rd, they urged their horses forward.

A large sigh escaped the marquis. "For reasons I do not

pretend to comprehend, you continually succeed in angering me and I continue to allow you to do so. If it weren't for the love I bear you uncle, I swear I would pull you off that horse and give you the thrashing that you so richly deserve." He flicked a glance at her. That small, telltale damp spot on her veiling which had so unmanned him was now dry. "I chose, however, to be magnanimous and make excuses for you since you have not ridden in what must be weeks. I will not be so forgiving in the future."

Though she recognized her behavior as shameful, Catherine's chest heaved at his effrontery to pass dispensation to her then claim he would not do so in the future, as if he had any say over her actions. "You odious, arr—"

"To prevent a recurrence of your reprehensible behavior," the marquis continued, ignoring her interruption, "we shall ride every afternoon. As this will be our daily habit, and as those seeing us leaving and returning to Harth House will soon ferret out your identity, you will in future dispense with the veil."

"Just who are you to dictate to me!" Catherine exclaimed hotly, urging Gwyneth forward, ready to return peremptorily to her aunt's home.

The marquis's hand was once again holding her bridle. "I am the gentleman," he said slowly, "who knows who you really are, who sees behind the masquerade. I am the gentleman who appreciates your talent, your wit, and your tenacity. I am the gentleman who can make or break you, and while doing so, break Burke's as well. Remember that, my headstrong miss, when next you think to defy me."

CHAPTER
TEN

As promised, Stefton appeared before Harth House every day at four o'clock. Most days he and Catherine rode

lence, for every time Catherine saw him dressed for
ding, a wild tingling surged through her, choking words
om her throat. In retaliation she'd whip up the anger she
ought she should feel, and practiced treating him with a
ool politeness.

When her identity became known among the *ton* and
ngues wagged over the headlong gallop across Hyde Park,
ere was renewed interest in her among the young bucks.
the clubs they claimed her "a great go" and muttered it
as a deuced shame that she'd not the fortune, face, nor
harm to complement her talent on horseback. Still specula-
on ran rife as to the marquis's continued interest in her
ntil it was observed at the balls, soirées, and routs both
tended, that though he danced with her, it was always a
ountry dance, never a waltz. He extended the courtesy to
l the Shreveton cousins and therefore did not single
atherine out for any more particular attentions than their
ternoon rides. It was also noted that Catherine Shreveton
d not use any flirting wiles upon the marquis. She seemed
accept his limited regard with studied coolness and never
essed to further his attentions.

This did have Society puzzled. Several young ladies who
esired Stefton's notice began to wonder if perhaps failing
try to capture his regard wouldn't be more successful than
e stratagems they currently employed: bullying their male
latives for an introduction, dropping their handkerchiefs in
ont of him, or artfully twisting their ankles upon his
oorstep. Accordingly, some did try to pretend he didn't
ist and his acquaintance was of no account. Unfortunately,
l that was achieved by aping what was seen as Catherine's
ratagem was the reflection on Stefton's part that the
rrent Season was refreshingly free of feminine devices
d schemes. The Earl of Soothcoor very rapidly disabused
s friend of this notion by elucidating to the stunned
arquis the nature of the new schemes. For a long moment
efton was nonplussed, a condition in which, the earl later
d friends, he never remembered seeing the marquis. A
ow smile spread across the face of the intended victim of
ese devious plans. He gave a great shout of laughter and
llapsed limply in his chair, continuing to laugh until his

gray eyes turned into liquid silver. This also was a condition
the dour earl had never seen grip his friend and so told his
enthralled auditors.

Redoubtable Society matrons were determined to solve
the mystery and descended upon the Countess of Seavernes
like locusts. That lady was equally redoubtable and held
court in the drawing room with arrogant equanimity (even
when she accidentally knocked the cane out from under
doddering Lady Quillerton's hand, spilled tea in the Honorable Mrs. Peckworth's lap, and knocked Lady Jersey's
bonnet askew). In hushed and quite scandalized tones, she
implied that the marquis's interest in her niece was due to
some mysterious obligation he owed Catherine's maternal
uncle. When questioned on the elegant habit and horse
owned by her niece, she replied that she often observed that
horse-mad people were wont to spend far beyond their
means in getting and keeping horses. The ladies obliged
Lady Harth by nodding sagely in agreement and passed on
the observation that it was a great deal too bad Miss
Shreveton was squandering what little portion she had in a
profligate manner.

Naturally, it was discovered eventually that Gwyneth was
a Burke horse. Some people were awed by Catherine's
ability to ride what was obviously a high-strung creature,
but most, fueled by Lady Harth's sad comments about the
spendthrift nature of the horse-mad, merely shook their
heads.

Catherine was only aware of the furor she was creating in
the way one would be aware of bees buzzing—a nuisance
nothing more. She was expending her energies in shoring up
the walls of her masquerade, despite Gwyneth and the habit.
She was quite content to allow her aunt magnanimously to
excuse it as an eccentricity of the horse-mad. Her mind had
more important problems to mull over—like her unaccount-
able reaction to the marquis, the insidious pleasure she took
in their afternoon rides, and her studious endeavor to remain
cool toward him.

In a move that she proudly thought of as a stroke of
genius, she insisted they include Susannah and Captain
Chilberlain in their afternoon outings. She informed Stefton

at she wanted to further her cousin's romance with the
ashing captain in a fashion Lady Harth could not object to.
or herself, she saw their company as chaperonage to
rotect her from the uncomfortable feelings Stefton was able
• rouse in her breast. Unfortunately, her scheme backfired.
istead of company for Catherine, Susannah and her captain
ways fell behind, leaving her again alone in Stefton's
ompany, a circumstance that caused no end of amusement
or the marquis, much to Catherine's chagrin.

But the worst consequence of the marquis's attention was
ie interest it generated in one gentleman in particular: Sir
hilip Kirkson. He began to pay assiduous suit to Catherine,
nused that good breeding prevented her from refusing to
onverse, if somewhat stiltedly, or from refusing to dance.
o irritate Catherine further, he began to make it a habit to
•proach her for a dance when he knew a waltz to be next
n the program. For her part, Catherine quickly learned to
• gone repairing a torn flounce at just that time.

So the game continued. Until the day the Marquis of
tefton happened to meet Raymond Dawes in the street and
ccompanied him back to the Burke offices.

"Relieved, I am, to run into you, my lord," Dawes said
•avily as he escorted his guest to the chair by the hearth.
e fidgeted a moment, poking the fire and adding more
imps of coal. "Considered calling on you."

The Marquis of Stefton drew his thick brows together
id leaned forward in the chair. He knew Raymond Dawes
ell enough to know it would not do to push the man for
iformation. He was the type to tell his story in a taciturn
ianner in his own good time. Knowing that, however, did
ot curb Stefton's sudden growing sense of unease.

"Recall that day you were at Fifefield?"

"Yes, perfectly."

"And that big bay horse?"

"The one Miss Shreveton was riding? Yes, very well. I
iderstand she schooled him." Stefton forced himself to
lax. He crossed his legs and steepled his fingertips as he
stened.

"Aye," Dawes said glumly, sitting down across from the
arquis.

"Has anything happened to the animal?"

"Sold 'm."

"I always supposed that was your purpose," Stefton sai
drily. "Don't tell me she wanted him for herself? He is
magnificent horse, but surely no match for her black."

"No, my lord." Dawes scratched the back of his nec
and grimaced. "That's not what has me perturbed like."

"Then what is it?" Stefton finally asked, frustrated wit
Dawes's slow manner.

"Sir Philip Kirkson bought 'm, my lord," he said baldly
"Miss Catherine will not like that."

"But surely if he paid a good price she should have n
prejudice. Business is business."

"Not to Miss Catherine, my lord."

"Ah, you're afraid she'll cut you up for selling one of he
darlings to that wastrel," Stefton said with a laugh.

"That's not all, my lord." The man looked painec
"He's been askin' questions."

"Questions about what?"

"Miss Catherine. Questions about how come she has
Burke horse at first, then more details on her and her famil
Didn't think to hush the men. Couple known her foreve
Proud of her."

"So they informed Kirkson of her being Sir Eugene
niece and heir."

"And 'bout her riding horses like a man."

The marquis rubbed his chin in thought. "I don't see ho
he could use that information to his advantage. He couldn
possibly persuade her to fly to the border with him. An
telling Society would serve no other purpose than to dra
every gadfly in town to her door with a bunch of posies an
a proposal."

"'Nother thing. Been questioning your man, too."

The marquis glanced sharply at Dawes, his thick blac
brows pulled down creating deep furrows between then
"Friarly?"

Dawes nodded. "I sent Ol' Jack—bandy-legged man yc
met here—to tip his elbow with him at the tavern. Seen
Kirkson's payin' your man. Handsomely."

The marquis's eyes narrowed, his visage darkening until Dawes was moved to continue hastily.

"Tain't what he's said. Seems he's to do something what in't done yet."

"Really? Interesting," the marquis drawled dangerously. "I hope Kirkson has paid him well. He'll need every penny when I'm through with him."

Dawes nodded, satisfied. "Knew you'd keep our Miss Catherine safe. Told the missus. She wouldn't listen. Wrote some tellin' about Miss Catherine's odd behavior."

"Damn."

Dawes nodded again, then stared down at his large hands, absently wringing them. He grimaced. "Don't know what will happen. Sir Eugene's demanding an explanation. Says as how he'll come to London himself, if need be."

"Egad, no! That's the last thing we want. Thankfully he's as far away as he is," Stefton said caustically.

"Thing is, he ain't. In Nottingham for a horse fair. Says oming here afterward."

"He could be a worse threat than Kirkson. I like and admire Sir Eugene a great deal, but if he comes to town bellowing like a stuck pig and demanding explanations, the resulting scandal will severely cripple Miss Shreveton's standing in Society!"

"I figured as much, my lord," Dawes said, shaking his head dolefully.

"The only thing for it is for me to go to Nottingham to head him off. I'll explain the situation to him and urge him return home. Failing that, at least he'll not bellow and all undue attention to his niece." He rose from the chair and grabbed his hat from the table. "Whatever you do, don't tell Miss Shreveton who purchased the bay—not even if she asks directly. Lie," he said bluntly. He fixed his hat on his head at a rakish angle, then swung wide the office door, taking the steps down at a near run and burst forth into the narrow lane below in a highly uncharacteristic rapid gait.

"Stefton! Ho, there, man!"

The marquis stopped in midstride, turning to see the Earl of Soothcoor hailing him. The grim expression on his face

relaxed a bit as he waited for the man to catch up with him
"What brings you to this part of town?" The two men
continued walking towards Pall Mall.

"Been to Tatt's to see Berner's breakdowns." The earl
made a face. "Faugh! Can't see how he came to buy th
team in the first place. A more awkward-gaited, ill-matche
pair I've never seen."

The marquis laughed thinly. "He didn't. He won them
cards off of Thackery. He certainly won't get for them wha
the bet was worth."

The earl sneered. "I've always thought Thackery doesn
know what *honor* means."

"Berner was a fool and I've no sympathy for fools. H
should never have accepted the bet without knowing th
pair."

Soothcoor nodded agreement, then changed the subjec
"And what were you doing at Burke's? Trying to buy horse
or employees?"

Stefton laughed shortly, remembering his conversatio
with Catherine on trying to hire employees away from S
Eugene. "Neither. I was learning," he said slowly,
crooked smile twisting his lips. He was contemplative for
moment, then he halted and looked at Soothcoor. "I have
go out of town for a few days."

"And?"

A brief frown pulled at Stefton's lips. "Keep an eye c
Miss Shreveton for me," he said slowly.

The earl whistled softly. "So that's they way the win
blows."

"Spare me your suppositions," Stefton said with a touc
of asperity. "You know nothing of the kind."

Soothcoor's eyebrows rose, his dark eyes protruding slightl
"As bad as that, is it?" He shook his head dolefully.

Stefton ground his teeth at Soothcoor's humor. "No, it
not," he said slowly, wondering why he felt a sudden pa
in his head. "Just do as I ask. There is more to Mi
Shreveton than any in London know," he said cryptically

Soothcoor looked speculatively at the marquis. Stefto
had a faraway contemplative look in his silvered eyes th
caused them to glitter more than was their wont. He shoc

his head at Stefton's strange behavior, but promised he'd do as the marquis asked.

"Catherine!" Lady Harth called, opening the door to her niece's room without knocking. "A note has just been delivered for you," she said severely, as if chastising Catherine for the occurrence. She held out the missive written on ivory-colored paper and addressed with a bold hand.

"Thank you, Aunt Alicia." Catherine took the note and turned back toward her dressing table.

"Well? Who is it from?"

"Aunt Alicia!" Catherine exclaimed, effrontery warring with amusement at her aunt's inordinate curiosity.

"I will not have any of you girls receiving strange notes from unknown persons. It's—it's unseemly," her aunt retorted self-righteously, though Catherine thought she detected two bright spots of color high on her cheekbones proclaiming a twinge of embarrassment.

"I see," Catherine responded slowly, her lips pursing to refrain from smiling. She broke open the wax seal and spread open the note.

Miss Shreveton,

I regret to inform you I shall be unable to join you for our daily ride. I have discovered urgent business out of town that necessitates my immediate departure from the metropolis. I do not know when I shall return, but I trust Captain Chilberlain will be delighted to carry on in my absence.

> *Your obedient servant,*
> *Stefton*

A cold lump settled in the pit of Catherine's stomach. "It's from the Marquis of Stefton!" she said with brittle brightness. "He merely writes to inform me he has been called out of the city and will not be able to ride until his return."

Lady Harth sniffed. "You do not seem unduly disappoint-

ed by the news," she said waspishly, dissatisfied with th
note's prosaic contents.

Catherine manufactured a careless shrug and casuall'
tossed the letter on the dressing table. "As you yourse
noted, the marquis has been fulfilling an obligation to m
uncle." She laughed. "It is not as if we have any form c
understanding, is it?"

"Definitely not. Does he say if he will be in town for ou
ball?"

"No, he doesn't mention it at all."

"Well, if that is all . . ." Lady Harth looked discomfited
She fidgeted with the toiletries on the dressing table, he
fingers inches from the note as she resisted an urge to pick
up and read it.

"Yes, Aunt Alicia, it is. No secret assignations or plan
for a midnight escape to Gretna Green," Catherine teased

Her aunt bristled. "I should hope not!" she exclaimed
turning to leave the room, her posture stiff, eloquent in he
displeasure at Catherine's levity.

Catherine smiled and shook her head as she watched he
leave. But when the door closed, a wave of depressio
swamped her. Sagging on the stool before the dressin
table, she picked up the note and slowly unfolded it agai
Upon rereading it, she searched for some trace of genuin
regret in its tone. There was none she could detect. I
remained a formal and proper missive.

She sighed and stared at her reflection in the mirror. Sh
had not realized, had never accepted the notion, that sh
looked forward to their daily rides. The cold lump in he
stomach turned into a heavy weight pressing upon her. Sh
felt she had been cut adrift and left to founder in the wind
seas of Society.

Though she practiced a strict formality in his presence
they shared a common sense of amusement at the foibles c
their fellow man. She laughed softly, remembering the man
occasions they exchanged glances or smiles at their observa
tions. Riding with Susannah and Captain Chilberlain woul
be lonely, for those two were too involved with each othe
to offer company. Perhaps she should invite the Earl c
Soothcoor to join their little party? He possessed wit an

nderstanding and—though he wasn't the Marquis of Stefton—
e was his friend.

Catherine frowned at her melancholy reflection. She did
ot care, couldn't possibly care for the arrogant, insufferable
an!

With an unladylike oath, she whirled away from the
irror and stood up, determined to seek out Susannah to
ivert her wayward, traitorous thoughts.

"Are you quite all right, cousin?" Susannah asked the
ext evening as they toured the assembly room at Almack's.

Catherine gave a wan smile. "If I'm not, I should be."

"What's troubling you? The Marquis of Stefton?"

"I don't know. Yes, partially, I suppose, if I must be
onest." Her face made a wry expression. "That is a very
owering idea. I had quite thought myself immune to our so
andsome, arrogant, infuriating marquis. To realize I am no
ifferent from the numerous ladies who fawn over him is
oublesome."

Susannah laid a sympathetic hand on her cousin's arm.
Think though, it is you who receives a modicum of his
egard, not they."

"But that is precisely it. It is a modicum, and it is always
roper."

"Would you wish him to make improper advances?"
usannah asked with a teasing laugh.

Catherine smiled, but answered seriously. "Sometimes, I
ink I would. I shudder at the memory of Kirkson's
athsome kisses, but then I wonder what Stefton's kisses
ould be like in comparison. And—and if they could wipe
e awful memories from my mind."

"Oh, dear."

"Precisely," Catherine said drily, a ghost of her normal
nergy and wit returning. "But it isn't just Stefton that has
e blue-deviled. I am beginning to understand how foolish
was to embark on this masquerade. If Aunt Alicia knew
f my true worth, she would not push unfortunate stammering
entlemen my way, nor would she encourage Kirkson's
ttentions over my protests. I am quite fatigued with devel-
ping stratagems to avoid that gentleman. I swear I will be

soon considered as clumsy as our aunt if I must contrive
tear any more of my dresses just as he approaches!''

Susannah giggled. ''Especially after Lord and Lady Riece
ball.''

Catherine looked chagrined. ''Yes, that rip did go beyon
the bounds of propriety. I never thought that fabric woul
tear so easily! It was almost up to my thigh.''

''I will admit, Cousin, it was most comical to see yc
walking around, clutching the side of your gown.''

''I forgot to replenish the packet of pins in my reticul
Admit it, though, it served its purpose. Under the circum
stances, there was no way I could waltz with Kirkson.''

They neared the refreshment table and accepted glasses
weak lemonade from a waiter, then sat in two of the chai
that lined the room.

''The other thing that makes me regret this abysm
masquerade is Mr. Dawes.''

''Your uncle's agent?''

''Yes. I went to see him today while you were sneakir
off to Gunther's with the captain.''

''Catherine, I never sneak!'' Susannah declared hotl
though a deep red blush colored her fair cheeks.

Catherine laughed. ''I'm sorry, I could not resist tweakir
you. Anyway, I went to see Mr. Dawes. He was extremel
reticent and taciturn. I'll admit he is taciturn by nature, b
this went beyond what is normal even for him. When
asked about the sale of horses we brought down, he brushe
me off. And he quite cut me off when I asked about n
favorite of the horses—Zephyros, a big bay. Said he didn
have time. The odd thing was, he would never look me
the eye. Then—and I don't know quite why—I asked him
he knew anything about the marquis's sudden departur
from town.''

''Did he?''

''He denied it, but he was strangely fidgety. I have know
Mr. Dawes all my life and I'd swear he was lying to me.''

''But to what purpose?''

''That I cannot say.'' She worried her bottom lip betwee
her teeth.

''Oh, look, Catherine!'' Susannah cried, grabbing he

rm, "Captain Chilberlain and Earl of Soothcoor have
rived!"

Catherine looked up dutifully, and though she saw the two
entlemen, she also saw Kirkson standing by the entrance
reeting two of Almack's formidable patronesses. She doubted
e'd seen her yet, but with the captain sure to capture
usannah's attention, she had to think of a way to stay clear
f the gentleman.

She rose from her chair, pulling Susannah along with her.
he Earl of Soothcoor didn't know it yet, she thought
rimly, but he was about to become her dress's savior.

"You watch the chit avidly. I swear I do not see what you
entlemen find of interest in her. She is such a tiny brown
vren, and just as common," Lady Welville said languidly,
awning delicately behind her fan.

Sir Philip Kirkson looked down at her and sneered. "And
fail to understand how you could possess a voucher to this
allowed hall of respectability."

Panthea laughed lightly, not in the least offended. "You
vould be amazed at the skeletons that reside in the closets
f some of our vaunted patronesses."

"Blackmail, hmm?"

She waved her fan slowly back and forth, smiling.

"Frankly, I don't know why you bother. It is such an
nsipid place."

"I don't often attend. Just enough to show I can if I
hoose to," she admitted. She tucked her arm through his.
'Walk with me to the refreshment table so I may pretend to
njoy lemonade, and tell me about Miss Shreveton."

"Why the interest?"

"Because Stefton displays interest."

"Gave you the go-bye, did he?"

"Only temporarily. See," she said, pointing to the diamond-
nd-sapphire necklace she wore, "he gave me this."

"It looks like a parting gift to me," Kirkson said drily.

"Nonsense," she denied haughtily. "We have an under-
tanding. He is merely drawing Society's attention from our
ffair. To save my reputation. Why else divert his attention
ɔ our little brown wren?"

"Possibly," drawled Kirkson, "because our little brown wren is the heiress of Sir Eugene Burke."

"Burke?"

"Of Burke horses, my dear. He is the best and most famous horse breeder in England."

"I know that," she said waspishly, "but why should that be of any interest to Stefton? He has more money than he can count. He scarcely needs to marry money."

"Because, my silly widgeon, Stefton has begun a breeding program of his own. I'll grant you he is more interested in racehorses than the carriage and riding stock of Burke's but it he were to marry our little brown wren, as you call her, he will have strong ties to Burke. With that connection and with virtually unlimited access to some of the best breeding stock in the country, he will be able to raise the finest racehorses around. He will dominate Newmarket."

Panthea frowned. What Kirkson said made sense—damn his eyes! "Why isn't her relationship to Sir Eugene more commonly known? This is the first I've heard of it, and would swear that would make juicy telling and have the fortune hunters dancing attendance upon her night and day."

"From what I have been able to discover from the people at Burke's establishment, Miss Shreveton has decided she doesn't wish to marry."

"How odd."

"To you, perhaps, but remember, she is endowed with an ample fortune. Miss Shreveton's family, however, does wish her to wed, and it is they who insisted she come to London. This deception of hers is a rebellion against them."

"She does not look like the type to have enough gumption for rebellion."

He watched Catherine laugh at something the Earl of Soothcoor said as they led down through a set in a lively contredanse. "There is more spirit in her than you suppose," he drawled, remembering how she fought him at the inn.

"I gather you wish to wed Miss Shreveton?"

"It is my intention. You see, I have suffered some—shall we say, less than trivial losses recently and need to effect

ecovery. Flight to the continent does not agree with me so I
lo not ignore the size of the wren's fortune.''

"From my observation, the little bird has taken you in
lislike.''

"An early misunderstanding, no more. I do not intend to
llow it to stand in my way,'' he said grimly.

Lady Welville's lips twitched. She took a glass of insipid
emonade from the waiter and raised it to Kirkson in salute.
'To your success!''

He inclined his head and smiled. "And may I wish you
he same?''

Panthea's darkened eyelashes descended over her eyes
ıntil she looked at Kirkson through narrow slits. Her smile
hinned enigmatically. "You may, sir. You will of course let
ne know if I may assist you in any way?''

"Of course,'' he replied with alacrity.

They looked at each other and smiled again in perfect
ınderstanding.

"My thanks to you, my lord,'' Catherine said breathlessly
ıs the Earl of Soothcoor led her off the dance floor. She
ınfurled her fan. "That has to be the most vigorous dance
ın existence.''

"Aye, I'll grant you that. May I fetch you a glass of
emonade, Miss Shreveton?''

"Yes, that would be grand, thank you,'' she said, smiling
ıp at him. Out of the corner of her eye she saw Kirkson
ook speculatively in her direction. "Then again, why don't
we go together? I would not have you think I am some
nissish young lady,'' she said in a rush, peremptorily taking
ıis arm.

The earl's this face registered surprise for a moment, then
ıe smiled at her, placing his other hand over hers. "I should
ɔe honored,'' he said. He had been curious all evening as to
Miss Shreveton's desire for his company, especially coming
ıard after the marquis's request that he watch over her.
Something, or rather someone, was causing her distress,
hat was obvious. Most likely importuning her for favors.
He thought himself an unlikely choice for a protector;

however, since both she and the marquis seemed to expect i
of him, he calmly accepted the mantle.

He looked about the room. Only one person seemed to be
watching her: Sir Philip Kirkson. A bad one that, but an odd
one to be pursuing Miss Shreveton.

"I don't mean to pry, but if we're to set the tabbies
tongues waggin' by remainin' together to protect you from
Kirkson, do you mind tellin' me why?"

A blush swept up Catherine's neck and face. "I—I'm
sorry, my lord. I know it is very bad of me." She tried to
remove her hand but he held it fast.

"Don't fratch yurself, lassie. I'm perfectly willing to be
of service."

She smiled wanly at him. "Again, I apologize. You are
right, but truthfully, I do not know why he persists. Unless i
is a matter of pride."

"And how is that?"

"I first met him during my journey to London. He took
me to be—well, you know, a certain type of lady."

He looked black. "I be understandin' you."

She sighed. "Yes, well, he was rather adamant that I
accept his regard and would not listen to any protestations
on my part."

They halted before the refreshment table. "And how did
you convince him of his error?" the earl asked as blandly as
possible, though his dark eyes were alertly watching Catherine's
face.

"It was the marquis who finally came to my rescue."

"Stefton?" he asked, jerking upright, lemonade sloshing
out of the glasses he held.

"Yes, and then Mr. Dawes, my uncle's agent. Thank
you." she said, accepting the glass he handed her.

"Dawes? Sir Eugene Burke's man? Burke is yur *uncle*?
So that explains it!"

"Catherine! What are you about?" demanded Lady Harth
in a strident whisper, sweeping down upon them before
Catherine could question the earl.

"I beg your pardon? Did you need me for something
Aunt?" She set her glass down on the table.

The Earl of Soothcoor lightly touched her arm. "I'll talk

with you later, lassie," he murmured. "Just you be remembering I'm here if you need me." He bowed perfunctorily to Lady Harth before walking away.

Lady Harth barely waited until he was out of hearing. "I demand that you tell me just what you mean, making a spectacle of yourself," her aunt hissed. "And have you no consideration for you dear cousin, Iris? You have an eminently respectable suitor whom you insist upon ignoring and instead make up to all manner of highly ineligible men. It is bad enough that you harass the Marquis of Stefton, but now you hang onto the Earl of Soothcoor in a frightfully forward manner, quite embarrassing your cousin. Iris has been enjoying his attentions and might have continued to do so in the future if not for you." Lady Harth's voice was becoming shrill, and several heads turned in their direction.

"Please, Aunt Alicia, it isn't at all as you suppose. Except," she said, pausing, her arms held rigidly to her sides, "that if you mean to consider Kirkson an eligible suitor, then you are correct, for I will resist any suggestion of a connection with that gentleman."

Lady Harth's narrow chest heaved and her thin frame quivered in anger. Her eyes grew wide and air whistled through her teeth. "Ungrateful wretch! After all the expense of clothing you and presenting you, this is how I am repaid!" she declared dramatically, her voice rising and her arms swinging wide as she stepped backward.

"Aunt Alicia, no!" Catherine cried, grabbing for her aunt.

Too late. Lady Harth's foot slipped on the spot of spilled lemonade, her flailing arms providing momentum and carrying her backward. Catherine watched in stunned horror as her aunt fell on the refreshment table, crushing cakes and upsetting pitchers of lemonade.

Cries of dismay echoed around the room and the musicians missed notes, coming to a discordant halt.

"Are you all right?" Catherine asked, trying to help her aunt to her feet.

Lady Harth pulled her hand free, refusing Catherine's assistance. "I was, until you descended upon my household." She shook crumbs from her dress and brushed at the

large wet spots on her skirt. She looked quellingly at the
murmuring crowd growing around them. She straightened
her shoulders and threw back her head. "We are leaving.
Inform your cousins."

The crowd parted before her like the Red Sea. Lady
Harth, two high spots of color flying on her cheeks, dis-
dained to recognize anyone who spoke to her as she made
her way across the room. The gathering was buzzing with
whispered exchanges, shock turning rapidly to amusement
at the sight of Lady Harth dripping lemonade and trailing
cake crumbs. A few went so far as to suggest it was
timely, for typically Lady Harth's clumsiness resulted in
disaster for others, never for herself. Others shook their
heads and clucked their tongues, for they were certain Lady
Harth would blame her niece Catherine for the mishap,
refusing, as she always did, to admit to her own clumsiness.

The same thought occurred to Catherine. And she wasn't
wrong. Barely had the carriage steps been put up before
Lady Harth launched into her tirade, punctuated by pitiful
sobs emanating from the twins. The cacophony of sound
made Catherine want to clamp her hands over her ears. She
clenched her teeth instead, endeavoring to allow the sound
to wash over her. Susannah glanced at her once in sympathy,
but had no power to halt the vituperative outpouring, so sat
in silent misery.

Aunt Alicia's harangue continued throughout the carriage
ride and showed no signs of abating as the carriage pulled
up before Harth House. She catalogued a library of Catherine's
failings, elucidating in no uncertain terms her disappointment
to the Shreveton family.

Catherine bore it all in long-suffering silence. Her head
docilely bowed in penitence.

"I shall not burden you with my presence for much
longer. I will instruct Bethie to pack my trunks in the
morning and then enquire as to posting charges to Yorkshire,"
she said softly when her aunt finally paused to draw a
breath.

"Do not be ridiculous," contradicted Lady Harth, leading her nieces into the drawing room. "To leave now would
create more scandal." She paced the floor. "I had my

reservations about including you this Season. I should have followed my inclinations. I knew when I met your mother that she was not worthy to be a Shreveton, and it's obvious you inherited more from her than from my dear brother. She was an insipid twit—most likely still is—who married Ralph for his family connections.''

A haze of red anger blurred Catherine's vision. ''You may say what you like about me, but you will not talk about my mother in that fashion!''

''How dare you talk back to me,'' Lady Harth said slowly in awful accents.

''I dare because you are wrong. Wrong in everything you think you know about my family.''

Lady Harth snorted. ''I doubt that,'' she said with calm certainty.

''Have you ever hear of Burke horses, Aunt Alicia?''

''Of course I have, you impertinent chit. What has that to do with your family?''

''I shall be heir to the Burke fortune.''

''Do not be ridiculous.''

''My mother, whom you so delight in degrading, is the twin sister of Sir Eugene Burke. When my parents married, it was your brother who could be called the fortune hunter, for his competence did not come near to meeting what my mother had—and still has—to command.''

''I don't believe you. Why would my own brother lead me to believe his bride was penniless?''

''He never led you to believe anything. You made it up out of whole cloth and never bothered to ask.''

''Well, how do you explain your attire?'' blurted out one of the twins.

''Yes,'' contributed the other haughtily. ''You certainly have not appeared the heiress.''

Catherine had the grace to blush.

Lady Harth, her eyes narrow slits and her lips pursed in consideration, stared at her niece. ''Iris and Dahlia are quite right. Well, what have you got to say for yourself?''

Catherine's shoulders sagged and she turned partially away from her relatives, staring unseeing at the gray-threaded marble fireplace. ''At home I was courted primarily for the money and property. When I came to London I had some half-formed notion of being courted for myself rather than for my dowry and expectancies." She smiled wanly and turned her head to look over her shoulder at her aunt. "I was also piqued at the letter you sent my mother. You assumed, without meeting me, that I would be without looks, accomplishments, or fortune. I decided to fulfill your expectations."

A muscle in Lady Harth's jaw twitched as she stared at her niece. She dabbed at her forehead with a lace-edged handkerchief and closed her eyes. "To think that I have nursed a viper to my breast these long weeks. I feel quite faint," she said, though her voice lacked any fainting quality. "Go to your room. We shall discuss this in the morning." She flung herself into a damask-covered chair. The delicate piece rocked precariously under her momentum, tottering on its slender back legs before tipping completely backwards, dumping the Countess of Seaverness on the floor.

CHAPTER
ELEVEN

"Maybe it would be best," Catherine mused the next afternoon as she moodily stared at the glowing coals in the fireplace in her bedroom, "if I cut my hair, bound my breasts, and ran away to be a groom."

Susannah shook out the flounces of the dress she was mending for her cousin. "You're becoming maudlin."

"No, I'm not," contradicted Catherine. "I can't become maudlin. I already am."

Susannah laughed and laid the dress on the bed. "Catherine, this is not like you. You're always so decisive and—and

lependent. I thought you didn't care a fig about what
int Alicia thinks of you."

"I lied. At least, I'm beginning to realize it was all a lie.
insubstantial as fairy dust."

"Goodness, such die-away airs. Perhaps your calling is
stage after all!"

That drew a reluctant smile. "All right. I stand properly
astised. I've finished feeling sorry for myself. Now if
ly Aunt Alicia would start talking to me again, even if it
is only to rail at me! Unfortunately, I don't think she will
til her back stops hurting."

"I'll admit, I've never seen anyone take a tumble in that
inner before—feet up in the air and petticoats down over
r head!"

"It's the screeching I'll not forget."

"Or how it increased when Pennymore burst into the
om to see what the uproar was about. The poor man. I've
ver seen him so flustered as when he realized it was Aunt
icia's drawers and petticoats he was seeing."

"I think it was Pennymore's seeing her in that predica-
nt that has fueled her anger against me," Catherine
ntured. "Truthfully, Susannah, I no longer know how I
ould go on."

"Excuse me, Miss Catherine," Bethie said from the
orway. "But this box just come for you." She laid a large
essmaker's box on the bed.

"That looks like it's from Madame Vaussard! I haven't
lered anything else from her," Catherine said, crossing to
 bed.

"Do you think the marquis would send anything?" suggested
sannah, moving the mended dress aside.

"Coo—but that would plop the fat in the fire," Bethie
d.

Catherine frowned and shook her head. "No, I don't
nk he would. He has too nice a sense of propriety." She
lled the lid off. On top of the white muslin covering the
ntents of the box was a letter. Catherine exchanged
rplexed glances with Susannah and Bethie before slowly
folding the note written with a fine, spidery scrawl.

*   *   *

My dearest Mademoiselle Shreveton,

On the day you visited my shop for your riding habit and told me of your circumstances, I knew you would on day need a gown befitting your true station. I took the liber of making such a gown. Since it was finished, I have bee waiting for a time when you would need it.

The world comes to my shop, and the world gossips. A wise businesswoman listens. When I heard of your contretemps with the Countess of Seaverness at Almack's I say to myself, "Augustine, the time has come. Miss Shreveton must now turn from the petite, ugly hatchling *to the glorious swan and so bemuse the* bon ton. *Now it is the time for this dress." Here it is, ma petite.*

Bon chance,

Augustine Vaussard

P.S. I have taken the liberty of forwarding the bill to yo uncle's place of business.

Catherine laughed at the postscript and silently hand the note to Susannah. With shaking fingers she pulled ba the covering material. The dress lying folded in the box w a shimmering blend of green, gold and white. Slowly s pulled it out of its nest of protective fabric.

"Oh, Miss Shreveton!" breathed Bethie. She help Catherine free it from the last of its covering and swept t box aside so Catherine could lay the dress out on the be

The dress was white lace over a white satin slip finish with a rouleau of pale green satin edged with gold cordin The lower third of the skirt was embroidered with bunch of gold grapes and shaded green leaves. The bodice was pale green satin cut square with a fall of white lace embro dered with gold lozenges set across the neckline. T sleeves of pale green satin were slashed with white lace a edged with gold cording and more lace embroidered wi gold.

Susannah grabbed her cousin's arm. "It's beautiful! I perfect!" she cried, giving a little jump.

A slow smile emerged on Catherine's face, her ey shining as she stared transfixed at Madame Vaussar

:ation. "It's not all white, which we know I look insipid
, but it is not so heavily colored as to offend Society
cklers—particularly given my age."

"A pox on comments about your age," scolded Susannah.
still, you are right, the amount of color is enough to
unteract the effect of stark white. And that green is a
illiant choice with your coloring!"

"Will you try it on now, Miss?" Bethie asked.

Catherine touched an embroidered grape motif with her
igertips. "Not right now, I think, Bethie. But just
:eiving this has put me in better spirits. It has certainly
ased away my depression and makes me feel ready to
:et the world again. Clever, clever Madame Vaussard..."
e murmured, shaking her head in wonder. "Bethie, put
e dress away. The ball is still several days away—time
ough to try it on. Right now I have to brave Aunt Alicia's
ath and see what comes. Shall we go downstairs,
sannah?"

For answer, Susannah picked up her shawl from the
nch at the end of the bed, draping its long length elegantly
er her arms and walked toward the door.

Laughing, Catherine quickly tossed her shawl about her
oulders and followed her cousin downstairs.

Hearing masculine voices in the drawing room, they
used by the door.

"Oh, Miss Catherine, Miss Susannah," loudly whispered
nnymore as he scurried toward them.

"Have we guests, Pennymore? Why weren't we informed?"
ked Susannah.

"Yes, miss. But I was told to tell any gentlemen who
led that you and Miss Catherine were indisposed," explained
ained Pennymore.

"Indisposed? Really? Well, I don't know about you,
sannah, but I seem to have just effected a miraculous
overy," Catherine said, a spark of mischief in her eyes.

"I don't know how it is cousin, but I also seem to be
ich recovered. What was ailing us, Pennymore?"

"I—I couldn't say, Miss," stammered the hapless butler.

"Whatever it was, it has passed. I think we are healthy
ough to entertain visitors," Catherine said, her hand on

the door latch. She smiled reassuringly at the butler as s
pushed open the door.

The Countess of Seaverness and Lady Iris and La
Dahlia were entertaining four gentlemen: Mr. Dabernath
Sir Richard Chartrist, the Earl of Soothcoor, and Capta
Chilberlain. The countess, in a nest of eiderdown pillow
was enthroned on a red damask chaise longue. She bare
turned at the sound of the opening door for she was bu
lamenting the absence of her other two nieces. She pro
ised she would convey the gentlemen's regards.

"That won't be necessary, Aunt Alicia," Catherine sa
brightly.

The twins gasped, Lady Harth scowled, and the gentlem
surged to their feet.

"You will be happy to know we are quite recovered," s
said, walking briskly into the room. She turned toward t
gentlemen. "You must know, Aunt Alicia is an inspirati
for Susannah and me. Look at her, in agony after a nas
fall, and still she insists on entertaining visitors whe
scarcely out of her bed of pain. She is an inspiration to
all," Catherine declared, coming forward to bestow a ki
on her aunt's cheek, then solicitously plumping up h
pillows.

Lady Harth compressed her lips, displeasure evident
the sharp glance she gave Catherine. Her niece mere
smiled blandly at her before sitting in a nearby chair.

"We were just proposing a walk in the park for th
afternoon," said Sir Richard. "If you ladies are feeli
better, might you consider joining us?"

"We should be delighted," Catherine said quickly, ign
ing the pouting faces of the twins.. She knew they would
disappointed that each would not command the attention
two gentlemen. No matter. For Catherine decided it w
more important that they all be seen together than to wor
over the twins' perceived injured sensibilities. "We w
leave you to entertain our dear aunt while we change.
won't be long." She quickly shepherded her cousins out
the room before anyone, particularly Lady Harth, co
think to comment.

"You always spoil everything," Iris accused as they ounted the stairs. "Now I suppose you'll monopolize the arl of Soothcoor again, leaving me with boring Mr. abernathy."

"Nonsense. But if you wish, I will confine my attentions whichever of the gentlemen you don't want," Catherine turned coolly.

"You would? Why—what have you to gain?" her cousin sked suspiciously.

"Nothing whatsoever. But neither do I wish to gain nything, as you so crudely put it. I was speaking the truth e other evening when I said I have no wish to marry. I ave financial independence, and quite frankly, I see noth-ng in the eligible bachelors I have met to recommend em."

"What about the Marquis of Stefton?" Dahlia asked yly. "You spend an inordinate amount of time in his ompany."

Catherine felt her heart jump in her chest at Dahlia's atement, but willed herself to maintain a calm manner. The marquis is a friend of my uncle's. He has spent much f the time we've been together berating me for pretending be something I am not. Does that sound like a gentleman out to make an offer? He seems more like another uncle to e!" She said the words lightly enough, but they twisted ainfully in her throat. The marquis's manner *was* akin to an ncle's, and that knowledge depressed her. She wished to ir other feelings in the marquis that were not at all those of relative.

She ducked quickly into her room, forestalling further omment. She leaned for a moment against the closed edroom door, struggling against the waves of emotion ulling her under to a dark sea of strange new feelings. She ughed drily, without humor. She didn't even know if tefton would return before Lady Harth's ball. She wanted m to. She wanted to show him the true Catherine Shreveton at he so often claimed he wished to see. Would it make a fference? Or after achieving his goals, would he forget her xistence?

She sighed, moving away from the door to ring the bell

for Bethie. No matter. The die was cast. She'd play th
scene to the end—whatever that might be. After the ba
she'd find a way to return to Yorkshire, for she would n
remain in London long after the truth of her wealth wa
known. She could not suffer the humiliation of being courte
merely for the gold guineas she would bring.

Bethie peeked in the door. "Did you ring, Miss Catherine?

"Yes. Fetch my brown-and-gold walking dress and hel
me change."

"The one Mrs. Scorby made, Miss? It's about time yo
wore those dresses. Now ain't it fortunate that I took t
pressing those just this morning, too."

Catherine laughed. "Bethie, you're a canny one. Ju
watch out that one of these days you don't outsmart yourself.

"No, Miss, certainly not."

The Marquis of Stefton, disdaining the knocker on th
front door of Harth House, impatiently rapped the bras
head of his cane against the carved oak panels. When Joh
opened the door, he pushed past him into the hall, asked
see Catherine and peremptorily handed the startled footma
his hat, gloves, and cane.

"B—but my lord, she isn't in at present. She gone for
walk in the park with the other young ladies."

"I see. Is the countess available, then? I bear messag
for her."

Almost instantly he was conducted to the drawing roo
where Lady Alicia still reclined in her pile of pillows.

"Lady Alicia, I hope I do not find you ill?" he sai
making his bow and claiming one of her hands in his.

"It is my back, that is all. I had the misfortune to suffer
fall yesterday, which has left me bruised."

"My dear lady, I am sorry to hear that. But perhaps th
news I bring you will cheer you up. I've come to tell yo
that Lady Orrick and the Earl of Seaverness will be return
ing to London later today."

"Seaverness is coming! But it lacks a week till the ball.
had not thought to see him before the day of the bal
impossible creature that he is."

The marquis laughed. "Yes, he bent my ear for over a

ur last evening with his antipathy for the frenzy of
ndon at the height of the Season.''

"But why is he returning early?"

"That you will have to ask him," advised the marquis,
s lips thinning. "Now if you'll excuse me, Lady Harth, I
ink I shall stroll toward Hyde Park and see if I may find
ur nieces. I understand from your footman that they've
ne for a walk there?"

"Yes," Lady Harth confirmed vaguely, her mind contem-
ating the advantages of the earl's and Penelope's early
turn. "They went there in company with Mr. Dabernathy,
r Richard, Lord Soothcoor, and Captain Chilberlain."

"Thank you. Don't bother ringing for the servants to
ow me out. I know my way."

Stefton had been anticipating seeing Catherine again al-
ost since he'd left London. Somehow the chit caught his
oughts more often than any other woman previously. He
adily admitted he enjoyed her company, for she talked to
m without artifice and was not afraid either to get angry
ith him or to contradict whatever he said. He grinned
ffishly. In fact, she did both things frequently, deliberately
ovoked a few times by him, for he enjoyed seeing sparks
ght her eyes and high color on her cheeks. It was at those
nes that, despite the plain dresses and hairstyles she
eadfastly wore, he was able to see what a beautiful woman
e was.

He swung his walking stick idly as he scanned the park's
otpaths. The Shreveton party was nowhere in sight, but
at did not perturb him unduly. He sauntered down the
ensington path, nodded at acquaintances as he went, and
anned how he would tell her he'd again saved her—this
ne from the justifiable wrath of her uncle. He had a hunch,
membering Sir Eugene Burke's anger and determination to
me to London to straighten out both his niece and Lady
arth, that this was one rescue she might even thank him
r.

And this may just be another, he thought disgustedly
hen he saw the group. He broke into a run.

* * *

At first, Catherine refused to believe the evidence befor
her eyes. It must be a coincidence—a horse similar i
appearance to the bay she'd schooled. It had to be, fo
surely Raymond Dawes would not sell Zephyros, or an
Burke horse, to Kirkson after his injury to Maureen. But i
any case it was a beautiful animal and did not deserve th
treatment it was receiving. Sir Philip, astride the sidling an
bucking animal, was making prodigious use of a wicke
looking crop that had already drawn a spot of blood
Catherine screamed and ran forward.

"Miss Shreveton! No!" called Soothcoor, echoed by S
Richard and the captain while Mr. Dabernathy looked frigh
ened and worried his hands. Soothcoor started forward on
to be halted by the anchor of Lady Iris's talon grip.

"Stop it! Stop it an once, I say!" cried Catherine. "Si
you are frightening the animal!"

"He's hasn't the brains to be frightened," growled Kirkso
scarcely glancing at Catherine. He raised his arm. "I'
teach this sluggard to obey me!" he vowed, bringing th
crop down on the horse's head.

"No!" screamed Catherine, grabbing the frightened horse
bridle and throwing up her other arm to block the blow.

The gentlemen yelled a warning to Kirkson, but he wa
deaf to their calls. The whip descended, the crack at i
impact loud in the air. Catherine cried out in pain, falling
a crumpled heap near the horse's hooves.

Susannah fainted and the twins screamed, covering the
faces and hanging on to their escorts. Soothcoor biting
lambasted Lady Iris while prying at her fingers, but sh
defeated him by sagging against him.

"Miss Shreveton! Are you all right?" Kirkson aske
visibly shaken. The crop fell from his hand as he quick
dismounted. "Miss Shreveton!" he cried, coming forwa
to help her up. Zephyros came between them, rearing an
pawing the air. "Damn you, back, you hell-spawned nag!
Kirkson rapidly retreated before the flailing hooves, h
arms raised to shield his head and face.

"Easy, boy, easy . . ." Soothcoor coaxed, attempting
approach. The horse whinnied, his eyes rolling as he kicke
at the earl. When all were far enough away, the animal can

own next to Catherine, instantly calmer, and nudged her
ith his nose. Catherine groaned.

A crowd was growing and suggestions were being made
rom all corners as to how to proceed, but no one could
enture near for the horse stood guard. Kirkson called for a
istol and young blood trotted off to a carriage where he
laimed he carried a brace of pistols under the seat. Soothcoor
nd Chilberlain argued against it while Susannah, revived
rom her faint, called to her cousin, pleading with her to
egain consciousness.

Catherine's eyes fluttered open and the horse gently
pped her face in the manner of a privileged dog. She
miled, knowing it was Zephyros, and reached up to stroke
nd animal's nose. A renewed cry of fear swept the crowd
nd she was enjoined to be careful for the horse was
bviously mad and needed to be destroyed. She laughed,
nd hanging on to the bridle, pulled herself up.

Kirkson took the pistol the young man brought from his
arriage and carefully loaded it. "Stand away, Miss Shreveton.
Move slowly so as not to startle him."

"Just what do you think you're going to do?"

"Destroy the beast."

"You will do nothing of the kind!" Catherine declared,
hrowing her arms around the horse.

"Stand away, lest you would have the animal's blood all
ver your gown," Kirkson coolly declared.

"Yu're mad, man," Soothcoor exclaimed.

"You could hit Miss Shreveton. Leave done. The animal
eems calm enough now," Chilberlain said.

A murmur of horror rose from the crowd.

"I believe Sir Philip's pride to be injured," drawled the
marquis, strolling casually in front of Catherine and the
orse. A sheen of sweat glistened on his brow. He turned to
ace Kirkson, his body directly in line with the pistol.

"Stefton, you're back," exclaimed Catherine stupidly.

He did not turn to look at her, his attention centered on
he gun. "As you see, little one." The marquis's words
ere spoken languidly enough, but every muscle in his
ody was tense and the expression on his face made words
f greeting from others in the area die within their throats.

The gray of his heavily-lidded eyes gleamed like a Damascu
steel sword while his black brows drew together—on
slightly elevated—and a sneering smile curled his thin lip

"Out of my way, Stefton. The horse is mine."

"Do not be a fool any more than you can help," Stefto
said in a measured, quiet voice that floated eerily in the ai
"Think, man. Shooting a horse in Hyde Park will scarcel
curry you favors with the *beau monde*. Not at all good *tor*
you know," he added in a bored tone.

Kirkson looked from the horse to the murmuring crow
and back, a heavy frown pulling down his handsome fea
ture, his eyes becoming beady and suspicious.

"I tell you what, Kirkson," the marquis said, drawing
snuffbox from his vest pocket and a taking a pinch of i
contents. "I will buy the horse from you at twice what yo
paid for him."

"Why?" Kirkson demanded, the gun beginning to sink

Stefton smiled enigmatically. "I remember the first time
saw that horse ridden by an excellent rider. I have fon
memories of that day, so I suppose purchasing the anima
might be seen as a quixotic gesture."

Kirkson stared suspiciously at the marquis for a momen
then he seemed to make some decision, for the gun ros
again. Seeing this, the crowd became agitated. Cries wer
heard from throughout the throng telling him to take th
marquis's money. Ladies were crying "For shame!" at hi
for wishing to shoot the animal in Hyde Park without regar
to their sensibilities (though it was later noted that none o
those same ladies took themselves off to avoid seeing th
shooting). Public sentiment ran strongly against him. Th
gun wavered uncertainly; then he threw it on the ground an
turned on his heel to stalk off, pushing his way angril
through the crowd.

"I'll send over a draft first thing in the morning," Stefto
called after him.

Kirkson raised his hand in curt acknowledgment b
otherwise did not turn around.

Catherine, smiling triumphantly, thanked the marquis whil
the crowd edged forward, but not too close, ever mindf
that minutes before the horse that now stood quietly next t

atherine was rearing and plunging. "Your arrival was most
rtuitous and I am extremely grateful," she said. "You will
t regret your purchase, either."

He slowly turned toward her, his expression now a blank
ask. "We must get you to a doctor. You were knocked
nseless for a few moments."

"Nonsense, my lord. I am perfectly fine, I assure you."

He ignored her assurances. "Will the animal take a rider
w?" His voice was strangely empty. His eyes drifted
wn to her arm and the ripped fabric of her sleeve from the
sh of the whip.

"What? Oh, yes, I think so." A puzzled expression
ptured her features. "Stefton—" she began.

"Soothcoor," the marquis barked, turning like a striking
ake toward his friend, "do you think you could disentan-
e yourself from Lady Iris long enough to aid me?"

Iris guiltily dropped her hold on the earl's arm, a bright
d blush staining her cheeks and neck. She looked daggers
the marquis, but he ignored her.

"Of course. How can I be of service?" Soothcoor asked
noothly, a faint hint of humor twisting his lips and his
orthumbrian accent sounding thicker than usual.

Stefton's eyes narrowed, but he did not respond to the
plied gibe. "I intend to take Miss Shreveton back to
arth House as swiftly as possible. A doctor must see to her
juries."

"My lord!" protested Catherine.

"I'll take her before me on the horse. You will help her to
ount in front of me."

"I will not!" Catherine declared. But as with Kirkson,
e crowd defeated her, for they approved of the marquis's
ggestions and urged him to make haste to see that she was
ated by a doctor.

The big bay horse was calm now and did not so much as
itch when Stefton mounted him. Wordlessly, the marquis
t far back on the saddle and caught Catherine as the earl
ew her up before him. His touch was impersonal, his
anner rigid and punctiliously formal.

"I suggest the rest of you return to Harth House immedi-
ly," he said as he gathered the reins. "The Earl of

Seaverness is returning today—he may be there already,''
added as he urged the horse toward the gate.

"My lord, this is hardly necessary," Catherine proteste

"Be quiet," Stefton returned evenly.

"You are causing undue talk! There is nothing the matt
with me, I assure you. I was merely winded for a moment

"Miss Shreveton, I do not suffer fools gladly. You cou
have been killed."

"This horse would never have killed me!"

"I was not speaking of the horse," he said repressive

"Oh," Catherine returned in a small voice.

"You, Catherine Shreveton, are an unprincipled hoyde
a complete ninnyhammer, and a menace to Society."

"I beg your pardon!"

"You may, but you shan't receive it. No horse—and
mean this without reservation—no horse anywhere is wo
risking life and limb. And that is something your un
would be the first to tell you."

"You behave as though you're trying to take the place
my uncle," Catherine said waspishly.

The marquis was silent until they reached Harth Hous
"I shall not waste my breath attempting to disabuse you
that notion," he finally said, the words spoken tightly in
throat, their meaning enigmatic. He dismounted and turn
to help her down.

Catherine resisted the petty urge to slide from the horse
back before he could reach for her. In his strange temper s
did not know what would be his reaction and did not tru
herself to press him further. She'd been delighted to see h
when he walked between her and Kirkson. She relax
then, confident in his ability to extricate her from t
uncomfortable situation. That he should offer to buy t
horse from Kirkson made her ecstatic, and the tingling
often aroused in her ran riotously through her body. Or
now she knew better than to pretend to herself that t
tingling was caused by antipathy. She glowed at his cons
eration until she realized his manner was not adopted sol
for dealing with Kirkson. She soon received quite t
opposite impression. It did not take a great leap of intell
to reason that *she* had something to do with his demean

e was so cold, so removed. What did it mean? Whatever it
eant, it frightened her in ways she hadn't begun to fathom.
 She stole a sideways glance at him as he punctiliously
corted her up the steps before Harth House. His features
ere sternly set, his eyes a dull tarnished silver. It was an
compromising expression and Catherine's heart plummeted
 her feet. She sighed.

"How is your head?" he asked, leading her into the hall.

"I don't know," she said lightly. "I don't know how
ything is now." The edge of hysteria crept into her voice
d overbright eyes.

The marquis frowned. "Fetch a doctor for Miss Shreveton.
e took a nasty fall in the park and may be concussed," he
structed the footman at the door.

"Is that you, Stefton?" called a tall man with receding
ay hair who came out of the drawing room.

"Good, you've arrived. Your niece met with an accident
 the park. I've taken the liberty of sending your footman
r a doctor. Now we must get her to bed to rest and hope
e is not badly hurt."

"Two invalids!" Lord Harth mocked. "What kind of a
usehold have I come home to? I beg pardon, my dear, I'm
ur Uncle William, and you must be my niece Catherine."

"How do you do, sir," she said shyly.

"Better than you, I daresay. Well, we'd best see you into
e tender hands of your maid before this young gentleman
lls me out for lack of family feeling."

The marquis raised a quelling eyebrow but the earl
nored him.

"Take her upstairs, Stefton. I'll have Pennymore fetch
r woman. If you get up there before the maid, I promise
t to tell a soul."

Catherine giggled, then stopped when she realized her
ad was beginning to hurt and laughing only aggravated it.
That is Lord Harth? Somehow I envisioned my uncle to be
ore formal, a dry old stick."

A reluctant smile pulled at the marquis's mouth. "I know
at you mean. But consider. Only a man with a sense of
mor could put up with your aunt."

"True," Catherine said sighing, but her thoughts were

already wandering for the slight pain in her head wa
steadily growing. She directed him to her room and allowe
him to lead her to the bed to lie down. She was on
marginally aware that he was removing her bonnet, glove
and calfskin boots before she heard Bethie's familiar voic
Then, through the haze of increasing pain, she thanked th
marquis for his assistance.

The marquis looked down at where she lay on the be
his face expressionless; then he nodded curtly to Bethie a
left the room.

CHAPTER
TWELVE

The Marquis of Stefton paced the cavernous length of th
library in Vauden Mansion, the London ancestral home
the Dukes of Vauden. The house was far too large for
bachelor's residence, but his mother had pleaded with hi
to make it his home so as not to displace the servants who
been with the family for years. It was typical of her to sho
concern for even the lowliest of their employees. It was on
of the traits he most admired and loved in his mother,
with affectionate good grace he'd acquiesced to her wishe

He'd grown used to rattling around the mansion and nev
gave its size a thought, though he did order most of th
furniture to be draped in holland covers. Now, however,
emptiness haunted him, grating on his nerves. He barked
his servants, scowled, and sneered, all to no seemi
purpose. The worst was that he knew why.

"Fool, fool, fool," he muttered, continuing his errat
pacing.

"I'll agree to that," the Earl of Soothcoor said mildly
The marquis looked at his friend, who sat in a wing cha

the fireplace, leaning forward to warm his hands. He ughed mirthlessly. "Alan, you are such a comfort."

"If it's comfort yu're truly wantin', I suggest you hie rself over to Upper Grosvenor Street."

"No!"

"And why not, may I be asking?" the earl said, leaning ck in the chair, staring sourly at the marquis.

"Egad, man, you know why. Surely you must."

"No. That's exactly what I don't know."

The marquis came toward his friend. "I'm much too old r her. She thinks of me as a meddlesome uncle, no more."

The earl snorted.

"It was a game, a way to amuse myself through another ring Season."

"Aye, just a game," said the earl harshly, a flare of anger itening his knuckles where they gripped the arms of the air. "You know, yu're not just a fool, yu're a blind fool!"

The marquis looked at him sharply. "Grant me the elligence to know I am not the proper mate for Miss reveton, even if she possessed any warm feeling for me, ich I assure you, she does not."

"Aye, I'll grant you intelligence. The intelligence of a eep. Och, I canna sit here any longer and listen to yur vel." He rose from the chair. "I think I'll be off to find ilberlain. Even though he's another lovesick dolt, at least 's honest, which is more'n I can say for you."

After the door closed behind Soothcoor, Stefton slammed fist into the chair arm. Damn the man's impudence! He se from the chair and crossed to the bell pull. Soothcoor l not know Catherine. Not the way he did. She deserved a unger man, one not so jaded by society. Besides, Sir gene was correct. He was not at all in her style. She might l some affection for him—as one would for an uncle, that s all. He never encouraged her to flirt with him, or to nk his attentions were any more than an obligation to gene. Besides, he steadfastly remained out of her orbit ve for their afternoon rides.

When the butler arrived in answer to the bell he ordered bottle of brandy be brought to the library—a full, new ttle. Noting his employer's expression, Kennilton hurried

down to the cellar and returned quickly with a dusty bott
that he hastily wiped clean, opened, and poured out the fir
glass before backing out of the room. He then set off
warn the rest of the household that the marquis was about
get badly dipped.

Stefton picked up the brandy glass and held it up to t
light of a flickering candle. He studied the glass's content
absently noting the play of colors off the crystal glass. Ho
could he have fallen in love with the chit? It was inconceiv
able. Yet love her he did. He didn't know when or how
happened, for he'd always considered himself unable
possess that weighty emotion. It wasn't that he didn't hav
an appreciation for love. He did. Perhaps too great a
appreciation, for he saw it best expressed in the love h
parents bore for each other—sometimes almost to his excl
sion. But he knew he loved her when he saw her thro
herself at Zephyros in an attempt to protect the horse fro
the blows Kirkson was raining down upon the animal. I
realized the depth of his feelings when Kirkson leveled t
gun at the horse and could have so easily hit her. Somethi
broke within him at that moment and he became possess
of a rage he'd never experienced in his life. He was su
prised he'd maintained enough sanity not to rend Kirks
limb from limb, and enough intelligence to realize publ
humiliation would go further to defeat the man than a
public brawl.

He took a sip of the brandy and closed his eyes. What
had not appreciated about love was the pain it could al
bring. As swiftly as he acknowledged his love for her,
also acknowledged their unsuitability. His was doomed to
an unrequited love. He could accept that. But it hurt like t
very devil.

He tossed off the rest of the brandy in the glass a
refilled it. Now all he could wish for was an emotion
numbing. He held up the glass in a silent toast to t
attribute of brandy. Then he laughed harshly, his laught
echoing eerily in the spacious room. He tossed off t
second glass of brandy and again reached for the bottle.
would be a long night.

*   *   *

Sir Philip Kirkson sprawled on the delicate settee in Lady
[M]elville's parlor, his hair disheveled, his cravat askew, and
[a] wineglass dangling from his long fingers.

"Made a fool of yourself?" Panthea goaded. She sat on a
[ma]tching settee placed at right angles to the first. A superior
[sm]ile turned up one corner of her mouth as she considered
[he]r unexpected guest.

"Oh, cut line!"

"My, my, aren't we touchy. The story, you know, is all
[ove]r London, and quite frankly, you are not in very good
[odo]r, my friend. I swear I must have heard the first tales of
[it] not half an hour after it transpired. It certainly would
[ap]pear you've lost your heiress—not that I believed you
[eve]r had her."

"I'll have my fortune and see that she continues to pay
[for] the rest of her life!" growled Kirkson.

"And just how do you intend to achieve this goal short of
[k]napping?"

[H]e looked up at her and smiled evilly causing a slight
[shi]ver of dread to skim her spine. "Why must it be short of
[k]napping? To my mind it's no more than she deserves.
[Sh]e has humiliated me enough. I'll see her good and
[pro]perly ruined first, and then I'll be generous and bestow
[my] name upon her. After that she may stay in Yorkshire if
[she] likes. I'll not need her cutting up my peace in London.
[On] the rare occasions I may venture north, she will be only
[too] happy to service me."

[P]anthea rhythmically tapped a long nail against the table
[at] her side. "So, what do you want of me? I do not believe
[this] is a mere social call."

"You know Panthea, we deal very well together, you and
[I. W]e understand each other. Perhaps after I have snared my
[heir]ess and you your marquis we should consider establishing
[a c]landestine relationship."

[S]he shrugged and smiled. "Tell me first what you have
[plan]ned and what is my role in all this."

[K]irkson rose and slid over next to her, placing one arm
[aro]und her shoulder, his hand skimming the edge of her low
[nec]kline. His other hand played with the ribbons on her
[bod]ice, the palm of his hand casually grazing the peaks of

her breasts until they stood out sharply against the fabri
Quietly, he told her his plan, his words interspersed wi
playful nips on her earlobe and neck. His sentences becam
more clipped, and as she covered his lips with hers furth
explanations and plans were saved for later.

Lady Orrick absently tucked a wayward silvery blon
lock of hair under her lace cap and snuggled into the p
green satin pillows of the Egyptian-style daybed. Dressed
a gold muslin day gown trimmed with white lace, her plu
figure looked extremely youthful and fragile, belying h
six-and-forty years. A colorful, long-fringed, paisley s
shawl was draped over her feet, its ends dangling to t
shaded green-and-ivory Oriental carpet. She sighed wistful
completing the girlish image, and only raised her eyes fo
moment from the book on her lap in order to grope absen
for a glass of Carnation ratafia set among several porcel
Pekinese dogs on the Chinese octagonal table at her elbo

She took a small sip of the sweet liqueur and turned
page of the leather-bound romance. She must remember
write Lady Bruckmaster and thank her for recommendi
the novel to her attention. Such excitement, and the bar
hint of the risqué! It was maddeningly frustrating to kn
she was more than halfway through the novel and had
notion as to how it would end.

She had begun reading the novel before she left Lond
to visit Marianne. Unfortunately, her daughter's househo
was so frenzied, she never had an opportunity to read m
than two pages during the entire length of her stay! T
peace and quiet of being once again in her own home v
particularly soothing. Time enough to become embroiled
the final preparations for her sister's ball. She chuckl
laying the book in her lap. And time enough, she mused,
unravel the skein of Catherine's mischief.

Penelope had never been more surprised than wh
Seaverness brought the marquis and Sir Eugene to talk
her. She'd had her suspicions about Catherine on the ni
of her arrival. Never, however, did she conceive the mag
tude of the error she and Alicia had made in their assur
tions concerning their fourth and eldest niece. The Cather

t Sir Eugene described was a far cry from the Catherine
e'd met—save perhaps for that gleam of challenge she'd
en in her niece's eyes as she looked at Alicia. She pitied
Eugene. He was clearly a man torn asunder. He held
de in Catherine and expected her to be the Belle of
ndon. He was thoroughly shaken to learn of the masquer-
e Catherine had adopted—doubly so when he learned of
wife's participation. He was grievously hurt, though he
opted a masquerade himself, one of cold anger. Once
nelope learned the entire story, she was quick to under-
nd Catherine's motivation, and, together with the marquis
l Seaverness, worked to convince the unhappy man that
therine was not completely to blame. She tried to place
brunt of the blame on herself and Alicia, but he would
e none of that. He would blame himself for allowing
therine too much independence, for encouraging her to
in the face of convention by donning male attire, and for
ating her as a son rather than a niece. The marquis broke
emotional tension by languidly disclaiming against these
ors on Sir Eugene's part. He said his only fault was not
he could control. Catherine inherited—full score—all
famous Burke stubbornness that evidently missed her
ther. Happily, then, while talking of inherited traits, they
ke of Ralph Shreveton and his role in beginning the
squerade by allowing his relatives to believe—without
r telling them the truth—that his bride was merely a
ng woman of a poor yet genteel family. It was the type
grand joke Ralph enjoyed, and if he were alive, he'd
ly applaud Catherine's masquerade as another facet of
joke. That notion drew a smile from Sir Eugene for he
to agree.

o calm Sir Eugene and keep him from hying down to
ndon had been the first step. To devise a method of
ifying the situation—for he refused to consider that
herine go on in the same manner—was a ticklish matter,
no conclusions were drawn. Seaverness diplomatically
gested that Penelope and he would be better able to
ise solutions when they were in London and could, at
hand, observe the current situation. This did not totally

appease Sir Eugene, but he promised to place his trust
them.

The only thing that still bothered Penelope—but she cou
think of no way to broach the subject—was the circu
stance of the marquis's involvement. It was so out
character for him to take any notice of, let alone interest i
any of the debutantes that yearly flocked to London. Penelo
gleefully wondered if she smelled a romance. That w
another situation that merited investigation—and perha
careful nurturing.

Now, however, she had a book to finish. Time enou
tomorrow to pick up the knotted skein of her niece's life a
begin untangling it.

An hour later Lady Orrick sighed and dabbed a la
edged handkerchief to her misting eyes. She'd just read
most heartrending confrontation and reconciliation scene
the close of the novel. Smiling, she ruefully considered
fortunate real life bore little resemblance to the occurren
between the covers of a romance, for she was sure s
would be a perpetual watering pot.

Hearing the distant thumping of her door knocker, s
looked up, setting the finished novel beside her. She
returned to London only a few hours ago. A brief frown
annoyance at the prospect of being disturbed pulled down
the corners of her pale lips. She'd anticipated at least
day's recovery from the exigencies of travel. It really w
not fair that she be disturbed so soon. She placed her rata
glass on the table. Annoyance quickly gave way to curios
when her butler entered the drawing room and made
elaborate show of closing the double doors softly beh
him.

"I beg your ladyship's pardon, but the Countess
Seaverness is below, desirous of seeing you." He stoop
down to move a large, blue Ming vase from the floor by
doorway to a more remote corner of the room.

"Alicia? Here?" Penelope asked, casting aside the pais
shawl and rising swiftly to her feet. She glanced around
drawing room in dismay. "Dare I ask her mood?"
inquired, picking up several of the china dogs from the ta
by the daybed and moving them to the mantelpiece.

"Begging your ladyship's pardon, I do not believe it is thin me to venture an assumption as to the countess's od; however . . ." Smythford removed precious china ces from the small tables which dotted the room and placed m in more out-of-the-way places. "However, I did note r ladyship's color to be a trifle high and she did set herself pacing the front salon immediately upon my conducting r there."

"Oh, dear," Penelope said with amused exasperation. ankfully her sister seldom visited her, preferring that nelope come to her home. Occasionally, however, some-ng would transpire and without warning Alicia would pear on her doorstep. The last visit she had enjoyed from r sister had cost her three figurines and a darling little vres vase her husband, Sir Harold Orrick, had procured ' her in France. This time it was the strong desire of Lady rick and Smythford to save all her pieces from chance struction. Working together, it took but a moment to ve the rest of the delicate porcelain statues to safety. hen they had finished, the mantle looked as cluttered as a ker's cart, but the fragile porcelains were safe.

Penelope patted another stray lock of hair back into place d nodded to Smythford. "I suppose I really should have icipated this. It would have been better if I'd gone ectly to Harth House on my arrival in town, but what's ne is done," she said shrugging philosophically. "Show sister up before she works herself into a rage."

"Very good, milady." Smythford bowed his way out of room, bestowing a quick last glance around as he did so assure himself all of her ladyship's fragile things were e.

Moments later, like a ship in full sail, her sister blew into room, her skirts swishing violently by the very spot ere Penelope's Ming vase had stood. The countess tossed heavy reticule and brown kid gloves onto a nearby table d turned to glare at her younger sister.

"All these weeks I have harbored a viper in my house!" said shrilly.

Penelope winced. "Please, Alicia," she said soothingly, t down and tell me what has you in such a pelter."

Alicia opened her mouth to speak, then shut it abruptl
glaring at Smythford still standing by the drawing roo
door.

Penelope's mouth twitched, though she gravely request
suitable refreshments be prepared and advised she wou
ring when they wished to be served. Then, dismissing h
butler with a wave of her hand, she turned toward her eld
sister, dispassionately noting how her high color clash
with her burnt orange gown.

The Countess perched herself on the edge of one of t
delicate green-and-gold chairs. "I should be abed. I injur
my back last night, but—"

"Oh, Alicia, what happened?"

Her sister scowled at her, not prepared to confide t
nature of the accident. "It does not matter. I am mere
trying to convey to you the seriousness of the situation
She paused and took a deep breath. "That—that creatu
has been bamboozling all of us—just as her mother
before her. It's unheard of! I have never been more shock
in my entire life!"

Penelope sighed. It appeared her sister was now aware
Catherine's true position, and obviously was not pleased
have been made to look the fool by treating her niece a
poor relation. This was not a contingency any of her fell
conspirators anticipated. It might be just as well that th
had not formulated any set plans.

It certainly wouldn't do to allow Alicia to know she w
conversant with Catherine's situation—that would most li
ly fan the flames of her sister's wrath. This might also be
opportunity to fill in the gaps of her knowledge ab
Catherine.

Penelope schooled her features to look at her sister
vague bewilderment. "Oh dear, I'm afraid I don't und
stand. Then how? No, wait—" her hand reached for the b
beside her. "I feel I am going to be in need of so
sustenance to fortify me *before* you begin."

Alicia inclined her head slightly in acknowledgment,
eyes were overly bright, her face flushed. Penelope wished
settle her sister a bit before she worked herself into apople

so, unless she calmed her sister, Penelope wryly doubted
e'd get any information she could understand.

As Smythford carefully passed biscuits to each, Lady
cia did relax in her chair, though it was evident from the
tlessly drumming fingertips on the satin chair arms that
    thoughts had not also relaxed. Pointedly ignoring
ythford's ministrations, she looked about the room. "Really,
 dear, must you keep such tawdry items as those cluttering
your mantle?"

Penelope and Smythford exchanged covert glances.

'All they do is gather dust. They're not even pretty, all
bled up like that," Alicia complained petulantly.

'Ah, but it keeps the servants busy," Penelope confided
hely.

Her sister, an arrested expression in her eyes, nodded
wly. Penelope, her eyes dancing, held her handkerchief
her lips and feigned a cough to hide a smile. Smythford,
intaining his rigidly impassive countenance acquired with
rs of practice, bowed himself out of the room, closing
 doors behind him with a snap before he allowed himself
rin. He wondered if Lady Harth would take up collecting
ues to keep her servants busy. Not that such items would
: long in her house, of course. Nonetheless, it would be
 her, he allowed, as he walked sedately away from the
wing room.

'All right, dear," Penelope said, taking a sip of tea.
lease tell me what has transpired, for I dare swear you
e intrigued me."

'Our niece, that you strongly encouraged me to include
my invitation for a London Season, is not the poor
tion we thought her to be! The baggage informs me her
ther's portion was always larger than dear Ralph's was,
 that she is to inherit the entire estate of Sir Eugene
ke—you know, that horse-breeder all the gentlemen
m is the best."

'I'm afraid I don't understand. A fortune, you say? Well,
, I suppose if she truly is Sir Eugene Burke's niece, that
lld be so. But is her possessing a fortune bad? I thought
 considered money to be the greatest cachet to a success-
London Season."

"Yes, yes," Alicia said testily, waving her arm wild
and scowling at her sister for interrupting. "But that
precisely the point. How can I now say to Society th
we've all been wrong about Catherine? She isn't a po
relation. What excuse can I make?"

"Why make an excuse?"

Alicia frowned at her severely. "Your levity simply w
not do, sister."

Penelope mumbled her apology while hiding a smile, th
swiftly diverted Alicia's attention by asking if she'd hea
from her son, Justin. She was only marginally successf
Her sister relayed the gist of her son's most recent lett
then returned to the subject of Catherine.

"When I consider the inquiries I have fielded when s
began to ride that black horse, I positively cringe! I te
simply *everyone* that she was horse-mad and implied s
squandered all her available funds on her habit."

"Why did you do that?"

"I didn't know what else to say! The Marquis of Stefto
peculiar friendship with her was inexplicable enough!"

"I'm sure you thought of something," Penelope suggest
drily.

"I merely suggested he was under some obligation to h
uncle—though at that time I never dreamed her uncle w
Sir Eugene Burke. Sir Eugene Burke! Just thinking of t
makes me feel faint. How could the girl be so heartless as
keep us uninformed! I could have used the knowledge
that relationship to advantage for them all. I have ne
been so aggravated!" With a loud clatter, she slammed
tea cup into its saucer, causing Penelope to wince and lo
anxiously at her delicate china.

Hoping her cup had survived intact, Lady Orrick look
at her sister. "I couldn't agree with you more. Those pe
dears, to think how all have suffered by that hide
information."

Lady Harth looked piercingly at her sister for traces
sarcasm. Penelope's guileless smile mollified her. "Precisel
she said self-righteously. "Knowledge of a connection to
Eugene Burke would draw another entire coterie of gentlem
to my house."

"Particularly all of London's fortune hunters."

Alicia sharply set down her cup and saucer, spilling some the contents across the little gilt table at her elbow. "I d not meant them," she said repressively.

"I know, but that is a nightmare you've avoided thus far. r the twins, while possessing an easy competence, do not ve fat enough purses to entice any dedicated fortune nter."

"Yes, but they have enticed quite eligible young men, :n they are in danger of losing to Catherine," Alicia said ly while disdainfully watching her sister nibble a biscuit, attering crumbs on her lap.

"If they are in danger of losing them, then they never had m in the first place," Lady Orrick said airily, absently ushing the crumbs away with her other hand. She leaned ck against the cushions. "But who are we speaking of?" e asked before taking another nibble from her biscuit.

Alicia rose and began to pace the room. "The Earl of othcoor has displayed an interest in our Iris," she said mplacently.

"Soothcoor? Alicia, you have windmills in your head! rely you don't believe he'll come up to scratch? The arquis of Stefton would be an easier mark than Soothcoor."

"Whenever the earl came to visit, he always spoke at gth with Iris," she said as she picked up and casually amined one of her sister's little figurines. "Or, at least he l until the marquis quite abruptly left town. Now Catherine commanding his attention in a fashion that is causing k!" She put the little china piece down abruptly.

Penelope sucked in her breath as she watched the piece ay, uncertain as to whether it would stay up or tip over. icia, unconcerned and without a backward glance, re- med her pacing.

"Alicia, does the earl come alone when he visits?" nelope shrewdly asked while keeping a ready eye out for aat else among her things might be in danger of her ter's passing.

"No, he arrives with Stefton and Captain Chilberlain. ptain Chilberlain has been assiduously courting our sannah. I am not convinced our brother would be happy

with such a match,'' she confided, returning to her chair. '
have tried to discourage him, but neither he nor Susanna
will listen to me; and that I also lay at Catherine's door f
she has been shamefully encouraging them.''

''Perhaps now that the marquis has returned, the earl w
not be monopolized by Catherine.''

Alicia reluctantly agreed. ''But I tell you, the girl is a
unprincipled hoyden. Stefton's obligation to Sir Euger
Burke must be great indeed for all the attention he gives he
I do not understand it!'' she said, waving her hands
mystification and nearly sweeping the teacup and saucer o
the side table.

''Neither do I, but I have my suspicions.'' Penelop
sipped her tea and turned to gaze out the tall narro
windows framed by pale green velvet drapes held bac
with gold tassels. In the square below she could see Lac
Harth's coachman walking the horses. How typical of her
make them wait instead of sending them round to the stab
in the mews until she was ready to leave. She turned bac
toward Alicia, suddenly realizing what this visit was a
about. Her sister was asking for help in the only way sl
knew how. ''Do you wish me to come and have a talk wi
Catherine?'' Lady Orrick asked as she moved Alicia
cup and saucer onto the tray by her side.

A tinge of color stained Lady Harth's cheeks. ''If yc
wish,'' she said, attempting nonchalance. ''But I wou
wait until tomorrow. Evidently Catherine took some fall
Hyde Park today. The marquis brought her home—he ev
had the effrontery to send for a doctor without consulting n
first! Can you imagine—''

''No, but I'm beginning to,'' Penelope said with a slig
smile.

''The physician assures us her injuries are minor—
didn't even bleed her—said she merely needs a good night
sleep, which he insured with a dose of laudanum.''

''That's reassuring. How did it happen?''

''I really can't say. Something about a horse and S
Philip Kirkson. Actually, if Sir Philip was involved, I'
surprised *he* did not bring Catherine home. He has be
quite particular in his attentions to her, you know.''

"Kirkson! And you've encouraged him? Alicia, it's said
: man's almost gone through his fortune and is hanging
t for a rich wife."

"I believe the rumors of his straitened circumstances to
all a hum. He has not the manner of a gazetted fortune
nter. And think, if believing Catherine to be poor he
uld still be interested in her, then the depths of his
otions must be genuine. I am not particularly heartless,
u know, Penelope. I may not read all the novels you do,
t I can appreciate true romance when I see it. Now I must
," she said, abruptly rising and gathering her gloves and
icule. "You will come tomorrow won't you? I am at a
ndstill over Catherine. Sometimes I just wish she'd quietly
nk off back north; she's been an irritation since she
ived," she declared. With that parting shot, Lady Harth
ept out the door with even more energy than when she
d entered, knocking over the small gilt table as she went.
Penelope held a hand over her eyes and shook her head.
e skein was tangled more than she'd imagined. She
finitely had her work cut out for her in the week before
: ball.

CHAPTER
THIRTEEN

Lady Orrick sighed and folded her hands in her lap as she
nsidered her niece's wan complexion. "I must admit, you
n't look well at all. Your skin appears to have a sallow
st except for those two bright feverish spots on your
eeks. Have you taken a chill?"

"No, I don't believe so," Catherine listlessly reassured
r, absently twitching a rug over her legs.

Lady Orrick got up and helped lay it in place, tucking
: ends around Catherine as she lounged back on the

daybed in her room. She touched the back of her hand again
Catherine's forehead briefly before resuming her seat. "Wh
you need is a good bracing cup of tea. And, I think,
sympathetic ear into which you can pour out your troubles.

Catherine laughed slightly. "What troubles I have are
my own creation. I fear I'm merely being punished for n
folly."

"In what way?" Lady Orrick asked, pouring out th
tea and handing a cup to her niece.

"Aunt Penelope, please do not patronize me. I've ha
enough of that from Aunt Alicia."

"Good. I'm glad to see you get angry. Maybe it w
shake you out of that pit of doldrums you've fallen into.

"It isn't the first time I've fallen into that pit. Only th
time I don't think a beautiful gown is going to be able
pull me out of it."

"What gown?"

Catherine laughed. "The gown Madame Vaussard mad
for me that I did not order. She made it because she thoug
there would come a time when I wished to end th
masquerade."

"She knew about it?"

"Oh, yes." Catherine smiled ruefully. "Perhaps I'd be
start at the beginning and tell you everything. It all starte
as you may have guessed, when Mother received the invit
tion from Aunt Alicia to bring me out."

It took Catherine almost an hour to tell her aunt the who
tale, punctuated as it was by little questions of clarificatio
laughter, and tears from Lady Orrick. When she was finishe
her aunt sat on the edge of the daybed and clasped Catherine
hands.

"You love him, don't you?" she said softly.

Catherine went very still. "Who?"

"The Marquis of Stefton," Lady Orrick said kindly.

Catherine blanched. "Don't be ridiculous," she toss
out shrilly. She tried to pull her hands out of her aun
grasp, but her aunt held them fast.

"That's nothing to be ashamed of."

"I'm not ashamed," she denied hotly, then capitulate
"It's just that—just that he doesn't love me. To him I'm ju

ir Eugene Burke's troublesome niece. And I refuse to be
ke the other young ladies who fawn over him, attempting
ll stratagems to gain at least his attention, if not his regard.
 didn't mean to fall in love with him at all. For the longest
me I found him to be the most arrogant, disagreeable man
f my acquaintance."

"But you did."

"Yes," Catherine said softly, bowing her head to hide the
parkle of unshed tears in her eyes. "And it hurts," she
hispered. "I wish I'd never come to London, or at least
ever instigated this awful masquerade. If I hadn't, he
ouldn't have felt compelled to bring me to Society's notice
nd therefore spend time in my company. What a fool I've
een. I see now why my family thought I should come to
ondon. I've been so naive."

"Now don't you start feeling sorry for yourself and
lling back into those doldrums," Penelope advised in a
otherly scold. She squeezed Catherine's hands, then re-
ased them. "How do you think I came to learn of this
ttle masquerade of yours?"

"From Aunt Alicia, I suppose."

"No. I learned it from your uncle and Stefton."

"I don't understand."

"Mrs. Dawes wrote to your relatives in Yorkshire about
our *hoydenish behavior*—that's her description, not mine."

Catherine grimaced. "I didn't even consider that possibility."

"It greatly upset Sir Eugene, for he is very proud of you.
nyway, he had to go to Nottingham to attend a horse fair, I
ather, and told Mr. Dawes he would come to London
terward. Dawes told the marquis of Sir Eugene's plans.
tefton, bless him, said that would be disastrous for you, so
 went to Nottingham to meet your uncle and stop him
om taking any rash action. Now why do you suppose he
id that? I've never known Stefton to do anything for
nyone." Lady Orrick looked pointedly at her niece.

Catherine shrugged. "I don't pretend to understand the
an. Evidently his obligation to my uncle is immense."

Her aunt clucked her tongue and shook her head. "You
e a very obstinate young woman."

"The marquis says it is a Burke trait evidenced by my

square chin,'' Catherine informed her aunt, chuckling. ''Still
you haven't yet explained how you became involved.''

''As luck would have it, when Stefton found your uncl
he was with Seaverness. Your uncle Seaverness is hunting
mad, you know. He went to Nottingham to meet Burke an
see about getting a new hunter. After he heard what wa
going on—all of which he could believe, knowing hi
wife—Seaverness convinced them to come and see me, fo
he reasoned that I would be the best person to—uh, educat
Alicia.''

Catherine laughed again. ''Something I had already don
in a rather brash manner that Stefton would say was ba
ton.''

Lady Orrick nodded. ''Very true. You seem to knov
him well.''

Laughter died on Catherine's lips. She sighed. ''That'
how I also know he has no interest in me.''

''I think you're wrong, Catherine.''

''Aunt Penelope, you don't know how I wish I were. Bu
you didn't see him yesterday. He was so cold and formal
He made me feel like a little girl caught in some prank wh
deserved a thunderous scold.''

Her aunt shook her head but smiled kindly. ''Then w
shall have to agree to disagree. But I propose a wager.''

''A wager?''

''Yes. I bet Stefton will make you an offer before th
Season is out. If I am correct, you will give me a pair c
Burke carriage horses. If I am wrong''—she shrugged—
''you set the terms.''

''If you are wrong . . .'' Catherine said slowly, trying t
think of a suitable stake. Unfortunately, she found hersel
trying to choose a suitable pair for her aunt. She wanted he
to be right. ''If you are wrong, you must have Aunt Alici
over to your home at least twice a week for a month.''

Lady Orrick closed her eyes and shuddered, visualizin
the havoc Alicia could create in her home among all he
china heirlooms. ''You drive a hard bargain. You should on
day do very well running Burke's, of that I have no doub
All right, done! I agree to your terms—but only because
know I won't lose.''

"Aunt Penelope, you are a romantic."
"I know, I know—isn't it wonderful?"

But in the week before the ball, it did seem as though ady Orrick would lose. On his return, the Marquis of efton resumed the habits he'd established prior to his trip Nottingham. He continued the afternoon rides with atherine, though now—at his invitation—their parties also cluded Soothcoor, the twins, and various of their suitors. such a large group, there was never the opportunity for ivate conversation, nor did the marquis appear to desire ivate discourse. Never again did he and Catherine ex-ange amused glances at the idiosyncrasies of people. At lls, routs, and other social events, he could be counted on for one dance, or a short conversation of social inanity aling with such subjects as Catherine's health and the alth of her cousins, the weather, Byron's poetry, or ummell's flight from his creditors.

In the face of Stefton's formality, Catherine retreated to e behavior, saving her smiles and laughs for others. And ere were plenty of others flocking around her, for all ciety soon learned of Catherine's wealth. At first there as displeasure among the *ton* and some people cut her quaintance. But they were in the minority, for the combi-tion of money and birth were the immediate tickets to the *au monde*. To assuage the old-guard sticklers who took fense at her dishonesty, Lady Orrick and Lord Harth t it about that Catherine's play-acting stemmed from a sire to avoid fortune hunters. They further said (to Catherine's agrin) that their niece was a great romantic who desired to loved for herself and had felt the only way to do so was pretend she didn't have money. Lady Harth was painted the innocent victim of Catherine's machinations. Their plomatic explanations soon caused even the strictest Soci-y matron to unbend toward Catherine. Many felt it be-oved them to deliver a lecture on the impropriety of her tions, but afterward they all forgave her, calling her a ever little puss and then chucked her under the chin or nched her cheeks. Catherine suffered it all with good ace, deeming it her penance. It was not the worst of her trials. Seeing the marquis every day was the worst. Her love for Stefton sat like a cold, oppressive lump in her chest. Sometimes the weight would get so heavy she felt out of breath and slowly suffocating. These feelings angered her, and she railed against them—sometimes she railed enough to even banish them for brief moments. But through it all she smiled and laughed, seeming to enjoy her newfound popularity.

Catherine worked at including the twins in all her activities and was always certain they were introduced to every gentleman she met. She kept them busy and active—so busy they had no opportunity to notice how much time Susanna and the captain were spending alone together. It was ironic, too, that with their own circles of friends and suitors increasing, they began to see the values of those gentlemen who early in the season came to call. It appeared that Dahlia was showing a marked preference for Sir Richard Chartris, a quiet-spoken man of impeccable manners and taste, who desired political involvement. Iris still hoped for the Earl of Soothcoor to evince interest in her, but she'd begun to flirt with other gentlemen such as Mr. Peter Howlitch and Mr. Dabernathy.

If by morning Catherine's pillow was often damp, Bethia never told anyone. Lady Orrick watched for the odd moments in repose when her niece's determinedly cheerful expression would sag. Not even the long-looked-for good news announcing her mother's betrothal to Squire Leftwic raised much of a response from Catherine. Her only comment was predictable. Now she could go home. Penelope shrewdly surmised that Catherine's former masquerade was nothing to the lie she currently lived. But there wasn't anything Penelope could do. Phlegmatically, she began to wonder how many of her beautiful china pieces would be destroyed by the time she'd paid her debt, and also if it was in the spirit of the wager for her to consider packing up her collection of figurines and relegating them to the attic until afterward. Regretfully, she knew it wasn't. Consequently, by the day of the ball, Penelope experienced a strong desire to throttle the marquis, and so she told his friend, the Earl of Soothcoor.

"Aye, I know what yu're sayin'. I've been experiencin' similar thoughts."

"I've never seen him consider anyone but himself before, I thought he held Catherine in some affection. I couldn't think of any other reason for his behavior. But now he's so cold and formal. Catherine told me his attentions were merely to fulfill an obligation to Sir Eugene, but frankly I didn't believe her."

"Donna believe it either," the earl growled.

Penelope looked at him in surprise.

Soothcoor scrutinized Lady Orrick, his eyes narrowing. "Are you sayin' the lassie holds some affection for him?"

"Some! The silly peagoose has fallen in love with him! However, she is determined not to show it."

The earl's lips twisted downward and he ruefully shook his head. "It's the same for him, the clodhead."

"He is? He does? Then why the—the—"

"Coldness?" Soothcoor asked, readily understanding her disjointed speech. "He says he's too old for her and claims he considers him an uncle. Won't believe otherwise, and we tried."

Lady Orrick's mouth opened and closed several times before she was able to speak. "But that's ridiculous!" She grabbed the earl's arm. "Soothcoor, we have to do something!"

"I've a mind to agree with you, but I canna think what that somethin' should be."

"You don't suppose you could make him jealous, could you?"

"Me! I'm not a man to be leg-shackled, and well he knows it."

"Or thinks he knows it. The most hard-bitten bachelor can suffer a reversal of feelings and become smitten with some lady's charms."

"Not me," the earl said firmly, attempting to back away, but Lady Orrick still held his arm fast.

"Only listen to me. You said one of Stefton's complaints was that he was too old for Catherine. You are older then . If you don't seem to mind the age difference—"

"And I wouldna if I were a marryin' man," interposed the earl.

"There, see. Dance with Catherine, take her down t
dinner, just be seen to spend time with her and no othe
lady. Catherine would welcome your company, you know
for she knows you're not one of those fortune hunters tha
are swarming around her. Then at sometime later, casuall
remark to Stefton of your interest. Meanwhile, I'll put th
bug in his ear that she has decided to accept the firs
creditable offer she receives. And by creditable, I mean an
gentleman who is *not* a gazetted fortune hunter. I believ
you fall into that category nicely."

The earl frowned. "I canna like it—"

"But you'll do it, won't you?" Penelope urged, squeez
ing his arm.

"Aye," he said heavily, "I'll do it, though I tell you
think it a daft scheme."

Lady Orrick released her grip on his arm and clappe
her hands. Soothcoor surreptitiously massaged his forearm
which she'd held tightly, and adopted the expression of th
long-suffering male.

"It will work, my lord," she said breezily. "It has to,
she finished in a whisper as the earl bowed to her an
strolled off in Catherine's direction.

"The little wren's new popularity will make it difficult t
draw her aside for private conversation," observed Lad
Welville. "Now that her wealth is known, you'd be
beware lest another unscrupulous character plans as yo
do."

"That I don't fear. They will first try to win her affec
tions," Kirkson said offhandedly as he scanned the room
"But you are right; engaging her in conversation without
least five hangers-on will be difficult. Nonetheless, I'm su
you're up to the task."

"Me!"

"Certainly. You stand a far better chance than I do."

"That is certainly true. What did you do to set her bac
up against you?"

He turned a tight-lipped smile toward her. "I importune
her for favors she wasn't inclined to grant." He shrugge
"I was drunk at the time."

"And typically lacking in finesse," suggested Panthea rily. He ignored her.

"Well, will you do it? Draw her into private conversation some empty anteroom. I'll follow you, discreetly, of urse. Afterward, we'll spirit her out of here. You did ring the laudanum, I trust?"

Panthea smiled slightly. "Of course. Where will you take er?"

"Ah—that I won't tell you, my pet. It's safer that way."

"You're certain Stefton does not care for her?"

Kirkson spread his hands wide. "It is as you said, merely ruse."

Panthea pursed her lips for a moment, then nodded greement. "All right. But if Stefton blames me, I'll kill ou."

"My dear Panthea, so full of doubts!" Kirkson chuckled.

She looked daggers at him, then slipped away among the rowd in the large room.

"I can't thank you enough for bringing Sir Eugene to see e and explaining Catherine's behavior. The poor child— hat a twisted path she has trod. I'm glad to see her settling own," Lady Penelope told Stefton later that evening.

The marquis, his arms crossed over his chest and his chin cked into his cravat, stared across the room at Catherine, ore beautiful than he could have imagined. The touches of reen and gold in the gown she wore gave it—and her—a chness in appearance that proclaimed the truth of her wealth. nd now, there she sat on a sofa, like a queen on her throne, rrounded by admiring suitors, most of whom Stefton knew be without a feather to fly with. At least Soothcoor was e of their number. He would keep some of the worst of the ngry hounds at bay, and so he told Lady Orrick.

"Yes, I think you're correct. And they do complement ch other, too," she said complacently.

The marquis shifted his attention from Catherine to Lady rrick. "I would not set your sights on Soothcoor, if I were ou. He is a confirmed bachelor," he said humorously.

"Umm," returned Penelope noncommittally. She sighed. But I think I'll keep hoping, for you should know that

Catherine has stated that since she must marry, she wi
accept the first offer that is creditable.''

''Creditable?''

''Why, yes, you know—not a man who desperately nee
a rich wife. Someone like Mr. Dabernathy. She says all sh
requires is a modest competence of at least five hundre
pounds per year to recommend a gentleman. Oh, and h
must not be known to be a gamester.''

''Five hundred pounds! Has she windmills in her head?'
he asked thunderously. He jerked his attention back t
Catherine, his arms falling to his sides. He watched her tur
her head upward to look at Soothcoor, laughing at some
thing he said. In the back of his head it struck him as od
that his dour friend could cause anyone to laugh. But h
allowed the idea to slide away, his thoughts on Catherine
matrimonial considerations.

''No, I don't think so,'' Penelope said. ''She merely
feeling remorseful for being a trial to everyone, and fo
some reason is apathetic concerning whom she marries. B
her behavior one would think she had suffered some disap
pointment in love! I don't know, and try as I may, I can n
get the child to confide in me,'' she said blithely with
patent disregard for the truth. ''Look, Captain Chilberlai
has arrived! I must go and see what news he brings. I'll te
you a secret. He rode down to Portsmouth today to ask m
brother Glendon for Susannah's hand in marriage. By h
expression, I'll wager he has it! Alicia will be furious!'' Sh
gleefully scurried across the room.

The Marquis of Stefton scarcely heard her, for his atten
tion was centered on Catherine, as it had been the entir
evening despite his efforts to the contrary. He was no bette
than a lovesick puppy, he thought disgustedly. He watched
little byplay where Catherine accepted an invitation to danc
from some gentleman quite unknown to him. The rest of th
gentlemen in her circle pretended to be devastated.

The Earl of Soothcoor looked up to note the marqui
intently watching the group. His eyes narrowed. Judging b
Stefton's expression, perhaps Lady Orrick's little plan wa
not bacon-brained after all. Now might be a good time t
enact his part, he decided, leisurely crossing the room.

"I think I preferred Catherine in her rags," grumbled the earl when he reached Stefton's side.

"Why? Don't tell me, my friend, that you are jealous of the attention she receives!" The marquis' smile was faintly sneering.

The earl scratched the side of his face and frowned. "Aye, and it's humorous even to me," he said matter-of-factly.

The marquis's smile faded and he looked closely at his friend, his eyes carefully hooded. "Perhaps as a fairy godfather I overplayed my hand," Stefton drawled.

Soothcoor looked across the ballroom floor to where Catherine was dancing. He paused a long moment. "Aye," he said finally, softly, "perhaps you did at that."

The dance ended then and Catherine's partner escorted her back to her throne and her circle of courtiers. Soothcoor murmured his excuses and quitted Stefton's side to return to Catherine. The marquis again crossed his arms on his chest and leaned back against the wall, hooking one foot across the other. A harsh frown carved deep furrows between his brows and alongside his nose, sharpening the planes of his face. His eyes were cold as stone.

He watched Susannah come to her side and whisper in her ear. Quickly Catherine rose and went off with her toward the library. Susannah was probably telling her of the betrothal, he thought angrily. Explosively, he came away from the wall and walked quickly, with the catlike grace that was typical of him, toward the staircase. He had to get outside for a breath of air.

"Oh, Susannah, I'm so happy for you!" Catherine hugged her cousin then stepped back to study her radiant features. "You deserve all the hapiness in the world."

"So do you," Susannah said softly.

Catherine laughed brittlely. If one looked closely, one could see faint smudges of gray under her eyes and an overbright, feverish quality in them. Susannah did, and her heart went out to her cousin.

"He's watched you all evening, you know."

"Yes, my uncle's loyal watchdog, undoubtedly on guard to protect my purse more than my virtue."

She tossed the words out casually, but the underlying bitterness twisted Susannah's heart. She wished there was something she might do to ease her cousin's pain. Catherine had done so much for her. Perhaps she should gather her courage in her hands and confront the arrogant marquis. He'd always frightened her and made her feel the stammering schoolgirl. But for Catherine, she'd surmount her fears.

Catherine leaned her forehead against the cool marble of the library mantle. "When is the wedding to be? I fear I shan't be able to attend as I am leaving for Yorkshire within the week."

"Catherine, no!" protested Susannah.

"Catherine, yes," she corrected, summoning yet another smile. She was so tired, tired of all the lies, the subterfuge, the sorrow. "My mother is also getting married soon, remember. I have to get back to wish her well, or she'll free herself right out of the engagement!" she said with a hollow laugh.

Susannah laid a comforting hand on Catherine's shoulder. "I understand," she murmured.

They stood there a moment, Catherine fighting back the same tears she'd fought against all week. Angrily, Catherine tossed her head back, willing the tears not to spill from her eyes. She gulped air almost hysterically, then ordered her breathing to relax. She closed her eyes. "If you don't mind, I think I'd like to be alone for a minute," Catherine said tightly.

Uncertainly, Susannah's hand slid from her shoulder. She gazed at Catherine anxiously, her teeth biting her lower lip until she tasted a drop of blood. "All right, if that is what you want. Just remember Catherine, you have many friends who care for you."

Catherine opened her eyes and smiled mistily at Susannah. "I know that, cousin, I know that, and believe me, it is appreciated."

Susannah nodded, looked as if she was going to speak again, then changed her mind and turned away, walking quietly out the door. Catherine watched her go, then sank down into her favorite armchair by the fireplace and let her head sink into her hands.

* * *

"Her cousin just came out of the library, but our little wren is still in there," Kirkson informed Panthea, as he walked past her.

"How convenient," she murmured. She continued down the hall, stopping by the library door and glancing back briefly. She smiled assurance, then pressed the latch and went inside.

From the mansion's deep shadow, Stefton cursorily watched the fidgety behavior of a team that drew up before Harth House. Soon, a woman and a man came down the steps of the town house escorting a swooning woman swathed in a voluminous dark cloak. They placed her in the carriage, then the gentleman jumped in leaning out for a brief word with the lady who had aided him, and ordered the driver on with a wave of his hands.

There was something about the stance and posture of the woman left behind that was familiar, but Stefton wouldn't place it however much it nagged at the fringes of his memories. He raked a hand through his thick, wavy black hair, causing several locks to fall and curl across his brow. The woman stood for a moment on the flagway, watching the carriage turn the corner at the end of Upper Grosvenor, before turning back to the house. It was then, by the light of the flambeau at the doorway, that Stefton saw her face. It was Lady Welville.

Suddenly, an awful, cold feeling grabbed at his insides and twisted them tight, the pain shooting down through his toes and upward into his brain. His breathing became harsh. He leaned out of the shadow and into the street light, his face transformed into a mask of steel and his eyes to obsidian. He ran back to Harth House, taking the steps two and three at a time.

No one was waiting by the door to let guests in and out, and the hall, shadowy and dark from guttered candles, was strangely deserted. The clutching cold feeling grew, spreading through his limbs. He fought against the lethargy it threatened. He ran across the hall and up the stairs to the ballroom. He stopped abruptly at the doorway, his breathing rapid now, sweat glistening on his brow. Panthea was just easing into a conversation with the dowagers. A nice touch that, Stefton thought grimly, but he was not one to b intimidated by haughty dowagers or public scenes. No now—there wasn't time for such niceties.

He strode over to Panthea and, grabbing her by th shoulder, twirled her around. "Where's he taking her?" h ground out, his face a death's-head white.

"Oh, la—Oliver, you startled me," began Panthea coyly batting her lashes at him.

His expression did not change. "Do not try it," th marquis warned softly. "Where is he taking her?"

"I don't know what you're talking about," Panthea sai with a touch of nervous asperity.

"Panthea, do not make me do something that you wil have cause to regret."

His unwavering gaze unnerved Panthea. She absentl plucked at the folds of her gown. "What do you see in he anyway?" Panthea demanded petulantly. "She is just a littl brown wren."

They were beginning to draw a crowd. Even the orchestr stopped playing. The marquis continue to stare silently.

"It was his idea," protested Panthea helplessly.

"I am warning you, Panthea, you'll tell me now what want to know or suffer the consequences as his accomplic in kidnapping."

"Easy, man," murmured the Earl of Soothcoor, coming up to his side.

She licked her lips nervously and looked around at th crowd. She was backed into a corner. "Oh, Stefton, it wa just that Miss Shreveton!" she said lightly. "She an Kirkson are just running off. They say they can't put up wit such formality any longer. I can't say that I blame them. is a pretty stuffy lot."

The marquis's fingers curled around her upper arm. "N games, Panthea," he said harshly, shaking her like a doll

The pressure of his fingers around her upper arm began t ache and it was soon obvious that all eyes were turned upo them.

Tears began to roll down Lady Panthea's cheeks, and fo once they were not artifice. "All right, all right," sh

iled weakly. "He is taking her, and not by her consent,
t I swear to you, I don't know where! He wouldn't tell
. He said it was safer if I did not know." Her hands
vered her weeping eyes.

A murmur of horror swept the company. Stefton flung her
m aside, his mouth working furiously before any words
uld come out. He turned and scanned the assembly.
oothcoor! Find Chilberlain and meet me at Vauden as
on as possible. We haven't a moment to loose!"

He turned back to glance briefly at Panthea, his eyes
pty. "I recommend you seek a warmer climate for your
alth, one where your devious charms can be appreciated."
Suddenly he was gone, and the muted whisperings in-
ased in volume.

Frantic, Panthea looked around for a sympathetic face.
ere were none. Each face read condemnation clearer than
last. Panthea whimpered, screamed, and fainted.

"I'm sorry, milord, but the gray's come up lame," the
om said when Stefton asked for his favorite mount.

"Lame! When did that happen?"

The man shrugged, suddenly nervous before the mar-
is's probing gaze. "I—I don't know, milord. Mr. Friarly
ok him out to exercise earlier and when he brought him
ck he was favoring that leg."

Seems Kirkson's payin' your man. The memory rang a
rning bell in the marquis's head. "Where's Friarly?"

"In his quarters, milord. Shall I fetch him?"

"Please," said the marquis equably as the captain and the
l arrived at the stables in the Vauden Mews.

"Do we ride together or split up to see if we can
termine which direction he took?" the captain asked,
inging down from his saddle.

"Together, for I believe we are about to discover not only
direction, but his destination," said the marquis, a cold
ile lifting the corners of his mouth. Behind him came the
tter of boots down the stairs. The marquis's smile broadened,
l he held up his hand to forestall further questions from
friends.

"You wished to see me, milord?" asked Friarly, s
tucking his shirttails into his breeches.

"Yes, Friarly. Tell me, how long have you been in
employ?"

Puzzled at the question, the groom's brows knitted
gether. "I don't rightly recall, milord. Five, maybe
years."

"And in that time, have I ever given you cause to distr
my judgment?"

"Oh, no, milord. Quite to the contrary."

"Good, for I am going to tell you what—in my judgmen
is the proper punishment for employees who take mor
from others to do some disservice to their employers."

The groom blanched. "Milord?" He backed up, runn
into a stall post.

"Particularly," the marquis went relentlessly on wh
moving to block the man's escape route, "if the disserv
also leads to the ruination of an innocent young lady."

Friarly looked anxiously from the marquis to the earl a
the captain, but they looked as forbidding as the marqu
They spread out to block his forward path of escape.
looked back at the marquis and extended a shaking hand
supplication. "Please, milord—" the man gabbled.

"Yes, Friarly? You wish to venture an opinion as to
punishment?"

"I didn't know what use he was going to make of it.
least, not until it were too late!"

"Ah, but I disagree with you. You could have come
me, revealed all, and been a hero. Instead of a wretch w
lames horses to prevent their being ridden in an effort
save a lady's virtue." The marquis grabbed the man by
shirt, slamming him up against the stall. "Where's he ta
her, you maw-worm!"

"Crowden Park! Crowden Park!" screeched the man,
eyes showing white all around. "Please, milord! H
mercy!"

"Crowden Park," murmured Stefton, stunned. His g
eased and the groom slid to the floor, sobbing apologies a
begging for mercy. "Stephen!" the marquis bellowed.

'Yes, milord,'' said a sandy-haired youth coming out of shadows.

'Saddle and bridle the bay, then lock Friarly in the tack ▸m until I return.'' He looked down at the gibbering ▸om. ''If I were you, I'd pray no harm has come to her.''

'Isn't Crowden one of yur properties?'' asked Soothcoor.

'Yes, on the road to Ilford.''

'East out of London. Not a direction we'd a been likely to searchin'.''

'Precisely.''

The gentlemen were grimly silent as they absorbed the ▸lications of that fact. Finally the earl stirred and threw reins he held back over his horse's neck and prepared to ▸unt. He paused and looked back at the marquis. ''Oliver, ▸e a piece of his hide for me,'' he said softly.

The marquis nodded curtly.

CHAPTER
FOURTEEN

▸atherine fought uselessly against the languor that drained muscles and the cotton-wool that filled her head. Her ▸s drooped, sleep threatening to obliterate the world. She ▸k deep breaths and blinked.

▸Aasculine laughter, reminding her she was not alone, was ▸ bellows to anger's coals. Kirkson. He was responsible, ▸ it was he who sat beside her now, laughing at her and ▸ating over his success.

'Wh-hat do you wa-ant?'' She struggled to get the words ▸, but they lacked the intensity of anger she felt.

'My dear Miss Shreveton, such naïveté! Why would any ▸tleman be reduced to kidnapping a young woman? Mar- ▸e, or course. Only in your case, not immediately. First I ▸nd to ruin you. Ruin you so thoroughly that no other

gentleman would possibly want my leavings. Then, afte
time, I shall marry you.''

''How mag-magna-a-animous.'' The word came out i
yawn. She tried to edge away from him, but her lir
refused to obey.

''Yes, I think so, considering the humiliation you h
caused me,'' he said harshly. ''No, don't try to slither aw
The laudanum will soon have you asleep.'' He grabbed l
pulling her against him.

Catherine tried to struggle, to call out for help, but it w
impossible. Never in her life had she felt so helpless—s
never so frightened. She fought to stay awake, but the d
spread through her body, insidiously inviting sleep with
peaceful oblivion. She pulled on her anger to keep her
awake and reminded herself that Lady Welville did not
all the laudanum down her throat.

What a fool she'd been to enter into conversation with
woman. Somehow Lady Welville maneuvered her so t
her back was to the door. She was not aware of Kirkso
presence until he grabbed her from behind and Lady Welv
shoved the bottle of laudanum into her mouth. She mana
to spit some of it out, hopefully enough to keep her fr
falling soundly asleep. She dreaded that, for she feared
liberties Kirkson might take with her in that condition
shudder ran through her body and her head lolled b
against the velvet squabs of Kirkson's carriage. *I must k
awake*. The litany echoed in her head, clanging like a b

She did not doubt that her absence would quickly
detected and a hue and cry would soon ensue. What
wondered was how long it would take the marquis to ded
that Kirkson was her abductor. Funny, though she had
reason to suppose he would, Catherine did not doubt t
Stefton would come to her rescue. It gave her a comforta
feeling inside and helped to mitigate the fear. The quest
was, how quickly would he discover her whereabou
Perhaps not quickly enough. She would have to do someth
to save herself.

A little hysterical laugh burbled up inside her. S
herself? She could scarcely move and didn't even kn
where she was or where she was going to be: on earth,

ven, or in hell. She laughed hysterically again, realizing
was partially the drug that caused her laughter, but it
ldn't be helped.

Kirkson looked at her askance. Vaguely Catherine knew it
s her drugged behavior that caused his disgust. He
bably wanted a somnolent woman. What he got was a
f-drugged, silly woman. She giggled again and threw
self to the left, her head resting in the corner. Kirkson
ore viciously, and in his diatribe Catherine hear Lady
lville's name mentioned, but he did not try to pull her
k. In the dark shadows of the carriage, Catherine smiled.
vas only a small victory, but it restored her heart.

When the carriage stopped at last, Catherine roused
self. Her mind felt a little clearer, though not much.
latedly she realized she must have dozed for a while, but
seemed Kirkson had as well. He unfolded his body,
tched, and looked out the window. A groom scurried
und to open the carriage door.

Quickly Catherine closed her eyes and willed her body to
limp, feigning sleep. She heard Kirkson swear softly;
n her wrist was grabbed and he was pulling her body
ard him. He caught her underneath the arms before she
ld slide to the floor. His touch made her skin crawl and
tinctively she began to stiffen. Angrily she fought the
ulse, and allowed him to toss her over his shoulder.

'Did you have much trouble?'' Kirkson asked the man
o opened the front door.

'None, sir. It was as Stefton's man said it would be. Just
caretaker and his wife. I've them locked in their quar-
, sir.''

'Excellent, excellent. Stefton will not think of looking
e, and in the future, when it becomes known I took her
one of his estates, Society will not believe he had no
wledge of my actions.''

Catherine stifled a gasp.

'Yes, sir. It is a small house. There are not many
rooms, but I think I have chosen one suitable for the
y. Shall I show you the way?''

"Yes, and quickly. She is no featherweight," Kirks
said as he moved toward the stairs.

Catherine's eyes flew open at his comment, but in
position, neither man noticed. She looked about as well
she could from her present position and the indifferent li
cast by the branch of candles the unknown man held. Th
were in a well-appointed country house. That it was
often used was evidenced by the Holland covers on all
furniture. If this was truly one of the marquis's estates, th
Kirkson was correct. There would be no reason for Stef
to suspect their location. The hope she'd held in her he
was snuffed out like a candle flame. She would have to r
upon herself.

Kirkson's henchman pushed open a door at the far end
the upstairs hallway. "Here, sir. I've taken the liberty
removing the Holland covers and starting a fire."

"Thank you, Jordon. In your investigation of the hor
did you discover if it possessed a wine cellar?"

"Yes sir, and I've already appropriated a few bottle
the man said as he circled the room, lighting candles.

"Excellent. I will meet you downstairs."

Kirkson waited until Jordan had left the room before
turned to dump Catherine on the bed.

She allowed herself to fall limply backward, one a
dangling off the edge of the bed.

"I know you're not asleep, Miss Shreveton. I felt y
stiffen when you heard this was Stefton's estate," Kirks
said in a mocking tone.

Catherine opened her eyes, her face a careful mask to
emotions she felt. She would not give him the satisfact
of seeing either her fear or her hate. Her body still
sluggish and her thoughts continued to be slow to form,
she was shaking off the effects of the drug.

"That's better. You'll find we'll deal much better toget
if you do not resort to artifice. Now, if you'll excuse m
have some—ah, letters to write, but we will be toget
very soon, that I promise you, my dear," he said, leer
down at her. In the flickering candlelight his expression w
demonic and Catherine felt an uncontrollable shudder

ugh her body. Abruptly he turned on his heel and left
room, locking the door behind him.

atherine stayed still, listening until she heard his tread
cend the stairs and all was quiet again. She struggled to
d, grabbing the bedpost for support. Her head spun, but
marshaled her energies toward her goal—the window. If
could get to the window and open it, perhaps the cold
would help revive her. Slowly she made her way to her
, stumbling and hanging on to furniture for support.
en finally she reached the window, she rested her fore-
d against the cool glass, a hand reaching up to fumble
the latch. It was stuck. A cry of frustration lodged in
herine's throat. She tilted her head back, her other hand
ing the first to increase the pressure. She panted as she
ssed on the latch. She could not give up! When it
ched open, she gave a whimper of relief. Shakily, she
hed the window open, allowing a cold night breeze to
w across her face.

he didn't know how long she stood there before she
ized two things: her head was definitely clearing, and
e was a narrow ledge of ornamental brickwork jutting
and extending horizontally from the bottom of her
dow to the next bedroom window. That window, directly
r the front door, sported a wrought-iron ornamental
ony under it. Further investigation revealed a similar
e at the top of the window also connecting to the other
dow.

he pulled her head in and sat down in a chair to think for
oment. Dare she try it? She'd rather die than submit to
slimy toad! What other recourse did she have? None,
she couldn't do it wearing a ballgown.

he got up and began to prowl the room, happy to
over that though her limbs were still shaky, they were
ying her and she could now move without stumbling. In
ardrobe in the corner she found men's clothing. Stefton's?
ran her hand down the fine material. Yes, it had to be.
t knowledge gave her a strange confidence.

he tore her dress off, ripping the beautiful material in her
e, then stepped out of the gown and tossed it aside. With
ing fingers she found a man's shirt and put it on, rolling

up the sleeves. Next she donned a pair of knee breeches
on her fell clear to her ankles. The waist was much too b
She held the trousers up with one hand as she anxiou
seared the room for something to tie them in place. Perha
she could rip a sheet—no, a cravat! She pawed throu
drawers until she found a stack of starched white ne
cloths. Quickly she tied one around her waist and cros
the room to the open window. She pulled a chair forward
she could climb up and stand on the window ledge. S
studied the narrow ledges then looked down at the sa
slippers on her feet. They would have to go. Swiftly
took them off and stuck them in her improvised belt. Th
taking a deep breath, she slid her foot out on the bott
ledge and grabbed the top ledge and edged herself out of
window and onto the wall. Suddenly all she was aware of w
a roaring sound in her own ears and the painful quiver
muscles that were not recovered from the dose of laudanu
She flattened herself as tightly against the wall as she dar
and continued inching forward—praying, cursing, and ho
ing the Marquis of Stefton's image in her mind as a pri

"Good God!" murmured the Marquis of Stefton as
Soothcoor and Chilberlain reined in before the house
Crowden Park. Silently the three men watched the fig
clinging precariously to the side of the house, all afraid
make a sound lest they break her concentration.

Stefton found himself standing in the stirrups, his t
curled within his boots and his fingers curled tightly ab
the reins as he willed her to cross safely. When her
found the balcony, his breath came out harshly whistl
between his teeth. Quickly he dismounted.

"The lass has spunk," whispered Soothcoor admirin
as he and Chilberlain followed suit.

"But you'll not have her," snarled Stefton savagely.

"I'm glad to see you've come to yur senses," the
returned blandly.

"Egad, what is she doing!" exclaimed Chilberlain.

Stefton and Soothcoor looked back up in time to see
break a pane of glass with the heel of her shoe and reach

open the latch. The window opened readily to her touch
d she was swiftly inside.

"Hurry, in case someone heard the glass break! Richard,
around to the side. There's a terrace with glass double
ors leading into the parlor. From there, there is a connecting
or into the library, where I'll wager Kirkson is. Alan and I
ill go through the front." Stefton was running toward the
use almost before he was finished speaking, his pistol
awn. Behind him came a grim-faced Earl of Soothcoor.

The marquis smiled. Obviously Kirkson thought himself
fe and well hidden, for the door was not locked.

"What's this—" demanded a wiry, rat-faced man coming
t of the butler's pantry carrying wine bottles in either
nd.

The marquis was upon him before he could say another
ord, his arm tight around his neck. Jordan's eyes bulged.
e tried to swing one of the wine bottles he held, but
efton saw it coming and ducked his head. The bottle
anced off his shoulder. Stefton winced, but he did not let
.

"None of that," Soothcoor whispered, wresting the bot-
s out of Jordan's hands. His struggles increased then until
othcoor rammed his pistol barrel against his skull.

"We can do this one of two ways," the marquis murmured
Jordan's ear. "My friend here may bring the butt of his
stol down on your head rather painfully, or you may
rrender peacefully. It's up to you."

Jordan's struggles ceased. "Oh, 'tis a canny one," said
othcoor approvingly as he grabbed the man's jaw and
uffed a handkerchief in his mouth. The marquis shifted his
ip and Soothcoor untied Jordan's neckcloth, using it to tie
s hands behind his back. The marquis, removing his own
ckcloth, tied his legs together. Then they shoved him back
to the butler's pantry.

At the library door they paused for a moment, Stefton
aving the earl to the side out of sight. He opened the door
ickly, his pistol at the ready.

"Ah, Stefton, I underestimated you. No matter," drawled
rkson, his own pistol trained on the marquis, "you'll be
ad soon."

The marquis shrugged. "I would say we are evenl
matched," he said, his pistol pointed directly at Kirkson
From the corner of his eye he saw Chilberlain glide silentl
into the room from the connecting parlor door. The captai
made no sound as he crossed the thick Oriental carpet.

Kirkson's eye's narrowed. "You wouldn't come alone.
know you, Stefton. Where are your faithful puppy fol
lowers?"

"Do you think he means me?" Soothcoor asked, comin
into view around the door frame, his pistol also trained o
Kirkson.

"Give it up, Kirkson. You've overplayed your hand, a
you have at all your encounters with Miss Shrevetor
Accept her as your nemesis," Stefton suggested.

"Where's the captain?" Kirkson suddenly demanded.

Neither gentleman responded, for Captain Chilberlai
was halfway across the room.

"Where's Chilberlain?" A terrified expression crosse
Kirkson's face. He suddenly whirled around, firing his gu
in Chilberlain's direction. The marquis lunged at him
spoiling his aim, and the two went crashing to the floo
Silently they struggled, rolling across the floor.

"Stefton!" warned Captain Chilberlain when he sa
Kirkson pull out a dagger.

But the marquis was already aware of the danger. With
surge of strength he pulled free and landed a smashing blo
to Kirkson's jaw. The man grunted, his head bangin
sharply against the floor, and lay still.

Stefton sat up slowly, breathing hard. "Tie him up an
toss him into the pantry with his cohort." He ran a han
wearily through his hair. "I'll send someone for them bot
later, to see they're escorted out of the country." H
staggered to his feet. "Now where do you think th
hoyden's gotten to?"

"Right here," came a soft voice from the doorway.

The three gentlemen turned to see Catherine by the doo
her face white and unshed tears standing in her eyes.

"Miss Shreveton!" exclaimed the earl.

"Thank God," swore the captain.

"Catherine," murmured the marquis, his face a study of
emotions chasing one after another over his normally impassive visage.

She looked at him closely, trying to read the meaning
behind his expression, hoping she was not wrong at what
she thought she saw there.

He held out his hand. With a little inarticulate cry, she ran
to him, tears flowing freely now as he caught her and held
her close.

"Oh, Catherine, my Catherine," he murmured into her
hair, cradling her close.

Behind them, Soothcoor nudged the captain and said
they'd best dispose of the filth. Quietly they carried the
unconscious man out of the room.

The marquis sat in a chair by the fireplace and pulled her
into his lap. "I never want to feel like that again," he
moaned, stroking her bright hair. "If it hadn't been for that
chance warning Dawes gave me two weeks ago, we wouldn't
have found you."

Catherine lifted her head from his shoulder. "What
warning?"

The marquis sighed, and explained what Dawes said and
his own groom's involvement.

"I'm glad you came. But it wouldn't have mattered. I
would have gotten away on my own."

"I know, we saw." Stefton looked at her fiercely. "I aged
ten years tonight, watching you traverse that narrow ledge."
He shook her. "You could have been killed!"

She smiled contentedly and snuggled back up to him. "But
I wasn't. Do you know why? Because I was thinking of you."

The marquis was silent for a moment, absorbing the
import of her words. "Catherine, I—"

She sat up quickly, placing her hand over his mouth. "I
don't want any more talk of obligation to my uncle. I love
you, Stefton, and I think, maybe, you love me a little too!"
she said aggressively, daring him to deny it.

"Oliver," he said calmly when she removed her hand.

"What?" She blinked at him, puzzled by his non sequitur.

"My Christian name is Oliver. I would like to hear you
call me that."

"Why?"

"Because, you silly peagoose, husbands and wives ofte[n] call each other by their Christian names, at least in private.["]

"Husbands and wi—wives?" repeated Catherine. The[n] her eyes widened. "Oh, Oliver," she breathed softly, h[is] name falling easily from her lips, just as it had in h[er] dreams.

His dark head came closer then, his lips covering h[er] own, first softly, tentatively, then with a crushing strengt[h.] The tingling Catherine always felt in his presence surge[d] through her, singing along her nerve endings. She moane[d] softly, lifting her arms to entwine her fingers through h[is] thick black hair and slide a hand around the strong colum[n] of his neck.

"My Catherine," he murmured against her lips when [he] finally ended the kiss. He nipped gently at her neck an[d] nuzzled her shell-like ears.

Catherine tilted her head back more fully to receive h[is] burning kiss. Suddenly she giggled and brought her hea[d] forward to kiss him and then rest her forehead against hi[s.]

"What is it, my love?" whispered the marquis, sti[ll] trailing soft kisses against her skin.

"A matched pair."

"I beg your pardon," he said, pausing to look at her.

"I owe Aunt Penelope a carriage team. A Burke team. [I] shall depend upon you to help me choose well."

At his quizzical expression, Catherine laughed aga[in] and told of her wager with Lady Orrick. Hearing the tal[e] the marquis also laughed, and they were still chuckli[ng] when the Earl of Soothcoor knocked on the door momen[ts] later.

"Kirkson's locked away and Chilberlain's brought t[he] horses to the door. We willna make London by daybrea[k] but like as not, it willna matter," he said, complacently. [He] turned to go.

"Alan," called the marquis after him, "wish me happy[."]

That dour Northumbrian gentleman genuinely grinned f[or] the first time in the marquis's memory. "Aye, with all [my] heart." He closed the door after him and stood shaking h[is] head for a moment, more than ever resolved to avoid t[he] matrimonial state. It made a man daft, it did. He continued o where the captain waited outside.

"Well, are they coming?"

"Aye," the earl said, nodding. He stopped to pull a snuffbox out of his vest pocket and sat down on the front steps. "Any year now, I'd say. Any year now."